Eric took the blanket and draped it over Guy's shoulders. He folded the kid's hands so they lay on his lap and packed ice at his sides so he would remain secure for the rough ride back to port. Reaching into the chest pocket of his own jacket, he removed a pack of cigarettes. His hand shook as he lit two.

"We smoke the same brand," he said, bending to wedge one in Guy's gray lips. He smoked the other cigarette, all the while talking to the kid as if his spirit lingered nearby. "What a bummer," he said, "dying so young." He told the kid he would be missed by someone and promised to get him home. Hearing his voice crack, Eric turned away as if he didn't want Guy to see him that way. Then he closed the freezer door.

Guy sat in the bait locker, the cigarette still hanging from his lips. The freezing temperature caused the saltwater on his eyelashes and beard to crystallize. He looked as if he were climbing Mt. Everest instead of sitting propped-up, dead in a fishing boat bait locker headed to Dutch Harbor, Alaska.

Praise for *Death in Dutch Harbor*, by D. MacNeill Parker

"A great read! Parker paints a picture of Dutch Harbor that captures the vibe of a small town isolated in Alaska's Aleutian chain of islands. From beer at a bar to a Council meeting, and a night of terror on the Bering Sea, she describes it perfectly. While reading *Death in Dutch Harbor*, I felt like I was back in Dutch trying to help the characters solve the mysteries."

> ~ Dan Hanson, Retired Captain after 42 years of operating vessels out of Dutch Harbor *National Fisherman* magazine's 2003 *Highliner Of The Year*

"D.M. Parker has cast a net in the sea and hauled back a stellar story that will have you hooked in no time. There's no substitute for first-hand experience and Parker shows she's got it on every page of *Death in Dutch Harbor*. Her description of a wave shattering the windows of a fishing boat wheelhouse brought back chilling memories of my time at the helm. Based on her vivid descriptions of boats and bars, I suspect she's weathered storms at sea and danced at least one night away at the Elbow Room."

> ~ Dave Fraser, Retired Captain, FV Muir Milach Member, Steller Sea Lion Recovery Team

"*Death in Dutch Harbor* grabbed me at the outset and did not let go. Right away you can tell Ms. Parker knows the issues facing the fishing industry in the Bering Sea. She weaves them into the tale and uses her characters to draw the reader deeper into the murder mystery, especially the veterinarian Maureen McMurtry, Arlo the

Captain and Police Chief St. George. If you're looking to be entertained, I highly recommend this book!"

"From the first scene, she evokes the real Dutch Harbor and the dynamic people who call it home. It's a roaring mystery that braids together oil rigs, fishing, sea lions and the kind of Russians we love to hate. *Death in Dutch Harbor* is a must read for anyone who wants to vicariously experience a rugged world on the edge of an unforgiving sea."

"Ms. Parker sets the hook straight away with a spot-on description of a harrowing landing at the Dutch Harbor airport. The tale told in *Death in Dutch Harbor* takes you on a roller coaster ride that *is* commercial fishing. And the shocking ending left me breathless and not wanting it to end. A must read!"

"After doing business in Dutch Harbor since the '70s, I've seen a lot of drama come out of this town. *Death In Dutch Harbor* captures the essence of one of our last fishing frontiers."

Death
in
Dutch Harbor

by

D. MacNeill Parker

Death in Dutch Harbor

Cover Art by *Kim Mendoza*

The Wild Rose Press, Inc.
PO Box 708
Adams Basin, NY 14410-0708
Visit us at www.thewildrosepress.com

Publishing History
First Edition, 2023
Trade Paperback ISBN 978-1-5092-5223-7
Digital ISBN 978-1-5092-5224-4

Published in the United States of America

Dedication

This book is dedicated to fishermen and women who work hard to bring sustainable seafood to our dinner tables, the port of Dutch Harbor/Unalaska that hosts the Bering Sea fleet, the U.S. Coast Guard that protects them at sea, the local and state police that protect them on land, the fishery managers that protect the resource, responsible environmentalists, and a plethora of plankton that keeps it all spinning.

Acknowledgments

I owe a passel of thanks to my crafty Seattle writing group and a gang of Beta readers that included fishermen, a veterinarian, a forensic scientist, and book lovers extraordinaire who were not shy about giving more than their two cents worth of feedback. And what about the Seattle police K-9 unit that invited me to its training grounds where deputy dog, CoCo, taught me a thing or two about police dogs? Woof, woof! And many thanks to The Wild Rose Press for taking a chance on this first-time author, and especially my editor who helped me step to the plate prepared to deliver a base hit. Finally, I simply could not have persisted in this endeavor without my amazing family, especially my husband, a fishing boat captain. Without his unceasing support, this book would not have been written.

Chapter 1

Knocked about by turbulence, the plane wove its way through Alaska's Valley of Ten Thousand Smokes. Dr. Maureen McMurtry pressed her head against the aging prop plane's porthole window. She eyed the jagged jaw of icy glaciers and active volcanoes that reached skyward, ripping holes in a fog that hovered in the lowlands. Leaning back, she propped her lanky jean-clad legs against the seat in front of her. Like most others on the plane, she'd been aboard her share of flights forced by fog to turn around for the roadless, eight-hundred-mile journey back to Anchorage. Her hand ran through rust-colored hair that lay in disarray along the collar of her worn leather jacket. In the shaft of sunlight pouring through the porthole, she looked like Amelia Earhart itching to pilot the plane.

"Damn," she said with flinty impatience, hoping the fog would not keep them from landing in Dutch Harbor. And she wondered which riled her more, the fog on the ground or the fog in her head. She might have a tough decision to make.

She'd just interviewed for a position at a veterinary hospital in Anchorage and was heading home to Dutch. If the job was offered, she'd have to decide whether to renew a four-year contract as the town's only veterinarian or move on. The job in Anchorage was more challenging than patching up cats and dogs in a fishing town, and it paid a lot better. But the sprawling city of Anchorage? It required at least an hour's drive to reach the *real* Alaska; the Alaska that still made her swoon.

"Shouldn't I have my life figured out by now?"

"Get a grip," she said, admonishing herself for letting the annoying chatter inside her head escape. This thinking-aloud business had snuck up on her. She'd have to rein it in. Get things in order. Ship-shape shit. Instantly ignoring her resolve, she laughed out-loud.

"Mo?" A willowy gal, her smile twisted into a question mark, stood in the aisle.

Maureen hoped she hadn't heard the pesky out-loud chatter, but so what, she thought. What are friends for? She flashed a grin and grabbed the folded newspaper and Red Sox baseball cap from the seat next to her. "Hey, Kate! What brings you to Dutch this time?"

Kate slid into the seat. As a biologist with the marine mammal lab in Seattle, she often traveled to Dutch Harbor. Wearing a sweatshirt, jeans, and deck boots, she looked dressed for field work.

"Dead sea lions," she said. Her lips folded into a frown. "We got a report this morning that some have washed ashore at the far end of Captains Bay."

When the plane ride got bumpy, Kate fumbled to secure her seat belt. Snapping the buckle shut, she looked up at Maureen. "I'm headed out there to investigate but couldn't get a four-wheel drive rental. How'd you and your truck like to tag along?"

The idea of tracking down decaying marine mammals at the end of a long, desolate drive to the head of Captains Bay wasn't working any magic on Maureen. She was tired. She wanted to go home, sit in front of the old diesel stove with her three-legged dog, and drink a cold beer. And endangered sea lions? They were a hair-on-fire issue between fishermen and environmentalists. Maureen didn't want to warm her hands on that bonfire.

"Generally," she said, trying to navigate away from the invitation, "my patients are still kicking." But watching her friend's face deflate, Maureen switched course. "But heck, count me in."

Kate's face lit up. "Thanks, Mo," she said. She pulled a packet of mints from her pocket and offered one to Maureen. "Discovering what killed the poor buggers is a big deal."

Maureen had a collection of names that signaled people's relationship to her. Friends tended toward "Mo," while folks in need of a veterinarian favored "Dr. Mo" or just plain "Doc." Practically no one called her "Maureen" except the new police chief who valued her forensic skills when he didn't want to wait a month to hear back from the state trooper's office in Anchorage and then to hear they'd taken over the investigation. The chief didn't cuss much, but he cussed plenty when it came to that issue.

When the plane's wings rocked again, the pilot announced they were approaching Dutch Harbor. "Winds are blowing southwest thirty-five with gusts to forty-five, so prepare for a white knuckler."

Maureen's hands tightened around the armrest like it might make a damn bit of difference. She calmed herself with thoughts unrelated to the plane crash last year. The plane, its nose punched in, still sat parked off to the side at the end of the runway. Instead, she considered Arlo Castle, a fishing boat captain who could fix anything. The smell of diesel fuel on his work clothes was intoxicating to a woman who lived in the Alaskan

Bush and valued competence. When the plane dropped suddenly, she thought about the tattoo on his upper right arm. It was of a ship breaking through a cresting wave. Like him, the ship seemed on course and unafraid. *Fearless or reckless*, she wondered, still trying to figure him out. A sour taste in Maureen's mouth reminded her she didn't want to make that mistake again.

The plane flew close to the water as they approached the runway. They were near enough to see whitecaps pound the rocks and swamp the channel buoys below. The runway was bordered by water at either end. A strong tailwind could cause the plane to overshoot the runway. It had happened before.

The plane's tilting wings caused Hog Island to jump in and out of view on the starboard side. Seat belts pressed hard against their stomachs. Maureen sucked in air. Kate choked down a moan. The mayor, sitting in the seat in front of them, hollered, "Holy shit!"

Now the plane pulled hard to the port side causing luggage in the overhead compartments to ram the doors. One flew open, discharging two duffle bags and some fishing gear. A tackle box bounced off a nearby seat, releasing a dozen hand-tied flies, including some wooly buggers and a Spey fly that hooked into the headrest in front of Maureen.

She eyed the blood-red feathers of the Spey. No, not blood. Think of something else, she thought. Anything but a crash landing. She closed her eyes, focusing on Arlo again. It had been a while since she'd allowed herself a romantic relationship, but she'd likely have to cut it loose if she moved to Anchorage. She hadn't yet told him it was an option. The notion of losing him, and her gang of friends who'd chosen this Bush town as home, stung. She was thirty-three and facing a fork in life's highway that came with costs.

"It's a damn toll road!"

"What?" It was Kate looking ghost-faced.

When the plane's tires gave a welcome-home screech upon hitting the tarmac, Maureen turned to look at Kate, who sat stiff-backed, her eyes still shut. Tapping Kate's white knuckles, she asked, "You okay?"

Kate nodded. Her smile had as much confidence as a flat tire. The mayor undid his seat belt and began chatting with the person next to him as if nothing had happened. Maureen knew that, like the other locals on board, he'd been through the drill before.

The plane taxied toward a small blue building where an airport ticket agent waved from the door.

The pilot leaned back in his seat, bringing a heavy metal microphone to his lips.

"Welcome to Dutch Harbor, Alaska," he said.

****

Straight-arming their way through the airport's double-glass doors, the duo headed across the dirt parking lot where an old gray pickup with rusting haunches stood waiting for them like a steed to a rail. They climbed aboard, tracking in mud that would dry and crumble onto the mat at their feet for delivery elsewhere. Maureen pumped the gas pedal and turned the key. The engine rumbled to life. She reached for the leather work gloves on the dash and tugged them on. Soon they were heading south on Airport Beach Road.

Fog licked the landscape making for lousy visibility. When they turned onto Captains Bay Road, they followed the contour of the beach. Passing by the Northward Seafoods plant, Maureen managed the steering wheel with just one hand.

"So, Steller sea lions?" she said. "I've seen steam explode from the ears of fishermen at the mere mention of those endangered pinnipeds."

Kate's eyebrows bunched together like caterpillars about to butt heads. She'd heard it all before. "The animals are nutritionally stressed. They have to compete with fishermen for prey. It's that simple."

"So sea lions in, fishermen out?" Maureen turned toward Kate, sharing a cockeyed grin.

"Yeah." Kate shrugged. "In areas where sea lions forage, they give fishermen the finger."

"You mean the flipper."

"Yeah, the middle one."

They both laughed.

The fog was too dense to see the International Shipping Inc.'s docks, but ISI's blue warehouse and cold storage facilities loomed like ghostly monoliths.

"Spooky," said Kate, turning to watch the buildings disappear into the fog as they navigated the pot-hole-pocked road.

Several more miles and the gravel road petered out, dumping the truck into a large mudflat that headed toward the beach. They were met by a bank of fog so thick that Maureen stomped on the brakes. Letting her foot ride the clutch, she coaxed the old truck forward until stacks of rusting metal pot frames emerged from the thick haze.

Kate leaned forward to see how high the pots towered above them. Perched atop the stacks, a half dozen bald eagles flapped their wings in alarm. "Holy smokes."

Maureen turned off the ignition, pushed open the

door, and stepped onto a thin glaze of ice-covered mud that cracked under her weight. Reaching behind the bench seat, she grabbed a pair of deck boots and her medical shoulder bag. She tossed Kate a flashlight and kept one for herself.

"Twilight time," she said, pulling on the boots. She tugged the Red Sox ball cap over her uncivilized hair.

Maureen led the way through the narrow passages of stockpiled crab pots, their metal frames strung with aging mesh. She explained to Kate that crabs were lured into the cage-like traps by hanging bait, usually rotting fish ripe with the scent of decay.

"Even discarded in a boneyard like this, the stink never really dies. The fog keeps it alive like a bad joke."

Emerging on the other side, the two women scanned the tideline. They walked to the water's edge where waves washed ashore, letting loose tongues of white foam that licked the sand. Maureen turned toward the sea, inhaling its salty, sweet scent. She listened to its retreating waves carry rolling grains of sand back to its lair. Beyond, she heard the barking of sea lions on a distant, rocky reef. No other sounds, nothing to remind her of human efforts to tame the wildness. She loved Alaska's rich emptiness.

"I was told the sea lions washed up just beyond the crab pot storage area," Kate said, "but it doesn't seem like they'll be easy to locate."

"Let's split up and go in opposite directions along the tideline."

Kate headed north and disappeared into the mist. Maureen turned toward the head of the bay, kicking at seaweed left behind when the tide took everything else. She spied what might be a heap of seaweed or driftwood.

Or a dead sea lion?

It growled. Maureen's shoulders shot back. She grabbed a stick big enough to take a swing at something. Approaching closer, she made out the silhouettes of pacing animals just beyond the heap. Three pairs of eyes stared back at her. She could see the outline of their pointed ears and snouts. Behind them, three fur-covered tails stood at attention. In a flash, the foxes were gone.

Maureen moved toward the seaweed that had attracted the vulpines' attention and poked it with her stick. She flipped off a clump. A swarm of flies exploded from the heap. Swatting them away, she let her eyes settle on the corpse of a dead sea lion. Its shape was twisted into an awkward position that caused one flipper to reach toward her.

"Hey, pal," she said, squatting beside the pungent corpse.

Judging from the size, the sea lion appeared to be a juvenile. Maybe three hundred pounds. Decomposition had begun around the muzzle area where its mouth welcomed agents of decay. Maureen hollered down the beach toward Kate, letting her know she'd found one.

Farther down the beach, she found a large female, perhaps six hundred pounds. The animal's head lay tossed back in the sand. Golden fur lay matted along her sleek body except where the enlarged teats of a lactating female pushed their way beyond the thick coat. Strands of kelp hung from her mouth.

Kate arrived and stood beside Maureen. "Any idea what caused her death?"

Kneeling beside the animal, Maureen lifted the flipper and looked for overt signs of damage. "So far, she's not talking to me."

The sea lion's long whiskers brushed against Maureen's wrist, sending chills up her spine. She stroked its face, letting her hand linger on one of its eyelids. She opened it. An eye looked up at her with the milky blue tint of death.

Marine mammals stink of organic marine matter on their best day. But when Maureen pried open the sea lion's mouth, the stench caused her to grimace. She knew immediately that the animal had been dead for at least forty-eight hours, maybe more. But the frigid sea water would make it a tough call.

Laying the animal's head down on the sand, she ran her fingers along the fur, searching for wounds. Buried beneath thick fur along the folds of its neck, she found a deep hole. She separated the fur around it. Looking up at Kate, she pointed to the area behind the ear. "Shine your flashlight here."

Maureen's fingers traced the edges of the wound. She poked her forefinger inside until she felt a hard surface. Using a pair of forceps she pulled from her medical kit, she worked it around the object until she was able to coax it loose. Clasped in the bite of the forceps, she held up a lead bullet. It was flattened at the top, so it looked like she'd pulled out a dull gray molar.

"Damn," she whispered, dropping the bullet in an empty latex glove and stashing it in her pocket.

"Jesus Christ!" Kate hollered. Her voice turned harsh. "Shooting an endangered marine mammal is a serious crime. Punishable with fines and jail time."

Maureen pulled a phone from her pocket and was surprised to see she had service. Punching in a number, she looked at Kate. "This is a crime scene now."

****

By the time Police Chief St. George and his two deputies, Chet and Michele, drove out the gravel road and located them on the beach, the two women had thoroughly examined both sea lions.

Maureen held up the lead slug she'd extracted and offered it to the chief. "I found bullet wounds in both the animals. Looks like it might be a .30-06."

The chief wore a bulky police parka over jeans. He held out a gloved hand.

She dropped the bullet in his palm and watched him roll it around there.

"Yeah, looks like a .30-06 or maybe a .308. Bag it," he said, passing it to Chet. "And get the GPS readings on the carcass locations before we move them."

"So, you know something about ballistics?" he said, turning again to Maureen.

"Brothers," she said. "Dad took us deer hunting."

"Really?"

Maureen could tell the chief was still trying to size her up. "Nothing worth talking about," she said, knowing it was nothing she wanted to talk about.

Michele was already down the beach taking photographs of the other corpse. They could see the camera's flash pop in clusters.

The chief turned back to Maureen, his eyes getting a bead on her from beneath a wide-brimmed western hat. His mouth was pressed shut. Maureen had learned that meant he was thinking and wanted to get it right before he spoke.

"I'd like you to remove all the bullets and give me an estimate on time of death." He hadn't asked her to take a scalpel to anything before, so the query was measured. Sure, she was a vet but the question came anyway. "Can you do it, Maureen?"

The city council had hired Ray St. George as its police chief five months earlier. Like most remote Alaskan communities, the town didn't have a medical examiner. And unless the community was lucky enough to have an appointed coroner to determine cause of death, the state police expected all evidence, including unexamined corpses, to be sent to Anchorage for forensic analysis. Dutch Harbor didn't have a coroner, and its lone doctor worked at the hectic clinic. Chief St. George had learned quickly that once state police took possession of a body, they also took possession of the investigation, often leaving the local police out of the loop. To Ray St. George, a retired Navy investigator, this protocol was unacceptable.

"Can you do it?" he asked again, watching her kneeling in the sand to get her medical kit back in order.

Looking up, she stated the obvious. "The cause of death seems pretty clear, Chief."

The chief waved it off. "I know these are sea lions, but it's still a crime I won't tolerate. I want to know how many shooters were involved. To do that, I need to know if the bullets were fired from the same or multiple weapons. And I can't begin to investigate properly without knowing if it happened this morning or last week."

"Well, not this morning." She lifted the flipper again and let it drop. "They've already passed through rigor."

Maureen closed the kit, stood up, and hung it over her shoulder. "They're gonna want to do their own necropsies," she said, nodding down the beach where Kate still knelt, taking notes by the other corpse.

The chief had three inches on Maureen, making him

about six feet tall. His face was clean shaven and his graying hair clipped short. His posture made you want to stand up straighter. She could tell by his expectant face that he was waiting for the wheels to turn in her head.

"Let me think about it," she said.

Chet stood over the corpse, entering its GPS location in his notebook. He looked over at the chief. "What now?" he asked.

The sea edged closer and surf shot foam their way. The chief pointed toward the tideline. "Look for shell casings," he said. "And there may be more animals washed up on the beach. I want to collect as much as we can before the tide takes it away."

Chet, young and with a gait that showed he was eager to please, pulled a yellow tide book from his pocket. "High tide's in less than two hours. We could lose them."

"Don't worry, Chet, we'll figure it out."

Michele offered to call the Northward plant and ask that they send out a flatbed truck to pick up the sea lions. An Aleut native, she'd served as the senior deputy for three years. Among her many duties, she penned the police log. Its droll language made it the favorite section of the town's weekly paper, *The Dutch Harbor News.* She'd already keyed in the fish plant's number and looked to the chief.

"Ask them to send the one with a crane," he said.

Maureen joined Kate, who'd begun to walk the tide line again. They were almost to the river when their roving flashlight beams landed on another mound of seaweed. Kicking away clumps of kelp, a hideous odor rose to scorch their nostrils.

Half buried in the sand lay a sneaker attached to a

white foot. It lay turned away from a twisted leg, its bruised skin exposed like a warning. Maureen knelt beside it and began to strip away the seaweed until she uncovered a shoulder. Following its sloping angle, she found strings of long hair that clung to a scalp like seaweed to a rock. The turned head revealed the nose ridge of a man.

Kate moved the flashlight beam to where the nose met the sand. The beam faltered, quaking as if the earth moved beneath it. But it was Kate, unable to quell her shaking hand.

Maureen hollered down the beach. "Chief, over here. Hurry!"

Their flashlights bobbing, the chief, Chet, and Michele loped their way to the spot where Maureen and Kate shined their lights. The chief knelt down. He reached for the man's shoulder and rolled him over.

Looking up was someone they all recognized. Some people called him One-Eye Ben. Most just called him One-Eye, a drunken drug addict who'd made Dutch Harbor his home for more than two decades. His lone eye was covered beneath a wrinkled purple lid. The other, an empty socket, overflowed with sand and seashell fragments. His signature black leather eye patch was nowhere in sight.

The chief looked out from beneath the brim of his hat again.

"Can you do it?"

Maureen studied the face that had already begun to decompose around the prominent features of its fleshy landscape. She recalled the box of apples One-Eye regularly left on the steps of her veterinary clinic. He'd known about the wild horses in Summer Bay. Everybody did. But he knew she looked after the herd when she could. The apples, she figured, were his contribution to their welfare.

Pulling strands of hair away from One-Eye's mottled face with an ungloved hand, she lifted the bill of her baseball cap and looked up at the chief.

"Yeah, I can do it."

Chapter 2

Maureen ran her hands down the torpedo shape on
the examination table. Two pectoral flippers designed to
propel the sea lion through the ocean fell limply away
from its body. Death had given them up to gravity.

"Ready?" said Maureen.

Kate nodded.

It was late, but they'd both decided it was better to
do it that night so it would be ready for the morning
flight.

Maureen had already removed slugs from the
juvenile sea lion on the beach. They'd both been fired
from a rifle. The fish plant had taken the animal and was
packing it in ice for morning shipment to the marine
mammal lab in Seattle. But this big female had too many
bullets. A necropsy was required to remove them.

Standing in her puppy-print smock and cap,
Maureen pressed the scalpel deep into the animal's upper
abdomen, where she'd shaved away its sleek golden fur.
Avoiding the enlarged teats that indicated she'd been
nursing a pup, Maureen's incision ran from beneath the
rib cage to its lower abdomen. The blubber was thick.
Tough to navigate, thought Maureen as she peeled open
the layer of fat.

The first thing Maureen noticed was how red the
organs and flesh were. "Much darker than ours."

"With all the body fat stored in its blubber, sea lion

flesh is lean." Kate patted its flank. "You know, the government once paid a bounty for killing these magnificent animals. If you brought in a sea lion jawbone, they paid a hundred bucks for it. Now that sea lions are endangered, there are severe penalties for doing the same thing. Ironic but necessary."

Maureen plunged a temperature gauge into the liver.

"And now I hear they want to kill Steller sea lions in the Lower Forty-Eight because they eat salmon." She pulled out the gauge and noted the temperature in her log book. "Seems crazy to me."

Kate eagerly reached for the stomach. "We think the animals may be nutritionally stressed," she said massaging the lumpy organ. "Feels like it's full of candlefish. Smelt," she said. She set it back in the abdominal cavity.

After recovering three accessible bullets, Maureen traced injured flesh to the spine and dislodged a bullet. It was larger than the others. She held it up to the light that hung above the table. "This one was fired close-up and personal."

Dropping the slug in a bowl with the other bullets, she looked at the clock. "Anything else you want to examine before I close her up?"

Kate shook her head. It had been a long night. And they were not done.

After stitching together the animal, Maureen stripped off her gloves and reached for the wall phone.

"Chief," she said when he answered on the other end. "This sea lion was dead for at least two days. Most likely longer, but it's hard to say based on water temperature in the bay. I'd put my money on four, but want to research it a bit more before a final verdict. The animal was healthy. Cause of death is clearly multiple gunshot wounds."

She stopped to listen. "Yeah, it's as if a couple of jerks were using these animals for target practice. Maybe out at the reef where sea lions hang out on the rocks."

She moved the phone between her head and shoulder and reached for the bowl. Four bullets rolled around in its concave embrace.

"No, the bullets were not the same. I found three rifle slugs and one that appears to have been fired from a large-caliber handgun. It severed her spine so seems fired at close range."

Maureen shifted in her boots. "Are you sure you want me to proceed with One-Eye?"

She hung up the phone and walked to the refrigerated drawers where she normally kept dead pets. Two drawers were built into the wall. She opened the one at waist height. When Maureen pulled out the stainless-steel drawer, the cold, dead body of One-Eye Ben looked up at her.

Compared to the sea lion, his body seemed ill-equipped to handle the sea. Maureen found plenty of scrapes and bruises from being tossed around in the surf. She opened his mouth and winced at the ripe smell of death.

Dr. Maureen McMurtry was a graduate of a veterinary school of medicine in Boston. Her parents had hoped she would practice medicine on human beings. She'd even attended medical school for a year, but Maureen felt more comfortable tending to animals. Dogs especially. Their faces tilt up toward you with that look of love, courage, patience, and loyalty that reminds you of what's important in a life well lived. Her own dog,

CoCo, had talked her through tough times. At least she barked in all the right places. Humans were more complicated, she thought, like chess. But dogs? They were like a game of tic-tac-toe. Becoming a veterinarian had been an easy choice for her in the end.

She tilted One-Eye's face sideways to wipe the sand from the eye socket. Underneath, she discovered an orbital implant. She pointed it out to Kate. But the ocular orb, or glass eye, a convex, shell-shaped prosthetic, was missing. She wasn't surprised to discover it gone since he'd worn a patch as long as she'd known of him. But, clearly, he'd once worn an expensive glass eye.

The clinic door opened upstairs. The familiar sound of CoCo exploding down the stairs was followed by slower, plodding steps.

"Hello, Mo, you down there?"

An enormous, three-legged German shepherd charged through the swinging double doors and came to a full stop at Maureen's knees. The dog's ears twitched, and its gaze lay on the doctor's masked face with the single-mindedness of a smitten ninja.

Maureen cocked her head. "Hey, girl!"

CoCo's tail wagged hard enough to create a mini windstorm. A determined woman swaggered into the room.

"Saw your truck out front," she said.

At five feet, two inches, the fit, energetic woman filled more than her share of a room. Her black hair, streaked with gray, was pulled back in a single braid that fell down the length of her back. Her eyes zigged and zagged from one exam table to other, sucking up information like a vacuum cleaner on the hunt. On one table lay a dead sea lion. On the other lay a naked man.

Her dark eyebrows pressed the ceiling in alarm.

"Holy crap!" she said, walking around the two tables. One hand covered her nose. The other carried a bottle of bourbon.

As a supervisor of the Bering Sea crab fisheries, Patsy Bonneville helped manage the largest crab fishery in the world. Barrel-chested crab fishermen learned not to mess with her. She'd been with the department for more than twenty years and could have retired with a nice pension, moved to California, and hung out poolside with her two grandchildren. But mixed cocktails and suntan lotion just weren't her thing. She liked her drinks, like her life, straight-up without the frou-frou trimmings. So, she stayed in Dutch, working in the office located across the parking lot from the veterinary clinic. It was no big deal for Patsy and Maureen to share a shot of whiskey together after work.

"Thanks for watching CoCo while I was in Anchorage," Maureen said.

They all looked at the three-legged German shepherd. Black as night and larger than most shepherds, she looked like the kind you saw patrolling the Berlin Wall in old Cold War movies. The dog had been gifted to Maureen by the Boston police after the animal was shot in the line of duty. Maureen had amputated the left front leg herself when others were ready to put the dog down.

"She's a hot shit," Patsy said. "My kind of girl." Then she eyed the naked corpse. She leaned over his head as if to confirm her first impression. Her lips tightened. "One-Eye?"

"We found him at the head of Captains Bay," said Maureen. "The chief asked me to determine cause of

19

death."

Patsy leaned over the pale face again. "You know," she said, sadness hobbling her words, "in the old days, he was one good-looking dude. Black wavy hair and a smile to kick you on your ass."

Patsy paced around the corpse. "He lost his eye early on when he first started fishing king crab." She pointed at the empty eye socket. "A grappling hook took it."

The three women fixated on the dark, empty hole.

"He wore a glass eye for several years, staying rock solid handsome through most of his twenties, but never seemed to sustain a relationship." She looked up. "I don't know if the kid ever fell in love."

Recognizing the question on their faces, Patsy raised her palm to stop them in their tracks. "No, no, no, no, no! I was too busy working for the department and raising three kids to have sex with anyone but my ex-husband."

She bent closer to his face. "By the time he was thirty, the pirate patch appeared. It was all downhill from there. He must be in his mid-forties by now."

"He looks more like sixty." It was Kate. "Drugs take a toll."

Patsy held up the half-empty bottle of bourbon. "I thought you two might need a drink when you're done." She put it on Maureen's desk. Then, yanking a handful of paper towels from its wall mount, she dropped them on One-Eye's exposed groin.

"Really, Mo. Some respect. Some modesty!" She laughed, then stopped to stand quietly at his cold, white feet. "His father's a business big-wig in Anchorage. Influential. If he gave a shit about One-Eye, he might want you to treat him with respect by covering his privates." She walked to the coffee pot on the shelf, grabbed a mug, and poured herself a shot of bourbon. "But the family gave up on him long ago. Except for his brother, Rob. Rob got a place for him not far from the Olympic Fisheries plant, but I hear it's more like a flop house these days."

All eyes were on One-Eye now. His stringy black hair framed angular ruddy cheeks. On a good day, he looked like a pirate with an eye patch. On most other days, a sad sack with a faded tattoo on his arm. One-Eye Benjamin Stokes. The expensive orbital implant in his empty eye socket seemed all he had left of his old life.

"See these contusions?" Maureen pointed to a massive bruise on his scalp. "He may have been struck on the head, but it doesn't seem to have done enough damage to kill him. Hard to tell without an autopsy. Perhaps he drowned, and the bruising occurred in the water. He could've been beaten up by the reef out there."

Maureen bent over a wounded area near the back of his head. With tweezers, she tried to remove what might be bits of shattered sea shells or coral. That failing, she clipped the tainted hair strands and laid them in a dish. An odd yellow color. *Paint chips?* she wondered.

Patsy rolled the dish of bullets around so that the metal slugs moved in a circular motion.

"Is there a relationship here?" she asked, indicating the two corpses.

"Perhaps," Maureen said, still culling through his hair. "They showed up together on the same beach. But the sea lions were shot..."

She stopped short. Clipping away the hair surrounding a wound behind his ear, she found a dark hole. She used narrow forceps to penetrate the wound until a hard surface would not let the tool go farther.

"Jesus. I think it's a bullet."

Maureen pulled back the forceps. Gooey matter dripped from the metal prongs to the floor. She stepped back, shaken. "I'm sorry, Ben."

Patsy rested a hand on her friend's shoulder. "Ben is dead," she said. "The best thing you can do for him is remove the bullet and help find out who killed him."

Maureen pressed the forceps back into Ben's brain. Coaxing it loose, she extracted the bullet. A big one. It looked like the same large-caliber slug she'd removed from the sea lion.

Kate gasped.

Patsy's face turned from sad to mad.

Maureen reached for the wall phone, and called the chief to report the dark turn of events.

"Okay, the door is open. Send them over." She hung up and turned to her friends. "The deputies will be here soon to take pictures and write a report."

Grabbing more mugs from next to the coffee pot, Patsy poured them a generous round. Together they raised their cups high over the cold dead body of Benjamin Stokes.

"One-Eye," she said. "May your raggedy looking self appear as handsome as you once were when you reach the pearly gates."

Maureen and Kate, still in blood-smeared smocks, raised their cups.

"Amen."

Chapter 3

Maureen approached a trawl vessel tied to the dock. Beyond it, a swath of snow-capped peaks slid into the tranquil waters of the bay. Arlo stood on the deck with his back to her, tending a BBQ grill. Careful not to alert him, Maureen raised a leg over the boat rail of the *Cape Kiska* and slipped onto the deck. The boat's loose lines sighed against the cleats.

Arlo lifted the metal poker straight up from the grill as if it were a stop sign. "What'd you bring, Mo?"

There is no sneaking up on this guy, but it was fun trying.

"A chardonnay." Maureen held the wine bottle over the grill for him to admire. The afternoon sun reflected off the glass.

"Hmmm," he said. "How'd you figure I'd be grilling rockfish?"

"Well…" Maureen moved past him, close enough to brush the folds of his denim jacket. "I figured you'd snag a few rockfish while fishing cod in the *Mushroom*."

Even she knew where the *Mushroom* fishing grounds were located on a navigational chart of the Bering Sea. Just southeast of the Pribilof Islands, where the continental shelf edge dropped off, the fathom depth contour lines drawn on a chart formed the unmistakable shape of its namesake.

"You know cod's not my thing," she said, "so I

figured, since you like me and probably want to ravish me, you'd cook up some rockfish to bolster your chance of success."

"You think you're smart." He poked the charcoals and spread them around the bottom of the grill. A lock of his darker-than-dirt hair fell across his forehead. The few silver strands there let you know he was no youngster.

"Yeah, I do want to ravish you." He looked her way with the hint of a grin that made her want to climb down his shirt. "But I don't like you much."

His jacket smelled of charcoal smoke and diesel fuel. She inhaled it, detecting a hint of fresh laundry detergent. Looking him up and down now, she noted the clean jeans and the crisp denim shirt he wore. He'd dressed up. Heady stuff.

"Figures," Maureen said, pushing past him as she headed toward the galley door.

Arlo called to her.

"What would you have brought if I was cooking up some cod?"

She stood in the doorway and looked at him as if he were born yesterday. "Beer, of course…lite beer."

"Lite beers are not your thing either."

"Right. So, I would have left early. *Before* the ravishing."

She returned moments later with a plate of marinated fish he'd filleted earlier and two cold bottles of craft ale. She set the plate on the fish sorting table and passed him one.

They both wore jackets to fend off the crisp fall air. The cuffs of his sheepskin-lined jacket were rolled back for cooking over the fire. His wrists were tanned and muscular. His large hands, calloused.

He took a long pull from the beer bottle. Condensation droplets rolled down its side and landed on his clean-shaven face. Man, he looked good. Yeah, she was warming up to him, but he seemed married to his boat, making her cautious. She smiled, letting it go for now.

"Fishing was a pain in the butt," he said. "The cod were spread out, so we did a lot of long tows. Not surprising for this time of year, but still, we didn't fill the boat."

"Bummer." Maureen looked at him, trying to imagine him at sea. It was sexy thinking of him at the helm.

"I've got a short survey charter with the fishery service that will bring in a few bucks."

She tipped the bottle of ale to her lips and swallowed. "A survey?"

"Yeah, the feds want to charter the boat and crew to make some tows over areas they believe might be skate nurseries. I'll be gone for five days. Nice and short, so I can be back in time for king crab season. I'll be leaving in a couple of days after a quick trip to Anchorage. Sully and a couple of greenhorn crew will do the survey with me while the regular crew gets the crab gear ready."

"Anchorage?"

He turned back to the grill and poked the charcoal again.

"Just some boat business."

She hadn't told him about her job interview in Anchorage since there hadn't been an offer to consider yet. But he seemed the evasive one now, something she'd encountered with him before.

Coaxing the poker from his grip, she took her turn

25

prodding the coals.

"One-Eye Ben." She said it slowly as if each word carried a load of baggage.

"Yeah, I heard about it."

She nudged the coals. "I dug a bullet out of his brain, Arlo. It shook me up."

Her gaze wandered toward the blue waters of the sea. "We found him washed ashore at the head of the bay. He was buried in sand and seaweed."

She eyed the hot coals again. "It's hard to make sense of it."

"Are you okay?"

She shrugged, not really knowing the answer except that she'd get over it. She was good at getting over bad things.

Arlo took the poker and the beer from her and set them aside. He rested his hands on her shoulders.

"Don't let it get personal, Mo. Let the police take care of it."

"It feels personal," she whispered.

He drew her close. She felt his chest rise and fall beneath her cheek. She felt his warmth. It's time he knows, she thought.

"I've been to Anchorage too." She told him about the job opening. "It would be challenging, and I'd be making real money." She waited for Arlo to say something. But he didn't, and she didn't want to prod him.

"Hey," she said turning toward the galley again, "I brought some asparagus to grill. I'll get it ready."

"Wait." He grabbed her hand. "I'd miss you."

She looked at him, letting her hand lie in his. "Me too. But there hasn't even been a job offer yet. I just didn't want to blindside you, should it come."

"So, wait and see. I get it." He let her hand slip away.

She headed toward the galley to fetch the food and was reaching for the door when a splash and a thundering skirmish caused her to spin around. Arlo, his poker extended, backed away from a thousand pounds of shaking blubber, fur, and whiskers that had flown up the stern ramp. Its muscular flippers propelled it across the deck toward the sorting table and the platter of marinating fish.

Barking and flashing its teeth, the sea lion flipped the platter into the air with its snout and arched its body to catch the glistening white fillets. Its toothy mouth, framed by long whiskers, swallowed them in a single gulp. It spun on its rear flippers, flopped across the deck, and slid down the stern ramp into the sea.

"Damn sea lions!" Arlo grabbed the bill of his cap and threw it on the deck.

Maureen bent over, laughing so hard it felt good.

"It's not funny! That animal could have killed us. They're nothing but trouble. Damn it! Damn it to hell, Mo! Stop laughing!"

Maureen could not strip the smile from her face. It was the most carefree she'd felt in days. "They're an endangered species, Arlo. Let them eat fish!"

"Let them eat fish?" He thrust the tip of the poker into the BBQ grill and slashed at the hot coals so that sparks flew. "We're booted from some of our most productive fishing grounds so sea lions can have all the fish to themselves. It doesn't make sense that we're taking food they need when there's more fish around than ever. It's always the same...blame the fishermen!"

She reached for his shoulder, the one powering

furious stabs of the poker. But it failed to calm him.

"The environmentalists are always trying to put us out of business." He turned toward the stern ramp where the animal had vanished into the sea and pointed the poker in its direction. "Did that sea lion look like it was starving to death to you?"

Maureen thought about the dead sea lions she'd examined. Minus the lead slugs, both had been in good health. "Kind of a fatso," she said, wanting to lighten things up.

Arlo bent to pick his hat off the deck. Fitting it squarely on top of his head, he looked at her. Wearing the half-grin that had won her heart, he'd transformed back into the Arlo she'd come to visit.

"How do you think that chardonnay will pair with peanut butter and jelly?" he said.

They found smoked salmon and cheese in the fridge and toasted a pair of bagels. With asparagus on the side, it was a decent meal. Sipping wine upstairs in the wheelhouse, they had a fine view as the sun set over Captains Bay.

Always on, radio chatter is the backdrop to every fisherman's life at sea. Arlo reached for a nob on VHF radio and lowered the volume.

"Anchorage, huh?"

"I haven't made up my mind to do it. Just exploring my options. Now that my contract is up with the city, I have to decide whether to re-up my commitment here." The contract had been to fulfill her veterinary school scholarship obligation to Alaska to help cover the hefty tuition. That responsibility had been met.

"What's wrong with Dutch?"

"You mean aside from the fact that it's the last

outpost of civilization?"

"That's one of its better qualities. You'll have to do better than that."

"How about the damn fog?"

"Yeah, the fog gets old, but it's pretty much gone a few miles offshore."

Maureen rolled her eyes, knowing he knew she rarely left shore. "Some days, it weighs me down. Some days, it wears me out."

Swallowing the last of her wine, Maureen walked to the array of windows that lined the front of the wheelhouse. She looked toward the mountains, appreciating that today, at least, they were not fog-bound.

She spread an arm toward Mt. Ballyhoo. "You know I love to climb that mountain."

"I do."

"But it's no longer challenging." She turned to face him. "That's how I feel about my job here." She took a deep breath. "But not you. I'm not bored with you. You make it difficult to leave."

She was surprised to hear herself say it.

Arlo reached for Maureen's glass and filled it with more wine. "Ballyhoo looks pretty good tonight." He passed the glass to her.

"Yes, tonight it looks good."

He sipped his wine and eyed her. "Am I supposed to find a new girlfriend?"

"You've got your boat." She gestured toward the map of the Bering Sea that lay on the large chart table.

She poked her finger on the small speck that marked Dutch Harbor, then let her hand spread across the map of the Bering Sea toward the coast of Russia. "You make a good living here. You love it."

"Yep, but it's not my girlfriend."

She raised her arms in the air as if exasperated. "I'm a talented veterinarian who's barely able to make ends meet. I'm thirty-three years old and live over my clinic with a three-legged dog, for God's sake."

Her chest heaved. She hadn't intended to get worked up. She looked away toward Ballyhoo again.

Arlo turned her face toward his. "There's the long-distance option."

"There's that," she said, letting her smile tempt him.

His hands wandered down her hips, hips that curved like the slow bend in a river. They came to rest on her butt, waiting like a question mark.

She felt the heat of his breath on her neck and let her fingers weave through the wave of his hair. Heck, she thought, long-distance relationships aren't always doomed to failure.

His hands traveled around her waist and lifted her onto the chart table. She leaned back letting her body stretch across the map of the Bering Sea. Strands of her fiery hair spread upward, smothering the coast of Siberia. He kissed her neck that arched over the Diomede Islands and, after they'd kicked free their jeans, his pelvis found hers in the tangle of contour lines that defined the *Mushroom*.

Radio chatter buzzed in the background.

Chapter 4

In an 1867 transaction called Seward's Folly, the Russians sold Alaska to the U.S. for $7.2 million. Russia needed the money in the aftermath of the Crimean War, and Americans needed to stoke the fires of Manifest Destiny. But the Russians never really left. In naming geographical formations and bodies of water after explorers like Vitus Bering, the Russians left a lasting imprint on Alaska. One of Alaska's most active volcanos, named for Russian Orthodox missionary priest Aleksandr Veniaminof, continues to spew ash twenty thousand feet in the air when magma breaks through its glaciated caldera. Cape Sarichef, where the most isolated lighthouse in North America is located in the Aleutian Islands, was named for Vice Admiral Andreivich Sarichef. Named for Commander Gavriil Pribilof, the Pribilof Islands are situated in the middle of the vast Bering Sea and are a famed breeding ground for fur seals and seabirds. And several geological landmarks are named for Russian navigator Aleksei Chirikov, who traveled with Captain Bering on the first Russian vessel to reach the northwest coast of North America.

****

Even a mile away, the thirty-story oil rig towered above the horizon of the Chukchi Sea. The structure lit up like a city block aloft in the sky. When it burned off excess gas, its fire-breathing profile took a bite out of the dark blue hue that signaled the onset of an arctic evening in early October. The sleek gray hull of the 170-foot *Cape Chirikof* moved toward the oil rig. In its wake, scattered discs of ice rose and fell on the water's surface.

Captain Rob Stokes stood at the open wheelhouse door. A black wool cap covered salt-and-pepper hair. He tossed a cigarette into the sea with a flick of his finger and watched it land on an ice disc. Polar winds would eventually propel the ice floe from the Chukchi Sea through the Bering Strait into the Bering Sea. Some years the ice ensnared both Pribilof Islands, elbowing fleets from their fishing grounds.

Rob figured the waters would remain navigable long enough to allow several more supply trips to the oil rigs. His charter with the oil company required that his boat provide transport of crew and supplies to and from Dutch Harbor as long as the waterway remained passable. Once it froze over, operations would cease until March.

Rob slid into the captain's seat high on the starboard side. Leaning back, he reached above his head to pluck the microphone from its perch. The vessel intercom system came alive. Rob brought the mic close to his mouth. He knew the crew were probably still drinking coffee in the galley.

"Suit up and get on deck for cargo transfer. And make sure the oil rig crew are out of their staterooms and ready to move to the rig." He hung the microphone on its hook and slowed the boat to five knots.

The sun hugged the northern horizon. It wouldn't be long before it didn't show itself again until February. The perpetual night would swallow the oil rig into three months of darkness. Only the crackling whip of the northern lights across the sky and the ignited gas burps of oil rigs would lighten the winter's polar eclipse.

Seeing that the crew was on deck outfitted in insulated, tractor-red work suits, he reached for the overhead microphone again.

"After we transfer the oil rig crew, we'll start with the machinery modules in the stern and work our way forward, so check the strapping and prepare them for the rig's crane."

The phone rang.

"*Cape Chirikof* wheelhouse, Stokes here," he answered, expecting it to be a call from the oil rig.

Instead, it was the police chief, Ray St. George.

"Yes, Chief St. George, this is Rob Stokes..." Perspiration dampened his hairline. "No, I'm not in Dutch. I'm in the Chukchi Sea pulling up to an oil rig."

He slowed the vessel to three knots.

"Is something wrong?"

Listening to the chief's response, Rob's face relaxed. "My brother? What's Ben got himself into now?"

He was used to his brother spending the night in jail. One-Eye had long ago transitioned from being a deckhand to a hopeless addict. But when the *Cape Chirikof* was in town, he generally showed up for a meal and some cash.

"Dead?" Rob choked it out.

He'd been bracing himself for this possibility for years, but he felt dizzy now as if slammed in the head.

His chin quivered. "What happened?"

Rob slowed the engine to an idle. The boat began to drift in the swells as he learned the fate of his younger brother, Benjamin One-Eye Stokes, found dead on the beach with sea lions.

He stood up. "Murdered?"

When Ben was younger, he'd worked as a crew member on the *Cape Chirikof*. Those were the days when king crab *was* king and ruled the docks from Dutch Harbor to Kodiak. But king crab had fallen from its throne, losing its feisty grip on thick wads of cash and gold nugget watches. Specially designed, the watch clock faces were framed by carefully crafted fourteen-carat gold king crabs. Those monied days, like gold strikes, were gone now, making the storied watches a rare sight.

Rob still owned his gold nugget watch but had nearly lost the *Cape Chirikof* to a wave of debt. So far, he hadn't had to sell the watch or the boat. The oil rig charter had been the life ring that saved the boat. But debt still strained its ability to stay afloat.

Rob could see the oil rig crane poised to reach down and secure the cargo from the approaching *Cape Chirikof*. He could see the crew on the rolling deck below looking up at the wheelhouse.

"Chief St. George, I'm gonna have to call you back after I make this delivery." He hung up the satellite phone and engaged the engine to move the boat under the rig deck high above.

The transfer of cargo progressed smoothly and oil rig crew heading back to Dutch Harbor boarded the boat. All the time he wondered why his brother had died. Ben, who had lived so far out on the edge for so long, murdered. Why?

Rob's attention moved to a module that had been lowered onto the deck. It was loaded with garbage destined for the Dutch Harbor landfill.

Still wearing a work suit, a crew member climbed

the deck ladder to the bridge and swung open the metal door. Cold air rushed into the wheelhouse. Rob turned toward him.

The thuggish man closed the door and studied Rob's face before speaking.

"You look bad," he said, using words thick with a Russian accent. Not waiting for a response, he reached into his coverall pocket. "Here." He threw a brown bag at the captain.

Stretching his hand to grab it in midair, Rob's eyes never left the man.

"Ben is dead, Viktor."

"Drugs kill, yes?"

"He was murdered."

Viktor said nothing.

Rob's eyes grew dark. "Did you kill him?"

Viktor walked with the hunched shoulders of a surly boxer until he was in the captain's face. His meaty forefinger poked Rob's chest. "Not kill brother."

He stepped back and folded his thick arms. "No more drug debts to pay for One-Eye," he said, looking at the brown bag. "More money for you."

"Get out!"

Giving Rob a mock salute, Viktor headed downstairs to the galley.

Standing at the array of wheelhouse windows, pain contorted Rob's face. Tears blurred his vision as he moved the vessel from beneath the rig toward the open sea. Clear of its shadow, Rob leaned out the starboard window, grabbed his wool cap, and tossed it toward the sea. It fluttered in an updraft of wind, then fell to land on a disc of ice. The cap lay limp, rising and falling with the motion of the sea.

Chapter 5

The morning sun was barely up when Maureen and CoCo stopped to catch their breath after a run that ended at Azalea's Café. The parking lot was already packed with pickup trucks, most bearing rusty bruises where they'd been battered by bad weather and salty air. Azalea's had the best eggs in town, pancake stacks a mile high, and homemade yogurt. And it was dog friendly, like most places in town.

Pushing the door open, she saw Blackie Maguire, the harbormaster, sitting in the far corner where he held court most mornings. He waved her over.

CoCo ambled ahead of Maureen, eager to find her place under Blackie's hand. He gave her ears a warm rub. "You are one big dog, CoCo." He patted her back and looked at Maureen, who'd pulled up a seat.

"Why is your shepherd so much bigger than mine?"

"Born in a place where they're bred to be big." She showed him the tattoo on CoCo's ear, indicating she'd been trained in Budapest. "A police dog with a mysterious past." She laughed. "But she understands English, even your brogue, Blackie."

A waitress swung by with two mugs of coffee. She looked at Maureen and Blackie. No order pad, just hands on her hips. "The usual?" she said, looking from one to the other.

Their heads nodded. "Thanks, Sparky," they said in

unison.

Blackie blew on the steaming cup of coffee. "So, water temperature?"

"Yeah, you know we found One-Eye Ben washed up on the beach last week. I'm trying to get a better read on when he died. To do that, I need a solid read on water temperature in Captains Bay."

Blackie sipped coffee from beneath a handlebar mustache so white it looked like walrus tusks. Then he pulled a folded paper from his chest pocket. He pushed it toward her. "Forty-one degrees," he said. "We monitor the air and water temperature regularly. Big tides flush the bay with incoming ocean seas, so the temperature is colder than you might think."

Maureen nodded. "I thought he'd been dead at least two days. But with a water temperature of forty-one degrees, I'm inclined to think it was longer."

"I suspect you'll be wanting me to think about the comings and goings of boats around that time. And I have. The troopers called me yesterday and asked what I might have seen two days before he was found."

"What did you tell them?"

"I had Marcus send them the manifest of vessels that were in town two days before you found him."

"Is it too much to ask for a list of vessels in town *four* days before we found him?"

He set his mug on the table and folded his arms across his chest.

She shrugged, knowing it was a big ask.

"Templeton sends his best, by the way," Blackie said.

The black and tan shepherd was almost always at the harbormaster's side but not today. He was recovering from a broken leg Maureen had set last week.

"Glad to hear it. He's a youngster and should be running up and down the docks in no time."

Sparky swung by, dropping off their breakfast. She slipped CoCo a Milk Bone.

Blackie perked-up when a plate of eggs and bacon nested in a mountain of home fries came to rest on the checkered tablecloth in front of him. He frowned at Maureen's plate. "Yogurt and fruit, eh? Are you some kind of health nut, Mo?" He looked at her as if he found this difficult to believe.

"Got to balance out my beer consumption, Blackie." She looked at his paunch and smiled.

He laughed and rubbed his belly. "Glad to see you're acknowledging the beauty of it."

They were flirting with the third cup of coffee poured when Maureen asked whether there was anyone she might speak to about goings-on at the far end of Captains Bay.

"Well, there's Mrs. Pynchon, who lives out on Levashef Island. She's not as daft as they say. But she's not got a phone and doesn't much care for company." He stirred his coffee slowly, looking at it like he was weighing whether or not a third cup would do more harm than good.

"She's got a small dock that's barely big enough for that monster skiff of hers." He dropped the spoon in the mug. "And there's a couple of tender tie-off buoys down at that end of the bay."

When Maureen started to speak, Blackie raised his hand and interrupted her. "I know. I know. You want the name of any cargo vessels tied to the buoys for the four days preceding the date you found One Eye. Come by the office and work with Marcus. He'll get you what you need."

Maureen was about to thank him when his hand flew up again. "Yes, I know. I'll send a copy to the chief too."

That's when Marla Mancuso entered the café. With an MBA earned at an East Coast university, she'd managed the Amchitka Shipping Company for several years. People wondered what brought a woman like Marla to Dutch and kept her there.

There's a joke played on greenhorn fishermen shipping out to Dutch for the first time. They're told there's a woman behind every tree. It doesn't take long for them to notice that the vast expanse of ocean and mountains are unobstructed by trees. Only a handful of Sitka spruce remain standing from a Russian colony's tree planting effort in 1805. The six stunted trees comprise a small city park just up the road from Azalea's. So, yeah, there's at least a woman for all six trees in Dutch, and Marla is the most striking.

Standing at the front counter sporting a red parka, blue jeans, and cowboy boots, she smiled at them. Maureen heard she'd dated Arlo once but that it had ended long ago. When she asked Arlo about it, he shrugged it off.

"Smart girl," Blackie said, waving Marla over to join them.

When she arrived, he gestured toward an empty seat at the table. "Pull up a chair," he said.

Noting they both seemed done with their breakfast, Marla said she'd come for just a scone and coffee. "Please don't let me hold you up. I have brought my reading material."

Marla dropped a copy of the *Anchorage News* on the

table and pointed to the headline above the front-page fold. "The price of oil jumped to over one hundred dollars a barrel this week. If it holds, I expect we'll see more interest in exploratory oil drilling in the Chukchi Sea."

A change in oil prices affects pocketbooks everywhere. But in Alaska, where most of state operating budget is funded by oil royalties, those revenues build roads and schools, fund agencies, and generally keep the lights on around the state.

"Hey," said an energized Blackie. "All that new revenue to state coffers might translate into an expanded city dock." He turned to Marla with a mischievous grin. "With all your oil rig support vessels we've had to accommodate this year, we could use more dock space."

Without bothering to take an order, Sparky delivered a mug of coffee and a blueberry scone to the table.

Marla was quick to bring the mug to her lips. She looked first at Maureen and then at Blackie. "So, what are you two up to? I hope I'm not interrupting a meeting?"

"Mo's helping the chief investigate the murder of One-Eye. She asked me for the water temperature readings in Captains Bay so she can better estimate his time of death."

Marla set her mug down. She looked at Maureen, who was doing her best to conceal her agitation with Blackie for sharing this information.

"Really?" said Marla. "I didn't know you were involved in police work, Mo."

"I'm not. The chief asked me to help him out on this small task. Nothing I'd call police work."

"I heard around town that One-Eye may have been murdered. Any clues about who might have killed him?"

"The investigation is just getting underway."

Marla's lips opened as if she were considering another question but fell shut as if knowing another query was best left alone.

Blackie looked from one woman to the other. "Whoa, I haven't stepped in it, I hope."

"Nah," said Maureen, making light of it. "But I'm the vet lady, not the lady detective."

They all laughed. Then, like everyone else in the café, they complained about the unseasonably warm weather.

"It truly sucks," Blackie said.

****

Nights later, the ocean rolled beneath a starry sky. A boat rode with it, its planks sighing in the gentle breeze. Above the boat, shimmering sheets of sapphire trailed off to meet the black horizon. Casey lit a cigarette and strode toward the stern. To him, the northern lights made the desolate ocean buffer between Alaska and Russia seem less empty.

A gust of wind caused sea spray to pelt his orange rain gear jacket and blue jeans. Passing a crane, Casey stopped alongside a crab pot that provided some shelter. He licked the salty sea spray from his lips. It was gritty and sweet. It felt romantic and, somehow, heroic. Yes, he thought, nodding his youthful bearded face, he *was* heroic.

He'd stumbled into a thicket of crime. It was not the environmental regulatory violations he'd hoped to uncover with his investigation. That would take more time. It was a tangled mess that had ensnared him personally. It was toxic enough that it might launch newspaper headlines and a public relations nightmare for the oil company. That excited him, but he would not use his discovery to make headlines. He took a long drag from his cigarette. He had a better plan, even if somewhat tarnished by blackmail. He'd use the money to help fund an end to offshore drilling and overfishing. Heroic stuff. Letting loose a trail of smoke rings, he grinned at the prospect. He knew he wouldn't be the first to do good by doing bad. His smile broadened beneath the starry sky as he turned to see whose hand had reached for his shoulder.

The smile slid from Casey's face when a fist rocketed toward him. He raised his forearm to block the punch and threw one of his own that landed on the chest of his attacker. Another punch came at him, an uppercut that rocked his chin skyward and sent him reeling until he hit the railing.

The man in green rain gear, a hood obscuring his face, walked purposefully toward Casey. He threw a punch to the right side of Casey's bearded face, followed by a pounding blow to the left side. It sent Casey down to the deck fast and hard. His head slammed back onto the base of the crane. *Crack.* His body went limp.

The man in green gear bent down and grabbed Casey by the collar. Yanking the kid's face toward his own, he shook him. He cursed the kid and hollered at him to wake up. But when the body responded like a rag doll, he dropped him. He felt for a pulse. Nothing. Looking out from beneath his hood, the man's eyes settled on the six-by-six foot crab pot.

The body was heavy. The man struggled to drag it to the pot's edge. Opening the pot door, he stuffed Casey inside and latched it closed. His fingers grabbed the pot webbing to take a last look at the kid's battered face. Finally, he turned away to take charge of the crane controls. The crane lifted the six-hundred-pound cage easily. The metal arm carried it high above deck and lowered it into the pot launcher on the starboard side. He watched it heave the pot over the side until the kid in the cage was swallowed by the sea.

Unknown to him, a face watched from the wheelhouse window above.

Chapter 6

Marcus was peculiar. Dressed in the clothes of a mechanic, he looked up from behind the counter when Maureen pushed open the door to the harbormaster's office. Running a hand through his rangy, carrot-red hair, he mumbled out of the side of his mouth.

"Morning, Doc."

"Hey, Marcus."

Everyone called him Marcus because he'd once worked in the Marcus Shipyard in Seattle. He talked about the vessels he helped build like they were his kids and checked up on them when they were tied up in town.

"Blackie told me to have our skiff waiting for you." He reached for one of the keys hanging on the wall behind him. "I'll walk you down."

They stopped at the first finger of the dock, the one closest to the harbormaster's office. Tied to the dock was a skiff with a large console at its center. Marcus stepped into it and reached to give Maureen a hand.

"Blackie says you know how to use it." He opened the console and held up a radio. "Give me a holler if you get stuck." Then he handed over the keys, giving her a squirrelly look.

"Thanks, Marcus," she said, dropping her knapsack under the seat.

"Gonna see the witch, huh?"

Maureen turned on the ignition. Marcus leaped onto

the dock. The engine rumbled to life.

"Yep."

****

Maureen's hair whipped in the wind as she powered past the harbor buoy and steered the skiff toward the head of Captains Bay. Blackie had lent her the boat after a skirmish of words about it being a reckless venture for her to tangle with Mrs. Pynchon. But persistence pays off, she thought. She throttled the boat up to fifteen knots, allowing it to skim across the cobalt surface of gentle waves. Ben's time of death was a tangled mess that needed fixing. And she wanted to be the one to sort it out because the state police didn't seem to be giving the death of a drug addict much priority. And, yeah, it was personal too. She thought she was right.

As she drove deeper into the bay, she heard sea lions barking on Swallow Reef. A buoy on its east side would guide her away from the dangerous shoals. Levashef Island would be a short hop from there.

The barking sea lions were close now. Thinking this might be where One Eye and the sea lions were shot, she slowed the engine to maneuver closer to the rocks. Calm seas licked the barnacle-clad rock piles, and water hissed as it navigated through small crevices. Several sea lions slid down the rocks and disappeared beneath the water's surface.

She knew the bottom dropped off quickly here, allowing good fishing for both sea lions and sport fishermen. Lots of rockfish were hooked along this reef. She let the boat bob in the water, thinking. She imagined someone shooting sea lions and One-Eye here. It seemed the most probable place. The beach where they were found was on the other side of Levashef Island, about a mile away. Four days seemed a reasonable time for the carcasses to drift there. Throttling up the engine again, she swung the bow around until it pointed toward the island and the small cove where she knew a dock waited.

Entering the cove at two knots, she navigated around unmarked rocks that Blackie had warned her about. She found just enough space to tie up aft of the power skiff that made hers look puny. Grabbing a small knapsack, she threw one strap over her shoulder and climbed stairs that ascended the rocky bank. She passed a flagpole. The state flag waved overhead. The eight gold stars against a field of blue was a sight far more common in Alaska than the flying of the Stars and Stripes.

She followed the weathered boardwalk through the forest and up another set of stairs until it ended in a clearing with a commanding view. At its center was a well-crafted cabin. Smoke curled from its stone chimney. A woman in jeans and an ivory-colored Irish fishermen's sweater waited at the open door. A shotgun lay across the crook of her arm.

Maureen slowed her step. She could turn and leave or persist. If she hadn't planned to follow through, she should have relented when Blackie tried to talk her down. But she'd gotten the keys, taken the skiff, and now she was here, facing down an old lady cradling a shotgun.

Maureen's heart quickened. She sized up the person that stood before her. She seemed strong and agile for a seventy-year-old woman. Her thick gray mane was cut squarely at her shoulders. Her eyebrows were black as night, and the eyes beneath them blue as ice.

Mrs. Pynchon patted the shotgun. "Did Blackie tell you about the time I greeted him with a blast to the sky?"

"Why didn't you fire one off above me?"

"I wanted to meet you," She looked Maureen in the eye. "If you got scared at the mere sight of a shotgun across my arm, well, I'd prefer not to waste my time."

"Here I am." Maureen unslung the knapsack from her shoulder and let it drop to the ground, making it clear she wasn't planning to hightail it back to the skiff.

The older woman eyed the knapsack noting a PVC pipe poking from beneath the flap.

It wasn't long before Maureen was sitting at the kitchen table with a cup of tea, and Mrs. Pynchon was stroking the pipe.

"I ordered this a month ago. It needed a special fitting." She drew aside a curtain under her sink, revealing a pot set there to catch leaking water. "That's my good pot. I'll be happy to have it back." She set the pipe in the sink and turned to Maureen. "Thank you, young lady."

Maureen smiled and set down her tea cup. "Why did you shoot when Blackie came by?"

"Ha! I wanted him to get a story circulated around town that would discourage visitors." She eyed Maureen. "But it didn't discourage you, Dr. McMurtry. Why is that?"

"You know my name?"

"I know all I need to know out here without having to know crap I don't want to know." She pointed to the VHF radio in the corner. The volume was turned down, but you could hear it spouting chatter like a babbling brook. "I know, for instance, that you're helping investigate the murder of One-Eye. But I don't know why."

"The chief needs my help."

"It's nice to be needed. But why are you here instead of the chief?"

"I'm trying to figure out his time of death. It's a medical question. The state police have made up their minds, but the chief and I agree it's worth further investigation." Then she shot Mrs. Pynchon a mischievous glance. "But if you saw or heard anything around that time, I'd be glad to hear it."

"As old as I am, I ought to know a few things."

Maureen sipped the tea again before continuing. "The tides, the currents, the water temperature, they make it hard to figure out the time of death. I thought that you, being so close to where it happened, might know something that could be helpful."

"I saw your skiff dawdling around Swallow Reef. Are you thinking that's where the killing came down?"

"Dead sea lions seem to point to a haul-out site. And that reef is the only one at this end of the bay."

"Good thinking, young lady. And the currents here move to the head of the bay."

"How long do you think it might take for the corpses to land there?"

"That's hard to say. It might take several days, but there were big tides about then, so it could have been just a couple of days."

Maureen frowned.

Mrs. Pynchon pushed a basket of fresh corn muffins her way. Then she stood and fetched a jar of honey. She set it in front of Maureen. "Mother Nature has her ways. They're not always predictable."

"I know the corpses were in the water at least two days, but I'm inclined to think it might have been as long as four. The water's so cold, it slowed the decay process."

Still standing, Mrs. Pynchon looked down at her. "Now you're going to ask me if I saw or heard shots in the days before you found him." She saw Maureen's surprised expression. "Oh yeah, I knew you found him. You'd be surprised the amount of gossip that passes over the fleet's radio waves when they're in town."

Maureen let herself smile. She cut open a muffin and drizzled honey on it. "Well," she said, "*did* you hear gunshots?"

The older woman sat down across from Maureen. "I hear all sorts of gunshots. People like to shoot things." She stopped, seeming to take care with her next words. "I did see a skiff out there about that time, but even with my binoculars, I couldn't make out who it was. It was near dusk."

"But you saw that it was a skiff?"

"Yes. It was definitely a skiff. I know my boats, young lady. It was a sizeable one with a center console. Not as big as mine, of course." She stopped to think about it like she was digging around in the back of her brain. "It had a yellow stripe around it near the water line. But that's not uncommon."

Maureen pulled a notebook from her knapsack and wrote down the details. She looked up, hopefully. "The date? Do you know when it was that you saw the skiff?"

"Time is a thing I don't much care for. And dates and days of the week are artifices I don't have much need for. Seasons are about as close as I like to get to giving a crap about time. But," she looked at Maureen, "I'd say it was more than two days before you found him."

Mrs. Pynchon looked at Maureen with some sympathy, knowing that she'd hoped for more precision.

She took a sip from her teacup and set it back on the saucer.

"May I call you Mo? I'd like to be frank, and for me, that means being on a first name basis."

"I'd like that."

"Call me, Rose," she said smearing more honey on the corn muffin. "I know you want to help find One-Eye's killer. And that's a good thing because others don't much give a damn about him."

Maureen looked over the lip of her teacup at the woman who seemed to know a lot more than she'd expected.

Mrs. Pynchon rose from the table and put her hand on Maureen's shoulder. "Well, caring about One-Eye is a good thing. But nosing around in murder is dangerous business. So be on the look out."

Maureen set down her teacup.

"You're right. I'll be careful."

Mrs. Pynchon nodded toward the knapsack. "Now don't you have something in there for me?"

Maureen had forgotten to give Mrs. Pynchon the five-pound slab of bacon Blackie had given her to pack for the visit.

She reached into the knapsack and pulled out the slab wrapped in butcher's paper and tied with a white string. Blackie had smoked the pork belly himself.

Walking back to the boat, Maureen stopped halfway down the dock. Looking at the harbormaster's skiff, she shook her head and laughed. There was a broad yellow stripe painted along its waterline.

Chapter 7

The *Viking King* thundered forward, its bow splitting open the next wave. Shots of spray hosed its windows, blurring the captain's vision from inside the wheelhouse.

"Aw, crap!" Jack slid from the captain's chair. He'd seen enough. Continued fishing in this weather was a fool's errand. He set a new course for the boat so that it turned away from the wind. It seemed a safer course for hauling back the net. The direction change would carry the boat off the edge into the deeper water of the *Mushroom*. He'd haul the net back as soon as it straightened out behind the boat.

He hadn't expected to find large schools of cod in October, but at forty cents a pound, it was worth chasing down roving gangs of smooth-scaled piscivores riding currents along the downward slope of the continental shelf. The shelf's edge spreads diagonally across the Bering Sea from the Alaska Peninsula toward the northern reaches of Siberia. Fish hang there waiting for the upwelling of food. And fishermen hang there for the same reason.

The hold wasn't half full of fish. Jack figured if they jogged into the wind for the night, they could resume fishing in the morning when the marine weather forecast said it would subside. He headed down the wheelhouse stairs to the galley, where he knew some of the crew were engaged in a cribbage match. Bill and Marty looked up from their card hands.

"Time to get wet, guys. We'll start hauling back in about ten minutes."

He ducked into the engine room where he knew the engineer was tending to the chillers that kept the sea water icy cold in the fish hold. He pounded the railing with a hammer to get his attention. The young engineer looked up from his work. He wore large insulated headphones meant to protect his eardrums from the thundering heartbeat of the seventeen-hundred-horsepower engine. Jack pointed aft and raised five fingers twice, indicating it would be time to get out on deck in ten minutes. Eric Petersen gave him a thumbs-up.

Pouring himself a cup of coffee in the galley, Jack headed up to the wheelhouse, where he checked the sensors. Seeing the net wire had straightened out behind the boat, he engaged the winches. Hauling back three hundred fathoms of wire had begun.

Eric wiped the grease from his hands, hung the headphones by the engine room door, and exchanged them for a billed cap smeared with fish gurry and grease. At twenty-nine, he already knew he would be captain one day. He climbed the stairs and pushed open the engine room door. Donning yellow vinyl coveralls and a jacket, he joined Marty and Bill on the pitching deck.

Deckhands counter the motion of a deck by shifting their weight. Not too dangerous for a crack fisherman with good sense, but the deepening wave troughs were challenging even to this crew. Loving the feisty weather, Eric lit a cigarette while waiting for the gear to pop above the surface. He smiled as the exhaled smoke disappeared into the wind. The salty spray clung to his beard. He inhaled the smoke again before tossing the butt over the side as the heavy metal doors approached the stern ramp.

High-powered sodium lights lit up the deck like a night game in a ballpark. The powerful propeller churned up the sea leaving a trailing path of green foam. Once the crew secured the doors to the blocks, the sweeps and bobbins popped to the surface followed by the nylon webbing of the trawl net. The gear slid up the stern ramp onto the deck.

"Shit!" The captain's jaw tightened at the sight on deck. He stopped the haul back and grabbed the microphone. "Crab pot?"

The crew looked up at the wheelhouse, signaling that the captain's grim query was correct.

"What's a crab pot doing here?" Eric wondered aloud, knowing they were in waters too deep to find much crab. But there it was, tangled in the net.

Marty and Bill hooked the net to the gilson and hauled the pot to the center of the deck.

The crew gathered around the unwelcomed catch. They knew that once they cut the pot loose, they would be out on deck for hours sewing the damaged web.

Eric pushed back his hat in disgust. Bad weather, okay. A torn-up net, not okay. He grabbed a knife from the sheaf strapped across his chest and joined Bill and Marty as they cut the pot loose.

Eric pulled the last layer of webbing aside.

"Holy shit, man-o-man!" he yelled, pointing his knife toward the net. "There's a fuck'n dead body in this fuck'n crab pot!"

Jack slowed the boat to jogging speed and hurried down the wheelhouse ladder to the deck.

"What's going on?" His eyes squinted into the sea spray.

Eric hollered over the howling wind. "There's a dead body in the crab pot!"

The captain moved closer to the twisted pile and pulled aside the cut webbing so he could reach inside the pot. Slowly he folded back the orange vinyl hood.

"Aw, jeez, he's just a kid."

The kid's face was drained of color. Dark bruises marked his cheek and chin. His lip was split open and one of his eyes, swollen shut. A codfish lay in his lap.

Jack moved the kid's head from one side to the other. "He looks badly beaten." He opened the kid's upper and lower lips. "There's some broken teeth in here."

He reached inside the jacket collar, hoping to find a scrawled name on the label. Nothing. He patted down pockets within easy reach, searching for a wallet. He found only a pack of cigarettes and a lighter. He stuffed them back in the kid's pocket and looked up at the crew.

"Okay, he's not badly decomposed," Jack said. "But we gotta get this body out of the net and off the deck. I don't want the catch contaminated. Let's wrap him in a tarp and put him in the bait locker."

The captain looked at each of his crew. "Treat this young man carefully and with respect. I'm gonna call the Coast Guard and report this now. After you stow him in the freezer, get the pot squared away and get the fish in the hold."

Heading across the deck, Jack started up the ladder. He turned back to the crew, his sweatshirt hanging heavy, soaked with sea spray. "Respect!" he said.

****

Stepping back, Eric surveyed the scene. Lit by deck lights and splashed by seawater, the limp body made him want to vomit. He held it down, not wanting to run to the rail. To the crew, he said, "Let's get this deck cleaned-up."

He watched Marty and Bill, each grabbing an arm and a leg. He could see in their faces they hoped the body would remain intact. Everyone was struggling to keep it together, he thought.

Climbing the ladder to the wheelhouse, he handed Jack the crab pot tag he'd dislodged from the steel cage. The tag had digits stamped on it that would identify its owner. They both knew it was important information. Without a word, Eric returned to the deck and headed down to the bait locker. He opened the freezer door. The five-foot square area was partially filled with loose ice. Half buried in the ice were several gallon containers of ice cream, two hams, five pounds of bacon, a stack of steaks, and a twelve-pound turkey. He could see some of it would have to be moved to make room for the new guy. Eric crammed as much as he could into a box for transfer to the galley freezer. The turkey, he put in the sink. It would take a couple of days to defrost.

Returning to the bait locker, he used a shovel to shape a bench area where he thought the new guy might sit for the ride to Dutch Harbor. He returned with a blanket from his bunk. Spreading it across the ice bench, he left it open so "Guy" could be seated there.

"Damn crazy," he muttered. But he knew if it were him, his folks would want his body handled with care. Seeing the frozen tomb was ready, he headed out on deck to get the body.

After the three crewmen rolled the kid's body up in

a tarp, Bill and Marty stood at either end of the long cylinder. Eric waited in the middle. At the end of a three count, they heaved the dead weight up on their shoulders.

At the bait locker, they unwound the kid from the tarp casing. At Eric's direction, they sat the kid on the ice bench. Bill and Marty headed for the deck. Eric took the blanket he had laid on the ice bench and draped it over Guy's shoulders. He folded the kid's hands so they lay neatly on his lap and packed ice at his sides so he would remain secure for the rough ride back to town. Reaching into the chest pocket of his own jacket, he removed a pack of cigarettes. His hand shook as he lit two.

"We smoke the same brand," he said, bending to wedge one in Guy's gray lips. He smoked the other cigarette, all the while talking to the kid as if his spirit lingered nearby. "What a bummer," he said, "dying so young." He told the kid he would be missed by someone and promised to get him home. Hearing his voice crack, Eric turned away as if he didn't want Guy to see him that way.

Then he closed the freezer door.

****

Guy sat in the bait locker, the cigarette still hanging from his lips. The freezing temperature had already caused the moisture on his eyelashes and beard to crystallize. He looked as if he were climbing Mt. Everest instead of sitting propped-up, dead in a fishing boat bait locker headed to Dutch Harbor, Alaska.

Chapter 8

Dutch Harbor has three names. On a map, it is identified as *Unalaska*, named for the large island on which it is located and originating from the Aleut word *Onalaska*, meaning *near the peninsula*. Cape Cheerful and Priest Rock face the Bering Sea and are the gateway landmarks to the protective waters of Unalaska Bay. And, not unlike an arrangement of Russian nesting dolls, Amaknak Island is nested inside Unalaska Bay, and the protected anchorage of Dutch Harbor is nestled in the crook of the smaller island's leeward coast. The seventy thousand servicemen stationed here in WWII called the town *Dutch Harbor* because the small harbor, named for a Dutch vessel believed to be the first boat to anchor there, was where they built the military airstrip. Today, Dutch Harbor is inhabited by forty-five hundred sturdy souls. The population explodes when fishing starts in January. Thousands of processing workers, marine vendors, and fishermen pour into town. They just call the place *Dutch*.

The smaller island defines Dutch with its welcoming coves and angular spit that swings out into the bay, tripping up ill-tempered weather. Perched along these protected waters are shipping and fuel docks, boat harbors that huddle together the steel hulls of hard-working fishing boats, and seafood plants where they deliver their hard-won catch. Down the road, on the inside perimeter, are the places that service the fleets and residential population, including the Aleutian Hotel, the grocery store, Azalea's Café, and The Rodent Saloon. Up the road sits the Bering Sea crab management office and, in the building next door to it, Dr. Mo's Veterinary Clinic. Maureen lives upstairs.

****

The kind of muscular coffee required to launch Maureen's day is not available in Dutch. So she purchased a complicated espresso machine with narrow pipes and nozzles in Anchorage and packed it back to her one-bedroom apartment above the clinic.

An overstuffed couch hogs up much of the living room which it shares with an armchair, an ottoman, and a small table framed by two paint-chipped chairs. A diesel stove in the corner heats the place. The galley kitchen is a cramped affair, but since she generally doesn't cook anything that exceeds a one-step process, she doesn't much care. The espresso contraption takes up a quarter of the kitchen counter space, a modest amount considering the importance of the frothy-rich latte greeting her there each morning.

"Oh yeah," she whispered into her mug as she inhaled its rich aroma. Rays of morning sun filtered through the old lace curtains hanging in her kitchen. The window looked out to the sea across the road. The view would be breathtaking if not blighted by a parking lot spread in front of it.

She made a second cup. Donning her leather jacket and expertly carrying the two steaming mugs with a single hand, she headed out the door with CoCo. Crossing the parking lot, the pair climbed the stairs of the large multi-use building. She pushed open the outer door and headed down the corridor with CoCo in tow. Stopping at the door marked *Bering Sea Crab Management,* she rapped it with her knuckles.

"I've got strong coffee, Patsy. You game?"

"Yeah, but come on in at your own peril."

Maureen opened the door and looked around cautiously.

Patsy punctuated her pronouncement by kicking over the garbage can at her desk. Papers flew out of the can and left a messy collage that spread halfway across her office floor.

"Nice." Maureen stepped over the papers to take the seat not offered. She placed a mug on the desk in front of Patsy. "You want to tell me about it?"

"Dead bodies make me grumpy." She brought the mug to her lips and downed half its contents. "A body was found in a crab pot hauled up near the Pribilof Islands."

"Oh, jeez. What happened?"

"I don't know."

"Have they identified the body?"

Patsy shook her head. "A kid in his twenties. Body's not too rotten, but no identification was found." She leaned back in her chair. "The pot is registered to the *Cape Kiska*, Mo. It's in the owner's name."

Maureen looked baffled.

"You mean Arlo?"

"I'm afraid so. Hard to imagine him as the culprit. Too good looking to be a bad guy." Patsy leaned farther back in her creaking swivel chair. "Like Ted Bundy."

"Cut the crap, Patsy. It's not funny."

"A trawler dragged the pot up southeast of the Pribs outta the *Mushroom*." Patsy sipped her coffee. "The boat's due in town tomorrow. They've got the body on ice."

CoCo pawed at the strewn paper and inspected a half-eaten muffin.

"Could it have been an accident?"

Patsy looked over the rim of her reading glasses. "There've been no reports of a man overboard in a crab pot. Besides, the season doesn't start until next week. And…they say he looked badly beaten."

Seeming to sense that something was wrong, CoCo rested her head on Maureen's knee. She stroked the dog's head. "How do they know it's one of Arlo's pots?"

"The permit tag was still attached to the pot. It's the *Cape Kiska*'s permit number."

Maureen contemplated the ceiling. Focusing on a crack there that spread across it like a river delta, she asked when the body was discovered. Finally, she looked at Patsy.

"Shouldn't you give the chief a call?"

"Chief St. George? He's the one who called me wanting to know whose tag it was." She swiveled the monitor screen around toward Maureen and pointed to a line on the spreadsheet. "Right here. Arlo Castle. *Cape Kiska.* Permit number, 95969."

The office went still like a set where actors had forgotten their lines.

Patsy leaned forward on her desk, both hands wrapped around the mug.

"It's just a crab pot, Mo. It's not a smoking gun."

****

Maureen parked alongside the Olympic Fisheries plant, where she knew Arlo's boat would be loading pots for the crab season. Behind a veil of falling snow, fishing boats lined the docks, their hulls straining against thick ropes that secured them to iron cleats. Forklifts carrying pallets of gear crisscrossed in front of Maureen as she made her way toward the *Cape Kiska.*

Pulling leather gloves from her pocket, she slipped her hands into the soft fur lining as she approached the blue hull of the fishing boat. Arlo stood on the bridge operating the crane. Chief St. George was already there, climbing over the rail and onto the boat.

She stopped short of the stern, where she saw the chief signaling to Arlo on the bridge that he wanted to talk. Arlo shut down the crane and hollered to the crew to take a break. Maureen could see him lift the billed cap from his head with one hand and wipe his brow with the back of his forearm. He gave the chief his full attention and didn't seem to notice she was there.

She watched Arlo's body language react to the chief. His hands rested on his hips. His head nodded as the chief spoke. He held the wheelhouse door open so the chief could enter first. Following the chief inside, he turned to look back over his shoulder at Maureen. Then he closed the door.

Maureen knew the *Cape Kiska* was the central compass in Arlo's life. Unlike most fishing boats, Arlo had the house painted every year. He chose a brilliant white that, together with the crisp navy blue of the hull, whisked away the rust wounds inflicted by the saltwater beating it took at sea. She'd once asked him why he, instead of the crew, repainted the boat's name on the stern and bow. "Therapeutic, my dear," he'd said after climbing down from the ladder and walking backwards along the dock to make sure he'd painted it straight and within the stenciled lines.

Arlo hadn't always stayed within the lines. In a barroom brawl seven years earlier, he'd broken a man's arm in two places and knocked him unconscious. He'd been out of control and paid for it by wasting six months of his life in jail. Since then, he'd not violated his self-imposed ban on drinking hard liquor, as far as anybody knew.

She swung her leg over the boat railing. "I hope you're not in trouble again, Arlo." It was that talking aloud shit again she thought shaking her head.

"What?" It was the boat's engineer, Sully. He looked up from the hold as she passed by. A cigarette hung from his lips and his hand held a wrench.

Startled, she waved at him. "It's snowing," she said. He shrugged and got back to work.

Maureen headed to the ladder where she climbed to the bridge. She found Arlo and the chief huddled over the chart table, thumbing through the log book. They looked up when the door opened.

"The chief just told me a dead body was pulled up in one of my crab pots," Arlo said.

"I know. Patsy told me." Looking at the chief, she said, "I thought you might be here. Is it okay if I'm here for this questioning?"

The chief's eyes wandered from one to the other. "Arlo and I are just talking."

Arlo's hand rested on the chart table where he'd ravished Maureen the week before. Pointing to a location on the map near the one-hundred-fathom curve south of the Pribilof Islands, he told the chief he'd just returned from a fishery survey that had lasted five days.

"They hired me and my crew to search for skate egg casing sites. Nurseries, some call them. They gave us the locations, and we did the work," he said.

The chief laid his notebook on the table where Maureen had wrapped her thighs around him. Arlo threw Maureen a glance that seemed to indicate he, too, recalled the intense lovemaking.

"Can you show me precisely where you were fishing during the survey, Arlo?"

They hunched over the table, and Arlo pointed to several locations on the chart, indicating a half dozen areas near the *Mushroom* and the *Horseshoe*. Then he opened a drawer and passed the chief a fishery service business card. "Ask them about it."

The chief took the card, looked at it, and stuffed it in his jacket pocket. "Thanks," he said.

Arlo crossed his arms at his chest. "Yeah, I could have done it. Killed the guy and stuffed him in a pot. But you'd think I'd be smart enough to remove my permit tag before doing that."

The chief nodded, seeming to acknowledge the logic of it as he scribbled in his notebook.

Arlo pointed toward the deck where dozens of pots had already been stacked. "Everyone's using fewer pots these days. The race to catch as many crabs as quickly as possible is over now that we've been issued individual quotas. Like lots of boats, I've got a stash of old pots stored out the road. Anyone could have taken one."

"When did you leave town for that trip?"

"Five days ago." He checked his log book. "We left the morning of October fifth and returned last night, the tenth." He looked at the chief. "So, we've got just a few days to gear up for the king crab opener. I'm hoping this investigation will not cause a delay."

Large snowflakes drifted past the wheelhouse

windows. Maureen knew Arlo had the strength to pummel a deckhand into submission. But not kill him, she thought. Not stuff him in a crab pot and abandon him to the ocean. Not possible, she thought, letting her eyes wander around the wheelhouse, wondering what it was like here when the boat was at sea. But she'd been wrong about men before and paid the price.

Arlo pointed out the precise beginning and end locations of each tow on the plotter. He handed a print-out of it to the chief.

"I see you stopped at St. Paul Island?" he asked. "What's that have to do with the survey."

"I've got a storage unit there and picked up a spare net."

The chief nodded and scribbled in his notebook.

"The trawler that hauled the pot up in its net is headed back to town," he said. "It should get in by tomorrow night. Reportedly, the body shows little sign of decomposition, so it was not in the water long. But, hopefully," he said, turning to Maureen, "we can get an estimate on time and cause of death when the ship gets in."

"And his identity, I hope," Arlo said. "I'd like to find out if I even know this guy who I'm suspected of killing."

The chief snapped his pen shut and put it in his pocket. "Calm down, Arlo. We've got to follow all the leads. I'm sending my deputies over to talk to your crew. Is this afternoon okay with you?"

"Sure, after we finish loading the pots. But, except for Sully, I didn't have my regular crew on board. A couple of greenhorns took their place while two of the regular crew stayed in town prepping the crab gear."

"Give the deputies their names and contact info. And," he said glancing at Arlo's beat-up left hand, "do you mind if the deputies take photos of your hand?"

Scabs had formed over his knuckles, and he'd fashioned a splint on his middle finger using a broken chopstick and some black electrical tape.

"Banged it up while working on the hydraulics." He held it up. "Talk to the crew all you want after we finish loading the pots, but I think I'll wait on having a mug shot taken of my fist until you find something more incriminating than a permit tag."

"Fair enough," said the chief turning to leave. He held the door open and turned to look at Maureen. "Are you coming?"

"I think I'll stay for lunch," she said, checking Arlo's expression to be sure it was okay.

The chief tipped his hat in a goodbye gesture.

Stopping at the bottom ladder, he looked up at Arlo, still at the door.

"The deputies will cover the basics with your crew later today. But we'll wait to see what we learn from the corpse before we climb any farther down your throat."

Arlo tucked his hands in the front pockets of his jeans. "Okay. Wait and see. I get it."

The chief looked at Maureen. "Call me," he said.

Chapter 9

Chief St. George parked his large SUV in front of the police station. Turning off the engine, he let his wrists rest on the steering wheel. The snow had turned to rain, and he could hear it pounding on the cab's roof. All he could see through the windshield was the blur of a gravel parking lot and a soaked landscape beneath an inky afternoon sky.

Three dead bodies in his town since he'd arrived. He paused to think about it. One, found on a beach with sea lions, had been shipped to troopers in Anchorage nine days ago. Another, found in a crab pot yesterday, should arrive by boat tomorrow night. And that body found floating in the small boat harbor two months ago, he suspected it was a drug overdose but hadn't yet heard back from Anchorage.

He wondered if he should be worried about Maureen and her apparent relationship with Arlo. He hadn't worked with her long, but her head seemed screwed on right. There wasn't much to pin on Arlo at this point, and he needed her assessment on cause and time of death before he released the body to state police. For now, she seemed a good fit, but he'd reassess as needed.

Opening the big SUV's door, he charged into the downpour, dodging mud holes as much as his long strides would allow.

Inside, deputy Chet looked up from his desk. He

held a phone in one hand and covered the mouthpiece with the other. "Chief, I've got a worried mother looking for her son on line two. Under the circumstances, I thought you might want to speak to her." He offered the phone to him.

"Okay, send the call to my office."

The chief hung his wet parka on a coat rack in the corner of his office, dropped his hat on the desk, and poured himself a cup of black coffee. He sat down and picked up the phone when it rang through. "Hello, this is Chief St. George."

Mrs. Elliot sounded concerned but not alarmed, he thought. Her son, Casey, had arrived in Dutch Harbor three months earlier, she told him. She generally communicated with him by phone or email about once a week, she said, but she'd not heard from him in more than three weeks and had been unable to reach him by phone.

"How old is your son, Mrs. Elliott?" He pushed his hat to the corner of the desk where droplets of water ran down its felt edge to puddle on the old varnished wood.

"Twenty-four," she said.

The chief picked up a framed picture on his desk. It was a photo of a young man dressed in Navy fatigues. His son, Tom. Next to it was a picture of himself, also in uniform. Though the captain stripes were clearly visible, you'd need a magnifying glass to make out the naval criminal investigation insignia. His arm was around a vibrant woman, her head tossed back in laughter. His wife, Libby. His career as a Navy investigator ended with retirement two years ago. They'd moved to a small spread near the Canadian border, just outside Republic, Washington. But after a year, it was clear he wasn't ready to retire. They'd landed in Dutch when he'd been selected to fill the seat at this desk.

"Okay," he said, opening a notepad. "Please describe him. Height, weight, eyes, hair, that sort of thing…" He jotted down the description and asked what brought Casey to Dutch Harbor.

"An environmentalist. Really?" The chief looked up at the map of Alaska on the wall across from his desk. It took up most of the wall. "And what was he doing in Dutch Harbor?"

He stopped taking notes. "Oh, really?" he said. "What was he investigating?

"Interesting." The chief took a swig of coffee. "Do you have an address and phone number for him? We could send someone around to check on him."

"Oh, I see. Living on a boat. Do you know the name of the boat?"

He stopped writing again. "No? Well, let us follow up on this information and get back to you, Mrs. Elliott."

He tapped his pencil on the desk while she spoke.

"No need for alarm. We get these types of inquiries all the time. Why don't you give me your number? We'll take a look around and get back to you." The chief scrawled the number in his notepad and circled it twice.

"Please let us know if you hear from Casey, Mrs. Elliot." He laid the pencil alongside the pad and tried to sound optimistic. "Yes, I'll call when we hear something. Goodbye."

It was true, calls from worried parents were not uncommon occurrences at the police station. Young people looking for adventure or running from something were not a rarity, he'd learned. But what the chief had not told Mrs. Elliott was that the dead body heading to town in a fishing boat fit the description of her son.

An environmentalist? He leaned back in his chair and looked at the map of Alaska again. Dutch Harbor was in the lower southwest section of the map, the nation's busiest fishing port. The Chukchi Sea was in the top center area of the map, Arctic oil exploration territory. He got up from his desk to examine the map more closely. Environmentalists were often at odds with both kinds of resource extraction.

Then he opened the door and called over to his deputy. "Chet, get Marla Mancuso at Amchitka Shipping on the phone."

The shipping company was a regional outfit owned by a big firm from somewhere back East. It serviced western Alaska villages as well as oil rigs up above the Arctic Circle. The company owned two large supply vessels that serviced deep water rigs and two smaller boats that could work shallower waters, including limited in-river navigation of the muddy Kuskokwim and Yukon rivers. Additional vessels were chartered by the shipping company as needed. The boats shared use of the neighboring ISI dock. Flanked by storage warehouses, the ISI dock was wider and longer than any other dock. You could drive trucks on it. Because of congestion at the city dock, most boats used the ISI dock at one time or another to transfer gear or fish, often both. Some tied up there when space was available because it was the best damn dock in town.

The chief looked down at his mud-caked shoes with disgust. After five months on the job, he still hadn't got the pesky weather thing down. First clear, then snowing, now pouring, almost always blowing. He opened a desk drawer, pulled out a whisk brush, and went to work on them. Brushing hard along the seams, he pondered the possibilities.

Mrs. Elliott from Chicago said her son, Casey, worked on a fishing boat but didn't know what kind. She said he worked with various environmental groups, but she didn't know what he was investigating.

He brushed his shoe harder.

These groups targeted all sorts of resource extraction operations, he knew: fishing, oil, mining, timber. Their approaches varied. Some were collaborative. Some litigious. At least one had litigated to halt fishing operations to protect sea lions. Another had organized demonstrations against offshore oil drilling.

He paused and looked at the map again.

Was she confused about Casey working on a fishing boat? Perhaps it was an oil rig or a support vessel? And he'd have to call the fishery service to find out more about its charter of Arlo's boat and crew.

The phone rang.

"I've got Marla on line two," Chet said. The chief took the call.

They exchanged some pleasantries before he asked her the question on his mind. "I've got a mother looking for her son and am wondering if you've had any new hires on your supply boats during the last three months. Especially any fellows in the mid-twenty range. His name might be Casey Elliot."

He put her on speakerphone.

"I'm sorry to hear it, Chief." Marla's voice filled the office. "The hiring of crew is generally done by the captains. But I will check it out and get back to you."

"You don't have to go back far in the hiring history.

Just the last three months should do it."

"Glad to help." Then she added. "Is there a problem?"

"We don't know yet. I'm hoping it's just a hiccup in the kid's life and that he'll be calling home soon. And maybe his mom will call back and say it was all nothing, nothing at all."

"Yeah." Marla sighed. "Nothing at all sounds good."

He hung up the phone and leaned back in the swivel chair, letting his eyes roam across the expansive map on his wall.

"Damn," was all he could manage. He reached for the bottom drawer in his desk and pulled out a lightweight foam basketball. Deftly launching it toward the hoop on the back of his office door, he watched it descend in its arc toward the basket.

Swish.

****

A bluetick coonhound lay on Maureen's examination table. Tears rolled down a six-year-old boy's cheeks. He wiped them away with his shirt sleeve and looked up at Maureen.

"Is Blue gonna die?" Toby said.

Maureen looked at the dog brought to her after being hit by a car. When she'd gotten the call, she'd rushed back from the *Cape Kiska* to meet them at the clinic. The mangled look of this loved and listless dog pressed down upon her heart like dirt in a shovel.

Except for the rise and fall of his chest, the dog lay motionless on her exam table. His right rear leg was twisted in an ugly position. Maureen ran her fingers along his spotted neck. Blue lifted his head and looked to see the unfamiliar hand there. Then he dropped his head, seemingly too dazed to care. She gently prodded areas in the abdomen area. There was no response until she got to his right hip. Even her light touch caused it to spasm. The dog let out a yelp of pain.

Toby's eyes bulged. "Oh Blue!"

At Maureen's direction, Toby's dad held the dog still while she administered a shot to numb the pained area. Then she squatted down so she could meet the boy face to face.

"We're going to take a look inside the area where it hurts and find out what's going on. Okay, Toby?"

She thought the boy was trying to look brave. His back straightened, but his lip quivered.

"Okay," he said.

"We're going to use an X-ray machine that takes pictures of his bones."

Directing Toby and his dad to step behind the screen, she gowned herself in a protective smock. Moving the ancient X-ray machine over the injured leg and hip, she struggled to get a good angle, all the while recalling the state-of-the-art equipment she'd seen in Anchorage.

Several minutes later, with four X-rays in hand, she walked over to the wall behind her desk and flicked on the viewing screen. She clipped the X-rays to the lightbox and offered Toby a seat on top of her desk so he could see them up close.

"It's pretty serious, Toby. It's what we call high-impact trauma, which is what happens when a dog gets hit by a car."

She pointed to the second picture. "This one shows it best. See these lines?"

She looked at the youngster to be sure he was following along. He nodded.

"There are three full breaks here." She indicated the femur bone. "And"—she moved her hand to the last picture— "his right hip has multiple fractures and is broken near the socket."

Toby's dad looked down at the floor.

Maureen called CoCo over from her bed in the corner. With an awkward gait, the shepherd eagerly loped across the room. Sitting at attention at Maureen's knee, her cocked head waited for a command. Maureen opened the lower desk drawer and grabbed a worn tennis ball. She tossed it at the far wall.

CoCo leaped across the room, her long legs stretching only twice before her teeth grabbed it from the air. Within seconds the ball rested at Maureen's feet. CoCo sat and waited.

"How many legs does she have?"

"Three," said Toby.

Maureen sat on the desk next to the boy.

"I'm going to recommend amputation of Blue's right hind leg. That means his injured leg will be removed. He's young and strong and, like CoCo, should learn how to get around just fine. What do you think?" Maureen looked from son to father, wishing she could fix Blue herself.

The boy did not hesitate. "Let's do it, Dad. It's the right thing."

His father nodded. "Okay. What's next?" he asked, looking at Maureen.

"Leave him with me tonight. Unfortunately, I don't have the equipment here to do the surgery myself. But I'll arrange for his transport to the animal hospital in

Anchorage that supports this type of care." She turned to the boy. "If all goes well, you'll have him home in no time."

On the way out, the boy turned back toward Maureen. "How did CoCo lose her front leg?"

"She used to be a police dog." The shepherd's tail wagged, knowing all eyes were on her. "She was hurt by a bad guy in the line of duty."

Maureen walked to CoCo's side. "She was in pretty bad shape, and they planned to put her down." She stroked the head of the shepherd, recalling she had first met the dog when police had been called to her home in Boston. "But I amputated her leg, just like they're going to fix up Blue."

Toby smiled. "CoCo's a hero," he said, raising his hand to salute the dog.

****

After they left, she knew she could no longer put off the chief's request to call him.

"Hello, Chief," she said when connected to his office.

He came to the point. He wanted her to examine the corpse heading to town in a fishing boat. But he wanted to hear whether she could do it without bias, knowing that Arlo was a potential suspect. In a small town where most everyone knows everyone, it was unavoidable. But the question had to be on the table.

"Can you do it?" he asked.

Chapter 10

The *Viking King* arrived in town with its frozen corpse the next day. It was afternoon by the time the ambulance backed up to the clinic entrance to deliver the body. Maureen clutched her sweater tight against the wind and made her way out the walkway to the ambulance. Two EMTs hopped out.

"Hey, Doc," Jeff said with a wave as he headed to the rear of the vehicle. He'd also delivered One-Eye Ben.

He swung open the two rear doors. With a practiced reach, the two workers pulled out the gurney. Its wheels dropped to the ground. On top of it lay a half-zipped body bag with a pair of bent legs extending beyond it as if escaping skyward.

"Interesting, huh?" Jeff said.

The chief's cruiser swung into the parking lot next to the ambulance.

Maureen turned to Jeff. "Can you guys bring the body downstairs? There's a table I've got set up for him."

She headed to meet the chief, her hair flying across her face.

He approached, his squinting eyes assessing her from beneath the rim of his hat.

"You're okay with this?"

Still clutching the sweater to her neck, she nodded. "Yeah, I'm okay. It's not like you have anything on Arlo other than a crab pot permit number. Right?"

She stopped and looked at him. "I want to do this, Chief. If it becomes a problem, I'll jump ship, or you can toss me overboard, whichever comes first."

They headed inside to the reception room and downstairs to the surgery area.

The two ambulance workers had just finished moving the body bag with the pop-up legs onto the exam table when the chief and Maureen descended the stairs.

"Is there anything more we can do?" Jeff asked.

"No, we can take it from here," she said.

The EMTs left, carrying the gurney up the stairs as if it were weightless.

Maureen poured two cups of coffee. She put cream and sugar in one cup. The other, she passed to the chief. "Black, right?"

They walked over to the body bag. The knees and ankles of the corpse, bent from being frozen in a sitting position, extended beyond the bag toward the surgical lamp above it.

Maureen sipped her coffee. "I'm not qualified to do a full autopsy, but there's a lot of information to be gained here without cutting anyone open."

"Cause and time of death are all I'm asking for."

"It presents a challenge," she said, passing him a pair of surgical gloves. "I like that."

He set his cup on the corner of the table and snapped on the gloves. "Is that why you're interested in the Anchorage job...more of a challenge?"

She turned to him. "How'd you know about that?"

"It's my job to know what's going on in this town."

"Do others know?"

"No, just me. The veterinary hospital called me to

ask for a reference since you didn't provide a local one. But it won't take long before it gets out. There are no secrets in a small town." He opened the body bag. "Does Arlo know?"

She stood across from him as they both began to roll the edges of the bag away from the body. "I told him before he left on the charter."

The chief tugged on the stiff vinyl hood frozen to the victim's head. "I figure that if you're able to leave Arlo behind to carve out a new career, you're not going to let feelings get in the way of examining this body."

"Ouch," she said, shooting him a pained expression.

He waved it off with a grin she'd begun to appreciate. Then he pushed down on the kid's legs. They didn't budge.

"Seems to be frozen solid," he said. "The crew told me they hauled the body out of the water the night before last and stowed it in the bait locker right away. So, it's been in the freezer close to forty-eight hours."

"I see."

"The freezer wasn't big enough to stretch him out." He took a sip of his coffee. "They thought a sitting position would be more...respectful."

"Interesting."

Her gaze scanned the victim from head to toe. He wore an orange vinyl jacket with a hood that extended over his head. The jacket was opened so that a flannel shirt beneath it was visible. His hands lay folded on his lap.

She tugged at the jacket to see if it moved or was frozen to the body. Frost fell from it at her touch. It was as pliable as a cardboard box.

"You know, this body will not defrost for days," she

said. "That should give us some time."

"Time for what?"

"Time to figure out what we're doing. They didn't train us in vet school using frozen cats and dogs."

The chief looked impatient. "We need answers now, Maureen. As it is, I'll be getting an earful of crap from the state trooper office for filing paperwork a day late. I don't much give a damn about that, but I suspect the message will be delivered in person by someone who'll come for the body...perhaps tomorrow."

"Okay." She began to flick crystals from the kid's hands with a small brush. Flaps of frozen flesh stuck up around the wounds on the knuckles of his right hand like potato chip fragments. "It appears he may have been in a fight."

The chief pulled reading glasses from his shirt pocket and bent to look at the hand. "We've got to get this body defrosted ASAP."

She looked up in time to see him adjusting the thermostat.

"No, don't do that!" she cried out. "Increasing decomposition of the outer layers may cause it to get out of sync with the core's decaying process."

His hand remained on the knob.

She threw her hands up and walked to the closet. "What the heck, freezing the body already screwed things up." She turned around holding a hair dryer.

The chief adjusted the thermostat regulator to its highest setting before crossing back to her side. Maureen directed the hair dryer toward the frozen jacket.

"What if we die of heat stroke?" she said. "What will our obits say? Oh, Michele will have fun writing that one up in the newspaper's Police Log. Died defrosting dead body."

"But we're not going to die for nothing." He motioned for her to help him pry open the warmed jacket to inspect for abdominal wounds. None found.

They were struggling to peel back the hood when deputies Chet and Michele came down the stairs.

"Holy mackerel!" Chet said eyeing the trajectory of the legs while pulling a notebook from his chest pocket.

Michele set her equipment bag on the bookshelf, grabbed the camera, and threw the strap over her head.

"What?" she said, looking at the chief and Maureen. "Why are you two looking at me as if I was up to no good?"

The chief told her to take a close-up of the hands. Michele bent near the body's mid-section, where the hands still lay folded. *Click, click, click.* Then she straightened up and joined the other three looking at the corpse. "You know," she said while chewing gum. "It's effing hot in here."

The kid's eyes were closed and sealed shut by heavily frosted eyelashes. Strands of his sandy brown hair and beard were frozen in brittle stick formations so that his face looked as if it poked from a thicket. Maureen waved the hair dryer over the thicket.

"Do you see what I see, Chief?"

"Looks pretty beat up."

Maureen used a small brush to dust away the remaining ice crystals from the kid's eyes and cheeks.

"There seems to be a cut below the right eye," she said. "And another flesh wound on the left cheek." Noting the smaller hematoma, she surmised it was a weaker punch. "But here's the big one." She pointed to his right jawline near the chin. "It probably broke his jaw and sent him flying."

The chief stepped back so Michele could move in to snap some close-ups. "The kid's face is more beat-up on the right side," he said, "making it likely a left-handed assailant was involved. But I doubt any of these wounds would have killed him."

Maureen aimed the hair dryer toward his mouth and tried to pry it open. When she pulled her finger back, an object flew out, hitting her on the chest and dropping to the floor.

Chet leaned over and picked it up. He held it up for everyone to see. A cigarette butt.

Maureen reached for the butt and rolled it between her thumb and forefinger. "Curious, it doesn't seem waterlogged." She dropped it in the dish.

The chief pried loose a half-empty pack of cigarettes from the kid's pocket. It was streaked brown with tobacco stains. Along with it were a cheap lighter and a ballpoint pen. He dropped them in a dish and continued to frisk the kid. Finding nothing else in the accessible pockets of his jacket and jeans, they worked together to tip the corpse on its side.

Using the hair dryer, they were able to peel the hood back and examine the back of his head where they discovered a big gash. "That's what killed him," Maureen said.

Michele circled around the table and took pictures of the four-inch crease in the skull.

When they rolled the kid on his back again, Maureen stopped suddenly.

"I saw it too," the chief said. He reached for the cuff at the left wrist. Pushing it back as far as he could, they all looked down at the exposed wristwatch.

Maureen took aim with the hairdryer and pulled the trigger.

Soon the watch was pliable enough to remove from the wrist. She laid the stainless-steel watch in the chief's palm.

Gold hands on its black face had stopped at 1:35 a.m. And, according to the small window located on its face, it had stopped on October 6th.

The chief pulled out his notepad and wrote down the date and time He looked up at Maureen, who met his gaze, both knowing it was the day after Arlo said he'd left Dutch to do the survey. It would have been easy to make it to the *Mushroom* during that time. Neither said a thing.

Michele snapped a close-up of the watch face while doing a calculation in her head. "That's eight days ago," she said.

"Time of death seems solved, Chief," Chet noted as he scribbled on his pad.

"Wait." Maureen reached for the watch and read its face. "This is an expensive, high precision watch. A very good one." She looked at the chief. "It's water resistant, so it probably wouldn't stop right away. It could have stopped hours, maybe days after being in the water."

She turned it over and read an inscription on the back. She handed it to the chief, who read it aloud.

"Congratulations, Casey. Good luck in life. Love, Mom and Dad."

Now that the kid had a name and a mother that had tried to track him down, it became a sadder business. Chet stopped taking notes. Michele let the camera swing from the strap around her neck. The chief bowed his head. Maureen thought not about a murder to solve but the family who had lost a son.

A wisp of rising steam hovered over the defrosting body.

Michele broke the silence by tearing open a stick of gum and popping it in her mouth. She'd already removed her jacket and stripped down to a T-shirt. "Wish I'd packed my bathing suit."

The chief stuffed a notepad in his pocket. "Let's call it a day," he said. "Except Michele. She seems best dressed to stay behind and get some fingerprints."

Michele, her jaw working on the gum like it was fighting back, examined the decaying fingers. "Don't get your hopes up, Chief."

Turning to Chet, the chief directed him to head back to the office and see if they could match the corpse's facial photo with a driver's license photo under the name of Casey Elliot. "Try Illinois, for starters. If that doesn't work, try Homeland Security to see if he has a port access identification photo. Let's confirm this is Casey Elliott before I have to make a very tough phone call to his mother."

The two men exited together.

Maureen snipped a lock of Casey's hair for DNA testing, bagged it, and dropped it in the bowl alongside the pack of cigarettes, a lighter, a ballpoint pen, the lone cigarette butt, and the inscribed watch. Then she stripped down to a T-shirt and helped Michele take the kid's prints.

"Nice bracelet," she said while watching Michele work.

Michele held up her hand so Maureen could get a closer look at the scrimshaw design on the walrus tusk bracelet. "My cousin made it," she said. "Only Alaska

Natives are allowed to sell the ivory. I'll get one for you if you want, but they're pricy."

Maureen held Casey's hand so Michele could blot it with ink. "Jewelry's not in my budget these days."

After Michele left, Maureen collapsed at her desk. And closed her eyes.

****

The bell over the front door of the clinic jingled, signaling someone had opened the clinic door upstairs. It woke her.

"Hello, anybody here?" A man's voice.

She looked at the wall clock. Nearly seven p.m. and hotter than hell. Wiping sweat from her forehead, she climbed the stairs to the waiting room, where she found a young man standing outside on the landing. Like Casey, he had a full beard. He wore the tall rubber boots of a fisherman. Snow fell on the wide brim of his Aussie outback hat.

"I'm looking for Dr. McMurtry."

"That would be me," Maureen said, rubbing one of her arms that had gone to sleep. "What can I do for you?"

He reached into his jacket pocket and removed two small plastic bags. He held them out, a contrite expression on his face.

"I was told they took the body from our boat to your clinic," he said. "I wanted to be sure these caught up with him."

Maureen took the two bags. One held two broken teeth. The other held a small notebook.

"These belonged to him?" she asked, looking at him again.

He wore a brown denim jacket, its corduroy collar turned up against the flurry of snow and the darkening night. She noted his hair, beard, eyes, even his wide-brimmed hat were all shades of brown. Against the backdrop of falling snow at dusk, he appeared to have stepped from an old sepia-shaded photograph.

"The notebook fell out of his pocket when we moved him into the freezer," he said. "I put it aside and forgot about it. It's waterlogged, and the writing runs together, but it was in a zip-locked bag, so might be legible in places. I thought I should return it to him."

He tilted his head to the side, looking at her. "Is he here?"

"Yes, he is." She said it warmly because he seemed to care.

"I just wanted to return his stuff. Should I have brought it to the police station?"

"You can leave it with me."

"We found the broken teeth in his mouth. I removed them before giving him a last smoke."

"A last smoke?"

A little embarrassed, he pulled a pack of cigarettes from his chest pocket. "We smoke the same brand. I gave him one for the trip home."

Maureen nodded, now understanding the broken cigarette butt.

"Thanks...?" she said hoping for a name.

"Eric. Eric Petersen."

"Thank you, Eric."

"What's *his* name?" he asked, nodding toward the clinic door.

Casey had been in this man's charge, thought Maureen. He'd helped rescue his corpse from the sea. Names are important when lives cross like that, she knew, but she couldn't tell him. Not yet, anyway.

"I'm sorry, his identification hasn't been established."

He raised his hat, about to bid her goodbye, but stopped.

"You know, he wasn't a fisherman."

"Why do you say that?"

He showed her his hands, turning them palms up in the falling snow. They were stained with grease that held fast to his heavily calloused hands.

"I just washed them," he said, stuffing his hands in his pockets and turning away.

"Wait," she said. He seemed kind, Maureen thought, and it was a long walk back to the docks. "Come inside." She waved him in when she saw him resist. "I'll fetch my boots and give you a lift to the boat."

Eric followed her inside, where CoCo was waiting. The dog's ears shot forward. Her muscles tightened. Eric held a hand in front of her muzzle, letting the shepherd sniff it. The dog took in all the man's sweat and toil, all the grime and grease, and the smell of the pumice-based solvent concocted to wash it all away and fail.

Then she licked his hand.

Chapter 11

Located on a gravel road halfway between the Olympic Fisheries plant and the Russian Orthodox Church, the boxy clapboard house doesn't look like much. Beneath the glow of a street lamp, a carved white fish hangs from a post. For those that follow the dirt path around the side of the paint-chipped building and push open the door, they'll find a room dimly lit by neon beer signs. Cigarette smoke hugs the low ceilings. Wooden booths line the walls. When the fleet is in town, the booths overflow with crew members sharing pitchers of beer and shots of whiskey. Famed for being Alaska's most dangerous bar, to regulars, it's a second home.

****

Maureen pushed open the saloon door. The wooden booths were mostly empty, signaling the fleet had left town for the crab season opener. Several patrons sat at the bar. And a country western songstress sang her heart out from the corner jukebox.

A big man stood behind the long wooden bar. At six-foot, four and weighing about 230 pounds, Andy Longstreet's frame was packed beneath a pair of anvil shoulders. No one's ever surprised to learn he once played linebacker for a professional football team. The practice squad but so what? He could still crush anyone like a saltine cracker looking for a bowl of soup.

He leaned on the bar, pressing his weight on

extended fingertips as big as sausages. A white rag hung over his shoulder. Long hair, pulled back into a ponytail, hung halfway down his back. Crow's feet stood sentinel at the corner of his eyes. Smiling eyes. Angry eyes. It didn't matter. The crows did all the talking.

"Hey, Mo." His eyes lay on her like a warm sweater. "Surprised to see you tonight. The World Series doesn't start till tomorrow."

"Yeah, I know." Maureen dropped her Red Sox cap on the bar. "The damn Yankees are in it again."

Maureen liked Andy from the start. Not just because, like her, he was from Boston and also like her, a devoted Red Sox fan. She did not share his fondness for poetry. Haiku only, but still, she was not among those who dove into Dutch Harbor's weekly newspaper in search of Andy's version of the Japanese poetic form. No, she liked the big guy because he made her laugh when there seemed nothing much to laugh about.

Seeing the glum look on Maureen's face, Andy leaned in and whispered, "Baseballs, white and round. Bounced across fields of green. Stitches hold them tight."

Maureen laughed. Haiku or not, he'd done it again. "If only the Red Sox could hold it together during the damn pennant race."

He popped the cap of her favorite beer and set it in front of her.

"Thanks."

"What's going on, Mo? It's not like you to show up alone or without a ballgame to watch. Is it the dead bodies?"

By now, only dead fish in Dutch didn't know the local vet had been tapped to help solve the mystery of two bodies spit from the sea.

"Yeah," she said, not really lying but not telling the truth either. It was Arlo. If he was involved in the death of Casey Elliot, she'd misread a man again. The price would be big. She'd lost sleep over it. Maybe she should walk away now. Leave him and the crime-solving to someone else. Move to Anchorage.

She looked at Andy. "I'm not thinking clearly these days. But I'll get over it."

He looked her over. Maureen could tell he was considering a response.

Laughing she said, "Not another haiku!" She kissed his forehead. "Thanks, buddy. I feel better already."

"So, you here alone or waiting for someone?"

"Patsy. We were supposed to meet here." She pulled a notepad from her jacket pocket and dropped it on the bar next to her beer. "Have you seen her?"

Andy pointed in the direction of the jukebox not far from the big picture window that looked out on the bay. Every ship entering or leaving Dutch had to pass through the array of buoys beyond the glass pane. At night, the buoy lights hung like red stars in the window as the moving mast lights of fishing boats passed them like planets untethered by gravity. Patsy stood next to the jukebox pouring quarters into the slot.

Andy indicated the glass tumbler on the bar with what appeared to be whiskey on the rocks. "That's hers."

She gave an appreciative pull on the beer. "The Yankees suck."

"Yes, they do." He slammed his big hand on the bar. "And your seat will be waiting here to watch them lose the Series."

She held up her bottle and tipped it in appreciation.

Andy raised a thumb before heading down the bar to tend to a demanding patron.

Once Patsy finished fueling the jukebox with coins, she bumped and jived her way across the floor dancing to a new tune until she slid onto the stool next to Maureen.

That's when Lillian came barreling out of the back room behind the bar shaking a can of soda like it was a fistful of dice. She and Andy shared ownership and barkeep duties at the saloon. Andy looked tough but Lillian was tougher. She plopped the shaken can of soda in front of a fellow sitting four bar stools down from Maureen. Leaning into the guy's face with a crocodile grin that regulars learned to relish, Lillian challenged him to open it.

"There's your silly-ass can of cola, you wuss."

The man looked up, horrified, like the can might explode in his face. Everybody within earshot laughed till their bellies ached. They all knew better than to order soda pop at this bar.

"Hi, girls," she said, passing Maureen and Patsy a bowl of nuts before delivering a pitcher of beer to a booth near the big window.

Turning to Patsy, Maureen got as serious as dark paint. "I need your help."

She explained that a notebook had turned up as one of Casey Elliot's belongings. "It's waterlogged, and most everything is illegible, but there's a few words and digits that remain readable. And it's bugging me."

She explained that among the dozen or so words she could decipher, there was the word *Cape* followed by a name she couldn't decipher, and the numbers *959*, followed by a few more digits she couldn't read.

"How common is it for a boat to be named *Cape* something and to have a permit number that starts with *959*?"

Patsy swirled the ice cubes and whiskey around in her glass and regarded Maureen with a mash-up of concern and amusement that only a bestie could get away with. "You're wondering if it might be a reference to Arlo's boat, the *Cape Kiska*?"

"Maybe. Just want to cross it off the list."

Patsy reminded her that *capes* were common geological features that dotted the Alaskan seacoast. And capes, she said, were often used in naming a fishing boat.

"There's probably a hundred capes along the Alaska coastline and many dozens of boats named after them. And you don't even know if it is being used as the name of a vessel. So go ahead, cross it off your list."

"And *959*?" Maureen asked, knowing those were the first three digits of the *Cape Kiska's* five-digit permit number. The *Cape Kiska* number was *95969*. Those digits appeared on the recovered permit tag attached to the crab pot hauled up with Casey Elliot inside. She knew the chief wouldn't miss the coincidence.

"I don't know how many federal or state permit numbers start with 959," Patsy said, tipping the glass of whiskey to her lips. "I'll check it out if it will make you feel better. But *959* could be referring to *anything*." She indicated Andy at the far end of the bar. "It might be the number of haiku syllables he's had published in the newspaper over all these years."

Maureen looked toward Andy, still unable to snap out of it. "There were two or three illegibly smeared digits that followed 959," she told Patsy. "Not even Andy could come up with that much poetry."

Patsy followed Maureen's gaze to the big guy, all clean-shaven like he didn't belong in Dutch, and waved him over. He seemed busy with an unruly customer who was speaking so loudly that his Russian accent chewed the air. Andy passed him two shot glasses of something and took his cash.

After working the register, he joined the two women. "What's up?"

"We're wondering how many syllables of haiku you've published."

He turned around and pulled out the drawer beneath the cash register. Inside lay a .22 automatic and this week's issue of the newspaper. He grabbed the paper and brought it to them. It was opened to the page where his weekly haiku was printed.

"Haiku consists of three lines, with five syllables in the first line, seven in the second, and five in the third. Seventeen syllables." He let his hand wave over the poem like a magic wand. "I've been writing poems for the paper for seven years." He pushed the newspaper in front of them.

"You do the math." His crow's feet did a tap dance of mischief. Then he headed back down the bar.

With zero time spent doing a calculation, Patsy scribbled on a cocktail napkin. She held it up for Maureen to read.

"I'm thinking 95,900 syllables."

Patsy shrugged with an expression on her face that begged Maureen to let it go. Then she signaled Andy for another round.

When he returned with the drinks, Maureen nodded her head in the direction of the loud Russians at the end of the bar.

"What's with those guys, Andy?"

"The Ruskies? That's Viktor and his brother, Arseny. Nothing but trouble when they drink too much. They're always loaded with cash, so maybe there's truth to rumors that they're dealing drugs. If I catch 'em at it, I'll…" He held up his arms, flexed his impressive biceps, and laughed. Then he looked at the scribbled-on napkin. "What's going on here anyway?"

"Not much," Maureen said, a bit embarrassed. "We were just trying to figure out what a five- or six-digit number that started with *959* might mean."

Patsy pleaded her case that it could mean *anything.*

Andy's palm flew up, like a stop signal. "No," he said, looking at Maureen, serious as a hammer hitting a nail. "Clearly, it's a starship federation number."

There, he'd done it again, thought Maureen, making her laugh when nothing seemed funny these days.

Ready to call it a night, the two women made quick work of their drinks. Patsy headed to the far end of the bar to fetch her jacket from one of the coat hooks. Her back to the two Russians still sitting there, she swung the jacket around her shoulders and punched her arms into the sleeves. One of the Russians jumped off his bar stool and spun Patsy around by her shoulder.

"I give you five hundred dollars in cash for jacket." He pulled a wad of bills from his pocket.

Pushing away his hand, Patsy smiled like she'd heard it a million times before. "Sorry, pal."

Undeterred, the big Russian stepped in front of her as she tried to head toward the door. He waved the money in her face. "You not be sorry," he said, a stupid grin hanging there as if to entice her.

Andy leaped over the bar. "Enough, Viktor!"

That's when the smaller Russian shot from his stool and made the mistake of reaching for Andy's arm to pull him away from his brother. Instead, the linebacker twisted his elbow into an ugly position, bringing the Russian to his knees.

Viktor backed up, both hands in the air. "We go," he said.

The two men moved toward the door, their palms up in surrender. Lillian held the door open, watching them go as if she was bored to death.

The few patrons left in the bar gathered around Patsy to see what had caused the ruckus. On the back of the black jacket, an embroidered puffin kept company with red stitched letters that read, *The Elbow Room*. Folks oohed over it and nodded in appreciation. They all knew the legendary saloon had closed. Its door and windows nailed shut as if trying to lock away the good ole days of untamed Alaska. Its fame and glory survived now in the minds of its former patrons and in outlandish stories told as if they were the last remaining tales of the Old West. The jacket hung on Patsy with the currency of a holster worn at the OK Corral.

Patsy saluted Andy on their way out. "Thanks, buddy," she said.

Climbing into her truck, Maureen primed the carburetor with a few pumps of the gas pedal, turned the key, and listened to it rumble to life. She pushed in the clutch and reached for the ball-topped gear shift that rose from the floor. Engaging it, she pulled the rig onto the road.

The number 959. It kept rolling around in her head.

Chapter 12

When a trooper appeared at the clinic door the next morning, his flat-brimmed hat was damp with melting snow, and his parka hung open so you could see his gold badge and his holstered pistol. His black shoes were covered with mud that climbed up the cuff of his dark blue uniform pants. The chief followed the trooper inside the veterinary clinic, careful to wipe the mud from his new work boots on the bristled welcome mat.

An elderly woman sat in the reception area, flipping through a magazine. She seemed agitated. The chief removed his hat to greet her.

"Hello, Mrs. Ivanoff," he said, his head cocked in an observant posture. "You seem distraught."

"Yes, Chief." She struggled to look composed. "My cockatoo, O'Henry. He flew out the front door this morning. A bald eagle grabbed him near the library. He's cut up pretty bad and might be blind if...if he survives." She gave the chief a brave smile and raised a suspicious eye to browse the stranger.

The chief rested his hand on her shoulder and gave it a slight squeeze before guiding the trooper and his muddy shoes down the stairs. He peered through the swinging double-door windows and saw Maureen in a surgery smock and cap bending over a large white bird at the far end of the long room.

"Okay to come in, Maureen?"

The chief had warned Maureen that the state police were pissed when they learned the body had not been sent directly to Anchorage but had been waylaid in a Dutch Harbor veterinary office for inspection. They'd sent a detective, Joe Franken, out on the afternoon plane to retrieve it. Casey still lay waiting on an exam table in the corner. His legs had begun to sag.

Maureen looked up from her feathered patient. "Yeah, sure, come on in, Chief."

The sedated cockatoo lay limply on its side, causing its yellow crest to lose its full fan display. Small specks of red blood still clung to its white feathers. Its black beak rested on a surgical pad.

With a sideward nod of her head, Maureen indicated they should go to the far end of the office where her desk was parked. "You know where the coffee is, Chief. I'll be with you in a few minutes."

The chief headed toward the coffee pot, speaking over his shoulder at Maureen. "This is Joe Franken. He's come for the body."

Her gloved right hand held a threaded needle that connected to the cockatoo's neck area. Checking out Franken, she figured him to be about six feet. His trim physique looked as if it managed a hundred sit-ups a day, but she didn't like the look of the mud he'd tracked into her office.

Ignoring Maureen's directions, Franken headed to the table where the thawing body of Casey Elliot lay on his back, his legs still extended in the air. Barely, even though she'd normalized the thermostat.

"What the hell?"

The chief sat on the corner of the desk drinking black coffee. "Meet Casey Elliot," he said. "Hauled from the ocean in a crab pot, frozen during the trip to town, and now defrosting. But you know that, right?"

Finally, he told him why Casey Elliot had been brought to the veterinary clinic.

"I need answers, Joe," the chief said, his new boot swinging over the garbage can at the desk's edge. "Before I hand him over to Anchorage, I want to understand the extent of injuries and cause and time of death. This one looks like a homicide."

Franken looked agitated. Condescension saturated his words. "We'll get you a report when we've done our investigation."

The chief stood up, matching Franken's height. "We still don't have the medical examiner's report on the body found floating in the small boat harbor two months ago."

"Look, I don't answer for what goes on in the medical examiner's office. They're backed up in cases, but..." he pointed his arm toward Casey, "that's no excuse for kidnapping our corpse."

The chief walked toward Franken. His work boots faced off with the trooper's muddy patent leathers. "Doing my job is not a crime," he said. "And I can't do my job without the facts. Without knowing cause and time of death as soon as possible, my hands are tied. I'm useless to you and..." the chief gestured toward the corpse, "the kid and his family."

Franken shook his head as if he couldn't believe he'd landed here and had to explain himself to a couple of yokels. "His parents are flying to Anchorage. They'll be looking for answers." Turning toward Maureen still working on the cockatoo at the far end of the room, he raised his voice. "I hope you haven't contaminated the body or compromised proper chain of custody protocols."

Still stitching the bird's wound, she ordered the cuss words charging up her throat to stop. She was mildly surprised when they did.

The chief approached the corpse. "Based on the watch found on Mr. Elliott, we believe his death may have occurred on October 6 or, perhaps, earlier. So approximately ten days ago. Thanks to Dr. McMurtry's examination, we believe death was likely caused by blows incurred during a fistfight. The fatal blow seems to have been blunt force trauma to the back of the head."

"Cut the *doctor* crap. She's a vet."

"You cut the crap, Joe. Thanks to Maureen's efforts, my investigation began yesterday instead of a month from now when we might get a report back from your office."

Franken's arms crossed in front of his chest. "The body was found in federal waters, so this case doesn't appear to be in your jurisdiction."

"Come on, Joe, the kid was found eighty miles offshore. We both know that's not within the state's jurisdiction either. I've spoken to the feds." He paused, seeming to let the weight of the federal agency have its full effect on Franken. "They want us to continue to investigate. They know the killer won't be found without a local inquiry. And they want us to cooperate with your office. We can make it work, Joe." He looked at Casey. "We owe it to this kid and his family."

Maureen cradled the sedated cockatoo in one arm while opening the recovery cage with the other. She laid it down, and she stripped off her gloves.

"I've prepared a report," she said, moving to the file

cabinet behind her desk. "I'm heading upstairs to let Mrs. Ivanoff know her cockatoo will recover." She pulled a typewritten page from a file folder and gave it to Franken. "We can discuss it when I get back."

Maureen returned from her good news meeting with Mrs. Ivanoff suddenly feeling grateful to be a small-town veterinarian. Would things be this personal working in an Anchorage animal hospital, she wondered?

She looked at Franken. "Any questions about the report?"

He turned toward the chief. "You can't be serious? You expect me to accept a report on what could be a homicide from an animal doctor?"

Maureen's mind ripped the report from his hands and hit him over the head with it. Her actions, not so much.

"Setting aside my years of medical school, use of my clinic, and my genuine desire to help, you might weigh the value of getting timely forensic information against the value of winning a jurisdictional dispute." She looked at the report in his hand. "Go ahead, toss it if you like."

The chief seemed to be admiring his new boots again. No one saw his ear-to-ear grin.

Franken opened the report and skimmed its findings. "Blunt force trauma, huh?"

"Yes, let me show you."

She slipped on fresh surgical gloves and tipped the body slightly, so the overhead light shone on the backside of Casey's head. Separating strands of hair, she exposed the nasty gash area that ran down the back of his head.

"That's what likely killed him," she said, circling

the area with her gloved finger. "Based on the wounds to the hands and face, he seems to have been in a fight."

The chief pointed to the lacerations around the right side of his face. "With someone who was likely left-handed. This shot to his jaw probably landed him on something hard."

"Or he could have been hit with something," Franken said.

"If the perpetrator had stopped there," observed the chief, "we might be looking at manslaughter. But once Casey was put to sea in a crab pot, the stakes went up."

Franken poked the victim's knees. "Murder One," he said.

Maureen excused herself to listen to the cockatoo's breathing with her stethoscope. Satisfied, she looked over at Franken. "What about Ben Stokes? Has the medical examiner finished that report?"

"Gunshot wound to the head. Not exactly rocket science," Franken said. "Just as your report said, he was shot at close range."

"Ballistics?" the chief asked.

"Not done yet, but a large caliber."

"And time of death?" asked Maureen.

"Two days before discovery of the body."

Maureen could see Franken did not like being questioned by her. So she persisted. "In my notes, I qualified that range, saying that it could have been as long as four days, depending on the water temperature. Since then, the harbormaster informed me—"

"Yeah, we got that memo. But the medical examiner's not buying it."

Maureen threw her arms up in in disbelief.

The chief looked at his watch. "You've got your

estimate, and we've got ours," he said. "We've expanded our investigation to include the additional days. No harm done, right?"

Maureen thought Franken looked unconvinced and peeved to be dealing with what he thought were amateurs. She figured he hadn't yet bothered to research the chief's record as a Navy investigator. *God, this guy is an ass.*

"So, when will you be removing the body from my office?"

"No more flights out today," Franken said. "I'll be by tomorrow in time to pack him out for the morning flight to Anchorage."

Maureen looked at the muddy shoe tracks left around the room. "How about wiping your feet next time."

Franken folded the report. He was tucking it in his chest pocket when the doors to the surgery flew open. Patsy looked grim.

"The *Cape Kiska*," she said between heaving breaths. "A mayday was sent."

Maureen froze. "Any word from Arlo?"

"Boats are searching the area, Mo. You can hear it on the radio in my office."

Maureen stripped off her smock and grabbed her jacket. CoCo was at her heels as she flew up the stairs.

Franken looked on. "The *Cape Kiska*?"

The chief picked up his hat. "Casey there," he said, gesturing toward the corpse, "was found in a crab pot permitted to the *Cape Kiska*." He positioned the hat on his head. "The captain of the boat is a friend of Dr. McMurtry's."

"The DA's not gonna like this. He's not gonna like

it one bit."

Maureen stopped at the top of the stairs and hollered down at the swinging doors that separated her from the cops below. "Anyone could have taken those pots!"

Chapter 13

Early sailors used a sextant to measure the sun's angle from the horizon at mid-day to calculate a latitude location. But because Earth rotates, longitude was a tougher nut to crack. After many navigational disasters, the British government offered a hefty reward for a method to accurately calculate longitude. John Harris won the competition in 1737. A clockmaker, he used time to calculate space as a distance from the British Royal Observatory in Greenwich, England. But few could afford the clock, and so most continued to rely on complex calculations that factored in curvature of the Earth and bending of light. A skilled navigator was required to be a master mathematician until 1801, when Nathaniel Bowditch published the *New American Practical Navigator.* So accurate were the mathematical tables that mariners bet their lives on them. To secure a Coast Guard masters license today, captains are still required to demonstrate proficiency in navigation using *Bowditch.* But in an emergency, most use *dead reckoning.*

****

The weather came up fast in the night, driving foam-blown streaks across the black sea. A wave lifted the *Cape Kiska* high into its curling crest causing sea water to charge the wheelhouse and explode against its windows. The boat hung there suspended until gravity dropped it into the trough below. Its hull trembled.

"Tie everything down, and get inside," Arlo told the crew over the vessel intercom. They scrambled beneath deck lights to secure the crab pots.

Another wave approached.

This wave knocked a book from the shelf above Arlo's head. He bent to pick up his copy of *Bowditch* and shoved it back on the shelf.

He checked the radar, noting that the closest boat, the *Petrel Prince*, was about five miles off his starboard quarter, fishing north and west of him like most of the fleet.

Sully called from the engine room, wondering about the marine forecast. "It's rocking and rolling down here," he said. "I've got water in the bilge. It's manageable for now, but what's the outlook?"

"Not much chance the weather will come down before dawn. But do your best to keep it dry enough to hang laundry down there, Sully."

"Roger that."

When the next wave struck, sea spray slammed the windows with a pounding force that caused books to fly clear across the wheelhouse. His coffee mug shattered when it hit the floor.

"Jesus!"

Arlo bent to retrieve the books and so did not see the colossal body of water climb high above the bow, its crest spitting foam as it hurled itself at the wheelhouse. An arm of green water punched through the windows. It slammed Arlo against the rear wall. Shattered navigational monitors swirled around him, cutting his forearms as he pushed them away. He struggled to stand in the waist-high backwash that rushed past him and down the steep stairs into the galley below. Anchoring himself to the captain's chair bolted to the floor, he reached above it for the single side band radio. Still dizzy, he brought the microphone to his lips.

"Mayday, Mayday. Mayday. *Cape Kiska* wheelhouse windows blown out. Wheelhouse overrun with seawater, but we're still under power."

All radio chatter ceased when the fleet heard the word, *mayday.*

"*Cape Kiska. Cape Kiska.* US Coast Guard here. Please give location. Over."

"Most wheelhouse electronics are down so can't give coordinates. But we are fishing king crab about twenty miles southeast of the Pribilof Islands. About fifty miles due north of Port Moller. The *Petral Prince* is about five miles northwest of my location and…" Another green wave stormed the wheelhouse. Unobstructed by windows this time, it stampeded into the wheelhouse with its unleashed power. Arlo grabbed hold of the captain's chair, but the torrent ripped him loose, submerging him in four feet of swirling water. When his head burst above the surface, he gasped for air and fought the river of water rushing down the stairs again.

The lights flickered. The radio went silent. The autopilot steerage failed. The boat went dark.

Mother Nature's violent fury is indifferent to man. Every mariner knows her. Every mariner dreads her wrath. But seduced by the wealth beneath her blue skirts and the blush of a pink sunrise she sometimes shares, they persist. *It's the risk we take*, Arlo told himself as he struggled to his feet again, ready to fight. But without steerage, Arlo knew Mother Nature would hammer the

Cape Kiska with waves that would turn her broadside for a final thrashing. Then she would roll.

****

The fishing fleet heard the mayday exchange with the Coast Guard. They heard the boat go silent. A circle of tossing deck lights on the horizon began to turn inward toward the reported location of the *Cape Kiska*. Every crew member on every vessel set their eyes on the horizon. All hands were on deck, their faces drenched in sea spray, their hearts beating faster for friends on the *Cape Kiska*, or just knowing it could be them.

Aboard the *Petrel Prince*, Captain Bob Donnelly asked himself how the captain of the *Cape Kiska* might handle a swamped boat. Arlo had once been the engineer on Bob's boat. He knew him well. What would he do?

****

The engine of the *Cape Kiska* throbbed like a beating heart. It's what would keep them alive if Arlo could reclaim steerage. He searched in the dark for a spoked, wooden steering wheel mounted like a relic just beneath the shattered windows at the center of the boat. It was standard back-up gear in most fishing boats but rarely used. In the darkness, he worked his way along the sill until his hand found the shafts of the wheel.

He waited for the next wave to rise. Up, up the boat climbed. Still, he waited, knowing he would need the wave's full power to turn the boat in the opposite direction. Froth spit from the cresting wave as he spun the wheel round and round, causing the boat to swivel to its port side. The momentum of the wave pushed it sideways and rained seawater over its railing. Arlo hung on the wheel, fighting to turn the boat farther so it would not roll in the rising wave. His teeth chattered. His heart pounded. At last, the *Cape Kiska* freed itself so that it surfed down the same wave that had raised it.

The seas were now following the boat, and waves rushed up its back deck rather than over the bow. They charged through the crab pots and throttled the bulkhead. Some splashed water into the exhaust stacks. He had to keep the waves at his stern and water out of the engine room. Killed power would kill them. It meant he was tied to the wheel.

In the darkness, Arlo wondered why the boat had gone dark? The electrical panel was in the engine room. Was it flooding? Where was the crew?

Arlo turned toward the stairs and yelled.

"Marley! Sully! Tom! Can you hear me?"

A lone reply; the hissing sea.

Then a headlamp popped above the stairwell.

"Everyone's okay, Arlo." The voice was tight, still struggling to breathe deeply.

"Jesus, Sully," said Arlo, seeing the shape of the engineer emerging from the stairs. "How's the engine room?"

"The main electrical panel is out. The generator is down, but the main engine is functioning for now."

Sully waded through ankle-deep water surveying the damage. The headlamp shone on the empty windows, their frames mangled and open to the storm.

"Holy shit."

Beneath the headlamp, Arlo could see Sully's mop of hair stretched across his blackened forehead. Smoke rose from the singed hair.

"The water pump?" asked Arlo.

"It's stowed in the fo'c'sle. I'm hoping it wasn't damaged. I'll fire it up but wanted to find you first."

Working the wheel, Arlo continued to adjust their course. "How bad is the flooding?"

"The galley's drained for now, but the bilge is filling with water."

They both knew that was the worst sorta news.

"I got a mayday out before the second wave killed the radio. Couldn't get them our precise location, but the fleet, they know we're here. They know we're in trouble." He nodded toward the chart table. "But we gotta get some flares up."

Sully lifted the lid of the table and shined the headlamp into the deep storage area. He pulled out a cluster of narrow, foot-long cylinders, a flashlight, and an oblong bag before dropping the lid back in place. Holding up the orange bag, he shined the headlamp on it.

"Your survival suit."

Arlo turned to look at Sully, the man he knew would help him keep the boat afloat. He felt a rush of relief knowing they were in this together.

Sea spray pelted both men. Their lips were purple. Their breathing shallow.

"Tom and Marley?"

"They're grabbing survival suits from beneath their bunks," Sully said, passing Arlo a found flashlight.

"Good. Get your suit too."

Now that he had a flashlight, he shone it on the mounted compass to check his bearings. He made a course correction so the boat headed southeast, keeping following seas on its stern.

"Anything else?" Sully said.

"Yeah. Send the guys up here with some mattresses and rope." He had a plan.

"Roger that," Sully said heading toward the stairs.

"Sully." Arlo turned to look over his shoulder at the engineer. "Let loose the first flare now."

Sully reached an arm through a busted window frame and fired off the flare. Both men leaned forward to watch the iridescent trail of smoke until it exploded high above them. Clouds racing across the night sky lit up as if struck by lightning.

****

Maureen and Patsy pushed open the door to Patsy's office, where the mayday exchange continued on the sideband radio. The *Petrel Prince* was giving its position. Both women jotted down the latitude and longitude numbers to be sure they got them right. Patsy walked to the Bering Sea chart on the wall behind her desk. She ran her fingers from the latitude and longitude markings on the bottom and side of the chart to where the two met in the southeast quadrant.

"Bring me a thumbtack, Mo. There's some in the top right-hand drawer."

Maureen found a box of multi-colored tacks and handed a blue one to Patsy, who pushed it into the chart. The two women stepped back. The radio had gone silent. They waited.

The radio crackled alive again. "I see a flare. I see a flare. *Ocean Wolf* here at 56 degrees, 16.7 minutes North and 164 degrees, 42.4 minutes West. Figure flare to be about five or six miles southeast of my position."

Maureen grabbed another blue tack and pushed it into the chart at the position given. Three more reported flare sightings came in, transforming the tack markings into a blue semi-circle around an empty space on the chart. Patsy stuck a red tack in its center.

"There he is, Mo."

Maureen stared at the red tack, not knowing what to think. Was Arlo really there, or was that where the boat had sunk? Pain and confusion contorted her face.

"I know what you're thinking," Patsy said. She sat on top of her desk and looked at Maureen. "You're thinking, *what's happening out there?* You're wanting to help but know there's nothing you can do. You're preparing yourself for the worst news but hoping for the best. Yup. You're not the first."

"I don't know what to think. This is *death-in-your-face-shit*. What kind of a life is that? Going to work and maybe never returning. How do they do it?"

"Fishermen are even more optimistic than you, girlfriend. They think they'll return deck-loaded every time they pull away from the dock. And bad luck like this..." She pointed to the radio. "Bad luck like this is something that always happens to someone else."

****

Sully's headlamp emerged from below. Soon Tom and Marley followed, each pulling a foam mattress and survival suit into the wheelhouse.

Still holding the wheel, Arlo talked to them over his shoulder. "We're gonna push the mattresses through the windows so that they weave in and out of the frames. Use as many as you need to get all but one of the windows covered. Rope them in as best you can. Leave the window over this wheel clear so we can see approaching vessels."

The boat shuddered, taking another wave against the bulkhead. Arlo turned to Tom. "You're the experienced man here, Tom. Put your survival suit on." And, turning to his nephew, Marley, Arlo told him to tie a line around the older crew member's waist and then his own.

Instead, Marley opened his survival suit bag and began pulling it out. Shots of icy sea spray whipped blond dreadlocks across his face. "Arlo, I'm the only one that can fit through these windows in a survival suit. As long as someone is tied to the other end of that line, I'm not going over the side, no matter how bad it is out there."

Arlo looked into the storm beyond the bow. Black as coal, it seemed to be looking back at them. Challenging them to make mistakes, he thought. Mistakes that could kill them, including his nephew.

"Please let me do this," Marley said.

Arlo looked at his crew. He saw fear but not panic in their eyes. He saw determination to work as a team.

"Okay," he said.

Unrolling the spongy, red neoprene suit, Marley navigated his feet into a pair of bulky legs. Pulling it up around his waist, he used a free arm to yank the hood over his thick knot of hair before stuffing his other arm inside. The mitten-like hand coverings caused him to struggle with the zipper. Tom reached for it and pulled it up to the kid's chin. Sully removed the headlamp from his own head and fitted it atop Marley's. A quarter-inch line trailed behind Marley as he climbed through one of the busted windows. Tom secured the other end of the line to his own waist. Soon the headlamp shone on an outstretched mitt that reached inside the wheelhouse to grab a corner of a mattress. He pulled it through the window frame.

Suddenly, the tethered line around Tom's waist went taut. Marley hollered and vanished from sight. All hands reached for the line and, hand-over-hand, pulled it in until Marley's mittened hand gripped the window frame. His chest heaved until he caught his breath.

"The bow's icing-up. I wasn't ready for it, but I am now."

A wave, bigger than others, roared up the back deck, ripping loose the remaining crab pots. Coiled lines and orange buoys stored inside exploded like swarms of angry snakes. They washed over the side. Water poured into the stack vents. Sully scurried down the stairs using another flashlight he'd found. He knew if he didn't get the water pump working the ship would succumb.

****

When Bob Donnelly saw the flare, he turned his vessel toward it, as did the rest of the fleet. But it didn't feel right. He picked up the radio mike and hailed his fishing pal, Erling Johansson, on the *Ocean Wolf.*

"If my windows were blown out, I'd want to be moving with following seas rather than having them crash into the wheelhouse. I think he's moving away from us, Erling."

Erling agreed. They could be wrong and so left the rest of the fleet to search in closer waters. They throttled up the engines full bore, letting following seas push them at a mighty clip.

****

Sully climbed the stairs to the wheel house to deliver the sickening news. "The water pump. I can't get it to turn over."

Arlo's heart sank, but keeping his voice afloat, he turned to Tom and Marley. "I'm gonna leave you two in charge here while I go help Sully. You've got to keep the boat in following seas, so keep it on a southeast bearing. Understand?"

Both men nodded.

"If the boat loses power and begins to list more than forty-five degrees, abandon ship. Is that clear?"

The two men nodded again.

Arlo pointed to the ceiling. Above it, the life raft was packed in a canister on the wheelhouse roof. When released, it would fly open and instantly inflate. "Remember to stand back when you release the raft. Once you swim to it and climb aboard, remember to cut the lanyard loose from the boat. Got it?"

"What about you and Sully?" Marley asked.

"We won't be long." He looked hard at his nephew and then at Tom. "You'll be fine if you do as I say."

Stepping outside the wheelhouse door, Arlo grabbed the emergency beacon mounted near the roof. Back inside, he flipped on the switch and left it on the chart table. A red light began to blink from its casing. It was now transmitting an emergency locating signal to the Coast Guard.

****

Maureen looked out the second-story window of Patsy's office and saw nothing. The wind-whipped rain on the glass pane made sure of that.

Patsy brought her a cup of steaming tea.

When the radio sputtered, both women turned toward it.

"*Ocean Wolf. Ocean Wolf,* here." Giving his location, the captain continued. "Coming alongside a loose buoy. Crew is bringing it aboard now. Numbers to follow. Over."

"Roger that, *Ocean Wolf.* This is the Coast Guard standing by for buoy number. Jayhawk helo launched thirty minutes ago from Cold Bay. Over."

Maureen and Patsy huddled at the radio, anxious to hear the number and news of the CG rescue helicopter. It was blowing sixty knots. How could they fly in this weather? Maureen imagined the crew members suited up, running across the tarmac, bent down beneath the rotating blades as they approached the Jayhawk. How did they get the courage to climb in, close the door, and strap themselves in for a ride that could kill them at any time? No wonder they were worshipped by the fishing fleet, she thought.

"*Ocean Wolf. Ocean Wolf,* here with buoy numbers. Permit number is 9,5,9, 6, 9. Over."

Patsy sat at her computer typing in the number. She looked over the screen at Maureen.

"I'm sorry," Patsy said. She walked to the radio and lifted the microphone to her mouth.

"Crab management office, Dutch Harbor. Over."

The Coast Guard was directing radio traffic now.

"Go ahead."

"Number 9,5,9, 6, 9 is the permit number for FV *Cape Kiska.*"

Silence filled the radio air, making way for the fleet's quiet prayer. Finding gear in the water meant the boat had probably rolled.

Nothing was said over the air for several minutes. All eyes strained to find floating red suits or a life raft rising in the tumbling waves that swept toward them.

Static suddenly erupted from the radio. Maureen strained her ears to make out the words spoken.

"This is the U.S. Coast Guard. We have a signal from an emergency locater device registered to the FV *Cape Kiska.* That position is about a mile due east of the *Ocean Wolf* and the *Petrel Prince.* The dispatched

Jayhawk is now heading to that location as follows…"

Maureen wondered what the Coast Guard would find. Would the crew be found alive or floating face down? What was Arlo doing? What was he thinking? She didn't know, causing a dark emptiness to swamp her.

****

Straddling a bench in the engine room, Arlo and Sully huddled over the water pump, their foreheads just inches apart. Sully's headlamp shined on it while Arlo worked a wrench on the pump's engine casing. Sweat dripped from Arlo's brow. He wiped it with his sleeve and looked at Sully.

"The threads might be stripped."

"It'll work, Arlo," said Sully giving it a whack with his hammer. Rust granules flew off the screw head.

Now that he had all the screws off, Arlo lifted the head cover. A spark plug was disconnected—an easy fix. He smiled at Sully. For the first time, it felt like they might make it.

"You know," Sully said, "it's gotta work because we gotta make our delivery."

Arlo looked up, confused. They hadn't pulled a single pot. They had no crab to deliver to the plant. He saw Sully nod toward the box stashed in the corner.

"You mean the walrus tusks we picked up in St. Paul?"

"It'll be crazy when we get back to town," Sully said. "Everyone coming aboard to share high fives."

"Can you deliver the ivory before it gets crazy?"

Sully passed him a new spark plug. "I'll have a skiff waiting."

They were both thinking about making it home now.

****

114

When Marley heard the approaching *wonk, wonk, wonk* of the powerful rotor blades, he opened the wheelhouse door. A helicopter hovered above them, its spotlight moving forward and aft to assess the vessel's condition. The light shone on the mattress-shuttered windows and a back deck strewn with mangled crab pots. Marley stepped out the wheelhouse door and waved his arms at the helicopter. Arlo was already climbing the stairs.

Most helicopter handoffs occur on the back deck of a boat. Clearly, that was not possible. The handoff would have to occur on the frozen triangle of the bucking bow. Arlo turned toward his nephew. But Marley was already halfway out the window.

The tethered line in tow, Marley crawled to the bow's forward cleat. He wrapped the line around it to hold him in place. Raising himself to his knees, he waved his arms in the air, signaling he was ready.

When the swinging package advanced toward him, he moved his upper body so that it was synchronous with its movement. The bundle just missed his head. He grabbed it on the back swing. Unhooking it, he crawled back to the wheelhouse.

Arlo opened the package. Inside was a hand-held VHF radio and a dewatering pump. He pulled up the radio antenna and turned it on. "*Cape Kiska,* here. Over."

"Hello, *Cape Kiska.* This is *Coast Guard Jayhawk 311.* Over."

"Thank you for the gift, *Jayhawk. Cape Kiska* hears you loud and clear."

The four men clad in red survival suits stood around the radio transmitter as if it were a warming campfire. Tom bowed his head. Marley wrapped his arms around

Tom. Sully howled like a coyote.

"Copy that, *Cape Kiska*. The *Ocean Wolf* is approaching your starboard quarter and the *Petrel Prince* is not far behind. Unless you are in danger of sinking, they plan to escort you to Dutch Harbor. You are clear to turn off your emergency beacon, *Cape Kiska*."

"Roger, roger, Coast Guard."

"Is there anything else you need, *Cape Kiska*?"

"No, sir," Arlo said, pushing open the wheelhouse door and waving to the helicopter above. "Thank you."

The helicopter pulled up and away from the boat. It was not long before the hand radio came alive with a familiar voice on the other end.

"*Cape Kiska. Cape Kiska*. Arlo, you there? It's Erling on the *Ocean Wolf*."

"Roger that, Erling." Arlo spun around and could see the *Ocean Wolf*, its lights ablaze, pull up from behind and travel forward along his starboard side.

A mile-wide grin spread across Arlo's face. "What took you so long, buddy?"

Soon the *Petrel Prince* pulled along his port side. Bob Donnelly pushed open the wheelhouse door, stepped out into the storm, and waved. His white hair flew wildly in the wind, and his face, even from a distance, did not conceal the joy he felt in finding his old friend alive.

****

Maureen's fist punched toward the ceiling in a victory salute.

Patsy pulled a pint bottle of bourbon from the bottom drawer of the desk. She poured them both a generous round, and held her cup high.

"Fuck'n A!"

Chapter 14

Heading home across the parking lot, CoCo raced ahead, looking over her shoulder like an outfielder chasing a fly ball. Maureen bent down, gathered up a fistful of snow, and packaged it into a ball shape. She launched it high above the German shepherd. The dog's speed accelerated, and her black muzzle opened to snatch it from the sky like a fielder's mitt shanghaiing fly balls headed toward the Green Monster in Fenway Park and saving a run. Just like the Coast Guard had saved the Cape Kiska, she thought, with skill and determination.

Leaving the imaginary ball game behind, Maureen headed inside the clinic and downstairs to turn off the lights in the surgery room. It smelled of decomposing flesh and she could see that Casey's legs had continued to sag. She was glad he'd be gone tomorrow. His belongings still lay in a bowl on her desk, including the fancy pants watch, a cheap lighter, waterlogged cigarettes, the notebook, and the broken teeth Eric had brought her. Reaching for the bagged watch, Maureen turned it over and read the inscription again. *Congratulations, Casey. Good luck in life!*

She held it so CoCo could see it. "Not so lucky," she said. It made her sad all over again.

CoCo followed Maureen up two flights of stairs to the apartment above the clinic. After feeding the dog,

Maureen was ready to collapse. She lay in bed, her flame of hair spread out on the white pillow case. Her thoughts turned to Arlo. It was a long journey home for a crippled ship in a storm. Her eyes closed. She turned to rest her cheek on the pillow. CoCo curled up on the rug and rested her head on the single front paw. Soon the sound of purring snores rose above the bed.

****

The shepherd pawed her arm. Barely conscious, Maureen struggled to open her eyes. The dog whimpered. Why? She sat up in bed and looked at the clock. It was *3:30 a.m. What's going on?* The shepherd headed out of the bedroom. Throwing on a bathrobe, Maureen was not far behind.

She found the dog at the kitchen door. The hair on her back stood up straight as a picket fence. Her ears twitched, hearing sounds that Maureen could not. The shepherd signaled to Maureen that something was on the other side. Maureen knew the dog was waiting for a command.

"Stay," Maureen whispered, easing open the door.

The stairs curved down around a small landing before opening into the clinic waiting room below. Still hearing nothing, she knew it did not mean there was nothing to hear. Something had alerted the dog.

Maureen closed the door. Turning on her heel, she headed back to the bedroom and into her closet. Reaching beneath a stack of folded sweaters on the closet's top shelf, she removed a .22 automatic pistol. She checked the clip to make sure it was loaded and chambered a round.

Maureen called the police, reporting a possible break-in. She asked that a siren not be used in approaching the clinic. If there was someone poking around her premises, she wanted the culprit caught, not scared away. She slipped on her sneakers and headed out to the kitchen again.

CoCo stood at the door, her nose hugging its edge. With a careful turn of the brass handle, Maureen quietly drew the door open enough to poke her head out. Then, there it was, the unmistakable swish of the swinging double doors to the surgery room two floors beneath her. A flashlight beam scaled the waiting room wall below. Whoever it was, was about to make their escape. *Damn it!*

Maureen pushed the door open, pointed down the stairs, and let loose the command. "Attack!"

CoCo leaped past Maureen and down the stairs, unimpaired by a missing leg.

Snarls. Thrashing about. The sound of shattered glass. A husky scream for help.

Maureen followed her outstretched arms down the stairs. The gun's safety was off. The barrel pointed firmly in front of her.

She reached for the light switch at the bottom of the stairs.

And there he was, the prowler. He lay face-up atop the smashed glass coffee table. A chaotic formation of magazines were spread out on the floor above his head. His forearm hung motionless in the grip of CoCo's jaw. Snarls boiled from deep within her throat, and saliva dripped from her fangs.

Maureen aimed her gun at the man. "Who are you?" she demanded.

His face red, his chest heaving, the man fought to catch his breath. "Call the dog off!"

"Not a chance, buddy." Her heart pounding, Maureen wondered how this would end.

"Please," he pleaded. "Call off the dog."

"Not before you tell me who you are and what you're up to."

A pair of headlights swung into the parking lot. Even without sirens blaring, Maureen could see through the window that it was a police cruiser. Two officers approached the clinic's front door. Michele and another officer entered the room, their guns drawn.

"You okay, Mo?" Michele asked.

"Yeah, thanks to CoCo." They all looked at the dog. Her jaw clenched the man's forearm like a piece of meat.

"Is this fellow alone?" the other deputy asked.

"As far as I know, but I haven't been down to the surgery yet." Maureen still aimed her blued-steel automatic at the stranger.

"You alone, pal?" Michele circled the man, trying to get a handle on whether he was packing a firearm. "Answer me. Now!"

"Get this dog off me!"

Another growl climbed up CoCo's throat, its hot air reaching the man's sweaty face.

"The dog! Call it off!"

Ignoring him, Michele directed the other officer to search downstairs.

CoCo's tail began to move back and forth like the slow, stern strokes of a metronome.

Michele turned to Maureen. "Keep him covered while I see what the guy's holding in his hand."

Then, giving her full attention to the prowler, Michele snapped on a pair of latex gloves "You gonna behave, mister? Your arm belongs to this dog until you agree to do exactly as we ask."

The man nodded.

Michele walked around to the man's extended hand and plucked a small notebook from his grip.

Circling back to Maureen, she held it up for examination.

"Recognize this?"

"You bet I do."

"Yours?"

"That notebook belongs to Casey Elliot." Maureen stepped closer to the man, the barrel of her gun aimed at his head. "This could be his killer."

Michele slipped it into an evidence bag and tucked it in her pocket.

"You have a right to remain silent, pal. Understand?"

"I want a lawyer!"

"Anything you say can be used in court against you. If you can't afford a lawyer, one will be provided for you. Understand?"

The man nodded.

"Okay then. You're under arrest." Michele pulled a set of handcuffs from her belt as the new deputy, Tyler, emerged from the basement surgery.

"All clear down there," he said.

Michele looked at Maureen. "You can call off the dog now."

"CoCo. Down!"

Michele cuffed the prowler and pulled him off the floor. She turned to the other officer.

"Get him in the cruiser, Tyler, while I take a last look around and make sure the clinic is secure."

When Michelle returned, Maureen stopped her at

the door. "Will this get a write-up in the newspaper's Police Log?"

The deputy popped a fresh stick of gum in her mouth and flashed a smile. Penned by Michele, she got to write pretty much what she wanted based on the facts of the police encounter and infused with a deft dose of dry humor. There were two camps about getting written up in the Police Log. One group feared it, and the other aspired to it.

The officer looked at CoCo, sensing which camp Maureen hailed from. "How about something like, *Faithful fanged friend foils felony*?"

"Nice."

Chapter 15

Maureen was still asleep when Chief St. George and Franken rang the doorbell in the morning. She hopped into her jeans and sweatshirt, pulled on her sneakers, and ran a brush through her hair so quickly that it looked like she'd raked a pile of leaves on her head. CoCo followed as she rushed down the stairs to greet the two men.

After last night's break-in, Maureen had used the bolt lock on the clinic door for the first time since she'd moved to Dutch. When she opened the door, she did her best to look as if she already had a cup of coffee under her belt.

The chief took one look at her and apologized for waking her up. "Sorry, Maureen, we heard what came down here last night, but Joe, here, has got a plane to catch."

Franken carried a couple of rolled-up body bags over his shoulder as he descended the stairs to where the body waited. Maureen noted he'd wiped his shoes this time.

The chief stood over the table, re-inspecting the body of Casey Elliot. One leg lay collapsed on the table. The other seemed close to joining it. Pools of bodily fluid had overflowed onto the floor.

Maureen was eager to see him go. She also wanted news about the prowler.

"Well, what did you learn about him? Who was he?

What did he want with the notebook? Is he linked to Casey's death?"

The two men looked at each other, then at Maureen. The chief spoke first.

"He's a private investigator from Anchorage. His name is Butch Bixby. Does the name seem familiar?"

"Never heard of him." The attachment of a person's name to the event made her feel more violated, like it was personal. "Do you know who he's working for?"

"He didn't tell us anything. He just waited for bond to be posted and was out first thing this morning."

"Who's his lawyer?

"Hal Lacey." The chief looked at her with an unhappy grin. "Yeah, I know. Lacey's a jerk, but he's smart enough to have well-heeled clients when they're in a pinch."

"So do we know who hired him?"

"No, but he's worked for the oil and fish companies. He may even have represented Amchitka Shipping. I'll ask Marla what she knows about him."

Franken interrupted. "That's all we know." He looked at the wilting body of Casey Elliot. "So can we get going on this?"

The door opened upstairs with a clatter as two emergency technicians navigated a wheeled gurney into the reception area. "Doctor Mo?"

"Yeah, come on down, Jeff."

Soon the gurney was parked next to the table where Casey lay. One leg remained extended above his body. The odor was raunchy enough that Maureen opened the lone window to air out the place.

"It will take two body bags," Franken said.

"And some duct tape," Maureen added.

"Definitely, duct tape," Jeff agreed.

Maureen grabbed tape, scissors, and gloves for everyone. "Masks, anyone?"

Jeff snapped on the gloves and made the first move by picking up the top half of Casey's body and asking someone to slip a body bag over it. "I think having the two bags meet in the middle is our best bet."

Standing alongside the corpse, the chief pushed down on the remaining raised leg. When it landed on table alongside the other, body fluids splashed onto the floor just missing his new boots.

"Well, that makes it a whole lot easier," Maureen said.

Once Casey was secured in the body bag, they all pitched-in to transfer him to the gurney.

"We'll bring him out to the airport," Jeff told Maureen. She indicated he should address Franken.

"He'll be loaded in the cargo section of the plane, where he'll be kept cold on the flight to Anchorage," said Jeff, backing out through the double doors.

The chief reached for the bowl still holding Casey Elliot's bagged possessions and poured them into an official evidence bag.

Franken approached Maureen, who now sat at her desk. He reached into his chest pocket, removed an envelope, and handed it to her.

"Please sign this, Dr. McMurtry. It's a chain of custody release form."

Maureen pulled the form from the envelope. After glancing it over, she looked for a pen but couldn't find one. Franken reached inside his uniform, removed one from his chest pocket, and handed it to her. First wiping his boots, now lending her a pen. Perhaps they could work together after all, she thought. Maureen looked up at him with an appreciative grin. But Franken was stone-faced.

"You've got a pretty interesting rap sheet, Doctor," he said.

Maureen signed the form, returned it to the envelope, and, looking Franken in the eye, handed it to him.

"Yes, I do," she said.

Chapter 16

It was after lunch when Patsy arrived at the clinic to announce that the *Cape Kiska* was just north of Amak Island and should get back to Dutch by dawn tomorrow.

"I just checked in with the *Ocean Wolf*," she said. "It's slow going, but the *Cape Kiska* is stable. The wind has died down to twenty knots, but the swells are still bigger than my house."

Cleaning up after her last patient, Maureen looked up from the exam table. Deprived of sleep, her face had all the vim and vigor of a hound dog's.

"How are the guys holding up?" she asked.

"You look like shit," Patsy said, crossing the room to rest her hand on Maureen's shoulder. She gave it a squeeze. "The water pump is working like a champ. They're still under escort by the two boats. Everyone on board is tired, but there's lots of coffee. And I hear they're taking turns doing the nap thing."

Maureen perked up, thinking about guys relaxed enough to sleep. "What's the forecast?"

"Northwest fifteen by dinner. Even the weather is rooting for them."

Maureen's tired face stretched itself into a smile.

"So, big girl with a bad gun taking down a burglar in the night? Did you get any sleep after the police took him off your hands?"

The smile melted away. "Not much. The police

came for Casey's body this morning." She nodded her head in the direction of the empty table stashed in the far corner. "And I just put down a family dog."

Patsy folded her arms in a scolding stance. "Next time, just call the cops. No need for stupid hero shit."

"No heroism on my part. CoCo did all the work."

Napping in the corner, CoCo's ears twitched at the sound of her name. One eye opened and scanned the room. When nothing seemed to require her attention, she dozed again.

"So, you had a bad night, and now you're having a bad day."

"Bad day?"

"I know you hate putting animals down," she said

"The Salingers loved their old dog Rusty but he was suffering. It's never easy."

Patsy sauntered back to Maureen's desk chair, where she made herself comfortable by putting her feet on the desk.

"That word *love* is a tricky thing," she said. "Are you tagging it to Arlo these days?"

Maureen didn't know the answer to the question. As far as loving relationships were concerned, she was out of practice, and it had been intentional. But there was a directness about him she admired, a sense of humor she found engaging, and he was a generous lover. But there was a part of him she felt was out of reach.

"I don't know what to call it. Love seems a bit of a stretch."

Patsy wasn't having it. "Give me a break. I watched you suffering through that mayday episode last night."

Maureen doubled down on wiping the examination table.

"My, how that table shines!" Patsy said, her boots still on the desk.

Maureen tossed her smock in the hamper and sat on the corner of the desk, refusing to take notice of Patsy's boots. "I don't want to talk about it now. But that's not why you dropped by, is it?"

"I've come to take you on a field trip. Not far, I promise."

"I'm beat, Patsy." Maureen gave her a look meant to conjure up guilt for even asking such a thing. "The mayday, the break-in... Did you know that jerk was a private investigator from Anchorage?"

"A private dick, huh?"

"I don't know if I should be scared or angry. What if he's Casey's killer? Even though it seems unlikely he could have been at sea, he may be working for the person who did. How did he know I had Casey's diary?"

"You're lucky I'm here to take your mind off this." Patsy swung her boots off the desk and stood up. "Think of it as a rescue mission."

She pushed Maureen through the double door and coaxed her up the stairs. "Come on. We're headed to a fishery meeting. They don't meet in Dutch often, so this is a real opportunity. The place swarms with fishermen and...*environmentalists*."

Patsy opened the front door. "That's why we're going, girlfriend. To talk to Casey Elliot's environmental friends and find out what the hell he was up to."

Maureen took a stand at the coat rack. "I'm too tired to care."

"Stop it. You do care." Patsy grabbed Maureen's jacket from a hook and pushed her out the front door. They climbed into Patsy's green truck.

Maureen turned to her buddy with a lightbulb-going-off expression. "Hey, the World Series started last night. Who won the game?"

Patsy shrugged. Baseball was not among her passions. "You'll have to ask Andy." But when a *wait a minute maybe I did hear something* expression crossed her face, Maureen looked hopeful. "Well?"

"Well, not the Yankees. That's all I know."

"Now you're talking! Okay, let's get outta here."

They were halfway to the Aleutian Hotel, where the week-long fishery meeting was being held, before Maureen asked what the meeting was about.

"Mostly fishery regulations. But, today, it's all about deep-sea corals. And that should attract a lot of environmentalists." She looked at Maureen as if she were sharing insider information. "They're not all assholes."

The truck pulled into the parking lot, leaving a whirlwind of flurries in its wake as it traveled to a spot at the far side of the building. They climbed out and made their way inside. The lobby had high ceilings, and comfy couches gathered around a large stone fireplace. An enormous moose head was mounted above it. A staircase headed up to a second-floor landing that circled above and looked down on the lobby below. The two women headed up the stairs.

Following the flow of traffic, they found the entrance to a large meeting room. A note taped to the door read, *Meeting in Session.*

"Can we go in?" asked Maureen.

"Yeah, sure, this is a public meeting. Just be quiet." Patsy nudged open the door. They walked to the back of the crowded room and leaned against the wall.

The cavernous room was packed with over a hundred people, some dressed in blue jeans and sweatshirts. In a hushed tone, Patsy identified them as fishermen and locals. Fishing trade group representatives were more buttoned-up, looking professional but not overdressed, meaning no ties or high heels. Environmentalists seemed either over or underdressed. Patsy pointed toward a young gal, her hair in twin braids that fell down the front of her flannel shirt. Then to an older woman with a streak of silver in her smartly cut hair. She was taking notes. "Smartest of the greenie bunch," Patsy said, "with a nose for finding common ground."

At the front of the room, sitting behind skirted tables and facing the crowd, were the fishery regulators. They sat in comfortable-looking swivel chairs, a microphone parked in front of each one.

Facing the panel was a small table where a man in a suit used a presentation on a large screen to make his case. He spoke about the need to protect deep-sea corals because they provided protective habitats for fish and other marine species.

Maureen leaned over to Patsy. "Very persuasive," she whispered.

"That's Jonathan Glass," Patsy said from the side of her mouth. "He works for some eco-greenie-save-the-something outfit. He's always here, arguing to close down fishing grounds and cut harvest levels."

One of the panel members signaled the chairman he'd like to ask a question.

"Go ahead, Mr. Gellhorn."

The man wore a tweed jacket and tie. In front of him, a large binder of documents lay open. It appeared to be marked up with multicolored sticky notes hanging off the pages. He leaned into his microphone.

"Thank you, Mr. Glass, for your desire to protect our marine environment."

The audience shifted in their seats.

"However, closing Pribilof Canyon may not be the best way to accomplish your goal. The camera survey of the ocean bottom shows few corals inhabit the area. When coral was found at all, its average density was comparable to a coral about the size of this pitcher of water in an area about the size of this room."

Patsy leaned into Maureen's shoulder and whispered, "They're talking about closing the *Mushroom* to fishing."

Gellhorn held up the pitcher in front of him and spread his other arm in a gesture to include the meeting room. "Hiding behind this pitcher would not make me feel safe from predators."

Audible laughter erupted from the audience.

Turning his attention back to the man before them, Gellhorn asked his question. "Is this the sort of coral density relationship you imagine will provide protective habitat to vulnerable marine species?"

Glass fingered the bright tie that flowed over his Santa-sized belly before leaning into the microphone. "Thank you for the question, Mr. Gellhorn. Ours is a precautionary approach. We believe that if we fail to take action now, the coral may someday be destroyed by fishing gear and lost forever. "

Gellhorn leaned into his microphone again. "Thank you, Mr. Glass. But I have to ask, *what coral*? The survey found few and none were damaged by gear. This *belief* of yours seems more religious than scientific."

Laughter again erupted from the audience.

"It's called the Precautionary Principle." Glass said it as if speaking to a child who didn't get the importance of its meaning.

Gellhorn ignored the tone. Instead he warmed up to his second question by reminding Mr. Glass that fishery managers had already restricted fishing in 1.3 million square miles in its Alaska jurisdiction. He continued to talk while pouring himself a glass of water. "Many more square miles than all the national parks combined. And not a single fish species is overfished."

"Mr. Gellhorn, your question, please." The chairman loosened his tie. People in the audience leaned forward in their seats. Gellhorn drank from his water glass and adjusted the angle of the microphone before speaking again.

"You know, Mr. Chairman. I am going to withdraw my question. I had planned to support discrete closures where high densities of corals were found. But none were discovered. So, unless Mr. Glass can point one out to me, I will not waste your time with another question." He began to lean away from the microphone but changed his mind. He spoke slowly. "Fishermen feed this nation, and they need access to fishing grounds to do it."

Fishermen jumped to their feet and clapped. Some just stared angrily at the back of Johnathan Glass's head.

The chairman pounded his gavel. "Enough!"

Public testimony continued for another hour before the chairman adjourned the meeting for the day, and most everyone moved to the hotel bar.

It was packed. Maureen could tell Patsy was searching for someone specific.

She nodded toward the far side of the barroom.

"C'mon, I've got someone I want you to meet."

They made their way to a table in the corner where the thoughtful-looking woman taking notes during the meeting sat quietly sipping a glass of wine. Her face lit up when she saw Patsy approach.

After a brief embrace, Patsy took charge of the introductions. "Sandra, this is Dr. McMurtry. Mo did the initial exam of Casey Elliot when his body was brought to town." She turned toward her eco-friend. "We were hoping to talk to you about Casey."

A waitress came by and took their orders.

"I'll cut to the chase, Sandra," said Patsy. "We're wondering if you knew Casey. His parents say he was doing work for environmental groups, and we're hoping to find out what he was up to."

Sandra took a deep breath. "I did know Casey. Not well. I was shocked to hear of his tragic death. He seemed to work as a freelancer. Not for us."

Letting her eyes drop to the glass of wine in front of her, she let her fingers rest on its stem as if carefully managing what she might say next. She looked up. "He was a passionate young man but pushed the edge of the envelope a bit too much for us."

"What does that mean?" asked Maureen.

"He was impatient. He wanted to save the world today, not tomorrow. He was sometimes fast and loose with the science." She frowned in a way that told Maureen she was troubled by the events. "Do you think his death was tied to his work?"

"That's what we're trying to figure out. What issues was he working on?"

"He talked about protecting fishery habitat. But he also talked about offshore drilling up north." Sandra's attention moved over Maureen's shoulder. "There's Jonathan Glass. He'll know more about Casey than I do. He hired him for a project last year. Shall I flag him over?"

Maureen nodded. "Please." She stretched her spine, in hopes that it might give her a second wind.

After introductions and some discussion of the brouhaha that ensued during Glass's testimony, they landed back on the topic of Casey Elliot's activities.

"He seemed interested in two issues," Glass began. "The first one was the protection of skate nurseries. The other was about a specific oil rig drilling process."

"Skate nurseries?" asked Maureen.

"Skates are a large flat species that resemble a giant ray," said Glass. "Casey thought he might land a job as a crew member on a boat that was doing skate research or on one of the oil rigs."

Maureen remembered the chief's questioning of Arlo on the *Cape Kiska*. She recalled his scraped knuckles and broken finger after he'd returned from the skate survey charter. She fought to focus her thoughts. Ask the right questions. Get the facts before jumping to conclusions.

"Do you know what boat he may have crewed on for the skate survey? Or if he even got the job."

"No, but the agency will know which boats were hired for the survey. I think it occurred earlier this month."

Maureen nodded. "What about the oil rig job?"

"I heard he may have landed a job on an oil rig and planned to return for another two-week shift. He seemed excited about something but didn't want to talk about it."

The waitress arrived with the drinks, including

Maureen's tea.

"When big oil quit offshore drilling in the Chukchi Sea, a few wildcat operations jumped in. Casey thought they might not be in compliance with extended-reach drilling regulations. He said he'd found a way to get more information about their operation."

Maureen stirred her tea. She was running out of gas. "Is there anything more you can tell us?"

He folded his hands on the table before continuing.

"Look, Casey was a good kid, and none of us want to tarnish his memory." He looked at Sandra, then back to Maureen. "What happened to him was terrible. But you should know he was out there…"

He twirled his hand in the air. "We all pretty much let him go his own way."

"Are you saying he was crazy?"

"I'm saying he had issues."

Shifting her gaze to Sandra, Maureen checked to see if she concurred. The woman's mouth turned down in a sad grimace.

Maureen stood up. "Thanks for your help," she said, pulling on her jacket.

"Wait," said Glass. "Should I be talking to the police?"

"Yes." Maureen leaned over the table and scribbled on a cocktail napkin. She passed it to him. "Call this number and ask for the police chief."

Patsy started to stand. Maureen pressed her shoulder.

"Sit down," she said. "I'm looking forward to the walk home. It will help me sleep."

She headed into the snow, wondering if sleep was waiting for her at home. Knowing she would be keeping company with a loaded gun under her pillow, she had her doubts.

Chapter 17

Maureen's hand hung over the side of the bed. Sleep had not been a stranger. She rolled over and looked at the shepherd knowing the dog, not the gun, was the reason she'd slept. Warm blood, she knew, was better than cold steel.

The *Cape Kiska* had made it back to town during the night and, according to the harbormaster's office, was tied-up at the ISI dock. Maureen stood on the dock, admiring the fresh snow that sparkled in the sunlight. She wore sunglasses and a cockeyed grin. The sea air smelled crisp, as if the storm had washed it clean and hung it out to dry. *Oh what magic a good night's sleep can do*, she thought.

The dog ran in circles and rolled in the fluffy white stuff. When it came to new snow, her police training pretty much went out the window. Maureen packed the snow into a ball and hurled it down the dock as if it were a line drive to first base. The shepherd took it down. "Out!" cried Maureen. Behind the dog, crystal peaks poked the sapphire sky.

"A perfect day!" she said to CoCo, who was begging for another ball. "But what about Casey Elliot and this skate survey shit?"

Dozens of boats were bound to the dock with long lines tied fore and aft. Some boats were as long as football fields, others a third that size, but all large enough to battle the Bering Sea. The harbormaster's office had told her the *Cape Kiska* was tied up at the eastern end of the dock. Her pace quickened. She couldn't wait to see Arlo. She couldn't wait to see that all the guys were safe.

As she approached, she saw a skiff pull away from the outer side of the boat. She thought it might be the harbormaster's boat. It looked like Marcus, and someone else was aboard. She doubted it was Arlo. He'd use a truck to get around. *Hey, maybe I know him better than I thought!* She was feeling good.

It was high tide, so easy to climb over the railing onto the boat. CoCo made it in a single leap. The back deck was littered with a half dozen bent and broken crab pots that hadn't been unloaded yet. In contrast, all the lines were neatly coiled. Alongside the house door, garbage bags were piled high. Inside, it was quiet, save for the rhythmic squeaking of the boat as it gently strained against the lines.

CoCo sniffed her way around the galley table and along the benches. She seemed to accept the rank odor of smoke and diesel fuel. Whatever garbage had been strewn about in the carnage had been picked up and packed into bags stacked on deck. Even the bench cushions were hanging out to dry. The *Cape Kiska* was as shipshape as circumstances would allow.

Maureen headed up the stairs toward the wheelhouse. CoCo's hind legs pushed her upward, the front leg rebalancing the shepherd's weight along the way.

The wheelhouse looked war weary. Mattresses blocked the broken windows like bandages applied on a battlefield.

Maureen headed to the captain's quarters just aft of the wheelhouse. Her boots left footprints on the soaked rug. Gently, she slid open the door. Arlo lay spread-eagle in his bunk. What a relief to see him safely tucked beneath a quilt. Deep snores erupted from his rising chest.

She leaned against the door. Did she really think he was capable of killing Casey, even accidentally? *No, not possible*. But the survey shit, the cut hand, the permit number, it kept getting in the way. *Damn it!* She wanted to cross it off the list and move on. Should she stay or go?

Shedding her clothes, Maureen slid into bed like a hand that's found its glove. She rested her head in the crook of his shoulder and stretched her arm over his T-shirt-wrapped chest. He rolled slightly, just enough to pull her closer. The snoring stopped long enough for him to whisper from a dream somewhere, "Oh yeah."

The snores seemed tamed by the touch of her body and returned as purrs, each one causing his upper lip to flutter as if catching a wind that set its course toward deep sleep. CoCo stretched out on the rug, a coat of thick fur protecting her from its dampness. She sniffed the air then laid her muzzle to rest on an extended front paw.

Three hours later, Maureen and Arlo sat naked at the edge of the bunk. Maureen rummaged through the tangled quilt in search of her underwear. Found, she began to dress.

"There's something we've got to talk about, Arlo."

"I don't talk about relationships unless I'm fully dressed. No exceptions." He kissed her neck.

"Hey, lips off the neck, please. This is serious." She stood up and stepped into her jeans, pulling them up and finishing with a tug on the zipper. Arlo handed her a coral-colored turtleneck. She slipped it over her head, tucked it into her jeans, and fastened a silver-tipped belt. "Can we talk about your skate survey, Arlo?"

Still sitting on the edge of the bunk, Arlo looked at her, the glow suddenly gone. "What's up?"

"I learned something while you were gone that could be...well, I'd like to ask you about it."

"Ask what?"

"Could Casey Elliot have worked on your boat for the survey? You said you had two greenhorns on board. Perhaps he used another name?"

He climbed into his jeans.

"That's your question? Really?"

He pulled a sweatshirt over his head.

"Look around." His arm swung around the room, indicating the whole shebang. "This boat nearly went down, taking me and the guys to the bottom. And all you want to know about is Casey Fuckin-What's-His-Name!"

He pulled deck boots over his socks and walked out of the state room.

"Wait. Please." She trailed after him. "You're safe, and that's what's important. But this is a simple question. One that you're going to have to answer at some point."

She reached for his arm, turning him to face her. "Casey told his friends he thought he had a job on a skate survey charter. I just want to know if it could have been on the *Cape Kiska*."

"You want to know if this murdered kid worked on my boat. Why?" He let it hang in the air. "You think I could have, might have, am capable of stuffing him into that crab pot and throwing him over the side? That's the real question."

His face changed. He looked like a different person. "Get off my boat, Mo!"

She backed away from him, her heart racing. A growl rumbled from between the shepherd's bared teeth. She reached for Coco's collar. By the time she climbed off the boat, Maureen's hair felt on fire.

Maybe she'd been wrong to ask the question. She looked up at the wheelhouse. *But I'm not going back.* It was a simple question, a question that would be asked by someone. No need to yell. No need to talk to her like that. *Asshole!*

****

She was halfway down the dock when a voice hailed her from a ship pulling alongside the dock. Maureen signaled the crew to toss her the bow line. She caught it mid-air and guided the boat to line up parallel with the dock. She hooked it around a cleat while a crew member jumped to the dock and secured the stern line. The captain leaned out the wheelhouse window and gave her a salute of appreciation. She recognized him. It was Rob Stokes, the brother of One-Eye Ben.

"Can I come aboard?" she hollered up toward the wheelhouse.

Stokes waved her onboard. Coco followed.

The deck was well ordered with stacks of blue plastic modules secured behind the house, some filled with garbage, others containing equipment from the oil rig. She pushed open the door, headed past the engine room entrance, and into an impressive galley that shone with new appliances. A crew member sat at one of the tables filling out paperwork. CoCo sniffed his jeans as she made her way under the table. Her snout passed by

the closed doors to the head and two staterooms but
stopped to sniff at the entry to the fo'c'sle. She pawed at
the door.

"What's in there?" asked Maureen.

The kid looked up from the food order form.
"Storage." He shrugged his shoulders and went back to
compiling his list.

CoCo continued to paw the door. Then she sat at
attention as a police dog is trained to do when smelling
contraband.

Maureen pursed her lips. It was not her job to police
the boat, she decided.

"All right if I leave the dog here?"

"Sure."

It was a big boat. She climbed up two sets of stairs
before reaching the wheelhouse. Rob Stokes was
standing over the chart table nursing a cup of coffee. He
looked over at her with a polite smile. All around him,
high-tech monitors seemed to be taking a siesta.

He reached out and shook her hand. "Thanks for
catching the line. I hear they call you Dr. Mo. Is that
right?"

His hands were clean. His shirt and pants seemed
newly laundered, and his combed-back hair freshly
washed. He'd be an attractive man, she thought, if not
for the dark circles under his eyes.

"Some call me Dr. Mo." Her voice was gentle, the
way you'd expect a person to speak to someone whose
brother had just died. "But you can drop the *Doctor,* if
you like."

He motioned toward a small table with a
wraparound bench and offered her a seat and a cup of
coffee.

Emptying a small canister of half & half into her coffee, she watched it swirl into the dark drink before looking up at him. She explained that she had been among those that had found Ben on the beach and that she'd done the initial medical examination.

"I know," he said.

"I'm sorry about your bother, Rob."

He accepted the condolence with a slow nod and nothing to say.

"I asked to come onboard to see if you had any questions about Ben's death." She stirred her coffee again. "I thought it might help."

He plucked a pack of cigarettes from his pocket. "I do," he said, lighting one.

Cigarette smoke gathered like a cloud over his head. Maureen waited, wanting to give the man some space.

"Chief St. George called me while I was up north dropping supplies at the oil rigs last week. He told me Ben was murdered."

Maureen nodded.

"He told me Ben was shot in the head and found on the beach with a bunch of sea lions. Do I have that right?"

"Yes."

Cigarette smoke drifted toward the open window.

"What caliber?"

"A large caliber, maybe a .44 or .45. The police don't have the ballistics report yet."

"Just one to the head?"

She nodded, not sure where to go with this. She had expected medical questions.

"What about the sea lions?"

"They were shot multiple times."

His eyes wandered toward the windows as if he were

thinking about how it might have come down.

Maureen stared down at her cup. She began to feel the visit had been a mistake.

"He owed people money. I tried to cover his debts." Suddenly, he was choked up. He stood and walked to an open window that overlooked the dock. "He had a big heart, you know."

A forklift drove past the boat with a full load of gear. When Rob spoke again, his back was still to her. "Ben was not a fighter. He never had a chance against whoever did this."

A crew member climbed the ladder and opened the door to the wheelhouse.

His thick shoulders hunched forward over a belly. He rubbed his hands together as if trying to build a small fire in his palms.

"Colt outside," he said, looking at Rob, his Russian accent easy to decipher. "We need you to operate crane."

"Okay, give me a few minutes."

"Who dis?" he said, turning toward Maureen, his smile so forced it pressed against his cheekbones like a push-up bra.

She recognized him immediately. He was the fellow who'd caused a ruckus at the bar because he wanted Patsy's jacket.

"This is Dr. McMurtry. She stopped by to talk about Ben."

Maureen raised a hand, as if to say "Hi" but not invite conversation.

Rob ground out his cigarette in an ashtray. "This is Viktor. One of the crew."

"So. You know One-Eye?"

She nodded. "A little."

"You know who kilt him?"

"Not yet."

"Get going, Viktor," Rob said. "Not your business."

Viktor shrugged off Rob's remarks and headed downstairs to the galley. "We wait for you," he said motioning toward the crane before he disappeared down the stairs.

An explosion of barking let loose like a barrel of ignited firecrackers. Maureen flew down to the galley to find Viktor pressed against the refrigerator by CoCo's aggressive stance. She commanded CoCo to stop. The barking ceased, and the dog sat at attention, but her focus lay on Viktor like a bear trap waiting to spring.

****

A rooster tail of gravel flew from beneath the tires of the old pickup as it sped out of the parking lot. Maureen looked at CoCo on the bench seat.

"What the heck was that all about?"

The shepherd's muzzle was closed tight as if to hold back a tirade that might go something like, "Why didn't you let me bring the bad-ass down?"

Maureen reached over and scratched under the dog's neck. "Damn," she said, wondering if she was more upset about the encounter on the *Cape Kiska* or the *Cape Chirikof.* She knew it was the former but preferred to focus on the latter. Perhaps Andy was right about the Russians dealing drugs?

She worked the truck's gears, downshifting as she turned onto Airport Beach Road and headed toward the Unalaska side of town. "Let's go have a chat with the chief."

Pulling into the police station lot, she parked next to a white truck. She recognized the insignia on the cab door.

"Stay here, CoCo."

The dog was breathing easier now, and her tongue hung over her bottom teeth. Nothing sloppy, just tucked out between the two canines. Maureen decided she saw a smile of relief on CoCo's face as she closed the door, leaving the big shepherd behind in the truck.

"Hi, Chet," she said, seeing the deputy working at his desk. "Is the chief in?"

"Yeah, he's in, but Marla Mancuso is with him now. Something about ships delivering supplies to oil rigs in the Chukchi Sea."

She swung over to Chet's desk and pulled up a chair. "How do you think I'd be received if I knocked on the door and invited myself in?"

Chet looked amused. "Nothing I'd try if I had my head screwed on straight."

"Well, I'm not so encumbered."

She stood up and headed toward the closed door, leaving the deputy to shake his head.

Maureen gave the door three taps. Not waiting for a reply from within, she opened it just wide enough to lean her head inside. "Hello, Chief. Sorry to interrupt."

She looked at Marla. "Can I join you two?"

Not waiting for an answer, she edged the door open wider. "Just stopped by to report something odd going on aboard the *Cape Chirikof*. You know, Rob Stokes' boat, One-Eye's brother."

The chief seemed to be waiting for more.

"The boat delivers supplies to rigs in the Chukchi. I thought that since you were talking to Marla, it might be pertinent."

The chief waved her in.

Maureen eased into the chair next to Marla. "Sorry about the interruption," she said again.

The chief leaned back in his swivel chair, his hands taking charge of the arm rests. "What's going on, Maureen?"

"There's a Russian crewing on that boat who made my skin crawl and caused CoCo to bark like a dog shot out of a cannon. And you know that's not like her."

"I'm not sure what you're saying. Why do you think CoCo's reaction is important here?"

"Two reasons, Chief. I learned from someone at a fishery meeting yesterday, an environmentalist fellow named Glass who worked with Casey Elliot, that the kid was nosing around two issues. Offshore drilling in the Chukchi Sea was one of them. It seems he may have had a job on one of the rigs. The *Cape Chirikof* services those rigs."

She turned to Marla. "Do I have that right?"

The chief and Marla gave each other a quick look seeming to recognize this as part of their earlier, pre-interrupted conversation.

Marla spoke first. "Yeah, Mo, the *Cape Chirikof* services the rigs. But Casey didn't work on the *Cape Chirikof.* You're not thinking the boat had anything to do with his death, are you?"

"I don't know what to think." Maureen pressed on, turning to the chief. "I told Glass to contact you with this information."

"I haven't heard from him."

"He's probably still at the Aleutian."

The chief leaned forward, both arms on his desk now, his hands folded together. "And the other reason?"

"Something aboard the boat triggered CoCo's police

training. Her nose was working the door to the fo'c'sle. Then she stopped and sat at attention just as she's trained to do when she locates contraband like drugs or explosives."

"What were you doing on the *Cape Chirikof*?"

"The boat pulled up to the dock as I was walking away from the *Cape Kiska*. Rob invited me aboard."

She leaned back in her chair. "I thought I might be able to answer some questions about his brother's death."

The chief looked dismayed. "Jesus, Maureen. That's police business. You could get hurt."

"You're right, of course. I don't always have my head screwed on right." She leaned forward, hoping a contrite tone would get her out of hot water. "I felt sorry for him. His brother is dead."

Marla turned toward Maureen. "Your dog might have smelled explosives used when production casings are installed to initiate the flow of petroleum. It's a supply vessel, so it makes sense."

Maureen considered Marla's take on what had happened. She looked from one to the other.

"I don't pretend to know much about drilling for oil. But I do know my dog. The reaction she had to this Viktor fellow was extreme."

She looked at Marla. "But maybe you're right. Explosives. It's something to consider."

The chief seemed to be adding things up, summing the totals, and maybe figuring out the square root of what it meant.

He looked at Marla.

"I still haven't received the crew and transport rosters for your supply ships. Would you mind rattling the cages in your HR department? And a list of the vessels and crew chartered by the oil companies, like the *Cape Chirikof*, would get us a lot further down this road of inquiry. You'd know who to call."

"Of course," said Marla. "What are we looking for, Chief?"

"We're looking for Casey Elliot's name on one of the crew rosters. Or maybe he was a passenger, a rig employee."

"What can I do, Chief?" Maureen asked.

"You?" He stood up and pulled on his blue-billed cap, the one emblazed with Police Chief across the front. "You can escort me to the fishery meeting and introduce me to this Glass fellow."

Chapter 18

Raymond St. George liked to wield an ice scraper across his windshield with care. He liked to stand on the running board, liberate the wiper from winter's icy grip, and use long strokes to expose the clear glass beneath. But not today. He and Maureen worked with quick strokes to get the job done and be on their way in search of Jonathan Glass, the environmentalist who seemed to know a few things about Casey Elliot.

With CoCo tucked away in the grilled back seat section, the chief pulled the big SUV onto the plowed road and headed toward the hotel, where the fishery meeting continued throughout the week. He took the road along the coast.

Maureen sat in silence. The struggle to make a decision about whether to stay in Dutch sometimes created a traffic jam in her head, hampering the progress of productive thoughts. Nobody just happens to end up in Dutch. She knew that. It costs a thousand bucks just to get here from Seattle and at least ten hours flying time if you aren't hung up in Anchorage for days by bad weather. It's easier and cheaper to get to Paris, France.

She looked out the window at the mountains across the bay. The vast emptiness still took her breath away.

While some folks come to Alaska *running from* something, most others make the trip because they're *looking for* something. Often it's adventure or a job in the oil fields or aboard a fishing boat. But for some, it's a calling to be swept back in time where anachronistic yearnings to feel untethered by civilization might thrive. When she was young, Maureen received a postcard from Alaska. It was an old black and white photograph of a woman dressed in a billowing Edwardian-style white blouse and riding pants. Her hair was piled into a loose bun. Wisps of it fell down across one cheek. She stood atop a mountain surrounded by peaks in the Chugach Range. A horse, its reins hanging loose, stood next to her. On her other side, an old wind-up gramophone, its metal sound horn pointing toward the sky, sat perched on a small folding table. Maureen imagined the woman listening to Enrico Caruso sing an aria. Perhaps one by Verdi, the one where Alfredo proclaims his love of beauty. The image still inspired Maureen on sleepless nights.

She knew the reasons for coming to Alaska hadn't changed since Caruso was singing his heart out and when Robert Service wrote *The Spell of the Yukon* in 1907 describing the allure of the far north. Like Service, she knew that if fortune was what called you here, it wasn't what made you stay. *Some say God was tired when he made it,* wrote Service. *Some say it's a fine land to shun. Maybe. But there's some as would trade it for no land on earth. And I'm one.*

Maureen wondered, *was she one not to trade it for another land?* Anchorage was not the real Alaska. Not to her, anyway.

The chief turned down the volume on the police radio.

"I spoke to the medical examiner's office in Anchorage and got an informal report about Casey," he said. "They got to him right away because he was pretty much defrosted by the time he arrived there. No gunshot or knife wounds. Just the blows to the face and the big hematoma on the back of his head. They feel pretty confident that death was caused by blunt force trauma, just as you thought. There was no indication of drowning in the crab pot."

Glad to shake off her mental traffic jam, Maureen jumped right in.

"So, we're looking for a regular run-of-the-mill killer rather than a sadist who dropped Casey in the ocean while he was still alive?"

"Seems so."

"What about time of death? Anything new on that?"

"They were as stumped as you were, Maureen. With ocean bottom temperatures around thirty-six degrees at that location, he could have been there a week without decomposing. So, they're going with the date on the watch face."

"October sixth?"

"It seems the reasonable course unless we learn something new. Why?"

Maureen opened the side window and let the cool breeze rustle through her hair.

"There's something I learned that I haven't had a chance to share with you." She looked at him. "This fellow Glass, that we hope to find at the meeting, said that Casey told him he thought he had a job on a vessel doing the skate survey."

"Go on."

"We know that Arlo left to do a skate survey on October fifth."

"Yes...."

"When I asked him this morning if one of the greenhorns he hired might have been Casey, he threw me off the boat."

She wasn't looking at the chief anymore. Her eyes followed the snow embankment along the side of the road.

"What are you saying, Maureen?"

"I'm saying Casey Elliot was pulled from the ocean in a crab pot registered to the *Cape Kiska*, that a notebook found in his possession included a series of numbers. Only three were legible, and they matched the first three digits of the permit number for the *Cape Kiska*. And when I asked Arlo this morning if Casey Elliot might have been on board for the skate survey, he threw me off the boat."

The chief pulled the cruiser to the side of the road elevating a tire in the snow bank.

"Look here, Maureen."

She turned her head slowly in his direction. It had been hard to share her monster fear with him, but she knew she had to, or lose his trust and, perhaps, her sanity. And she hoped he would tell her there was nothing to it.

"We've known about the crab pot permit match-up since the beginning," he said. "Anyone could have taken a pot from the storage area. You said so yourself, as I recall. And the three-digit match-up could mean anything. We don't even know if the digits translate into a permit number. Now, it seems, we may have a skate survey in the mix."

She hesitated. "When Arlo got back, his left hand was pretty beat-up, including a broken finger. You saw it yourself. And some of the survey drops were in the *Mushroom* near where Casey was found."

Averting the chief's questioning gaze, Maureen looked out the window again. "I simply asked Arlo if Casey might have worked on the boat when it did the skate survey. Simple question, right?"

Maureen flinched, hearing herself say it aloud again. She knew her fears were pointing a finger at Arlo.

The chief's wrists rested on the top of the steering wheel. His attention seemed focused on the well-plowed road that stretched before them. The engine hummed in neutral. The heater pushed out warm air, countering the brisk temperatures invited in by Maureen's open window. At least the windows weren't fogged.

"Look at me." His voice was patient. "Really, look at me, Maureen."

Her facial muscles tightened. Some might say her face looked defiant, but it was not. Slowly, she turned to face him.

He spoke warmly. "Those guys on the *Cape Kiska* are damn lucky to be alive. So, for a minute, let's give Arlo the benefit of the doubt, knowing he's just been through a traumatic experience."

He waited for her to acknowledge that approach. "You know why I am willing to go there, Maureen?" He paused, allowing the question to sink in. "Because there's no motive. Why would Arlo murder a crew member? And maybe he's pissed that you think he could."

Feeling her face overheat, she turned toward the open window.

"You're probably right." The breeze felt good. "All I wanted to do was rule it out and move on. Instead, I got my head handed to me."

"Let's leave ruling out suspects to me. We do need

answers to those questions from Arlo, but they're for me to ask. Okay?"

She leaned her head back, nodded in agreement, and wound up the window. The chief shifted into first gear and powered the vehicle out of the snowbank and onto plowed ground again.

"It was a damn good watch," she said. "A watch that wouldn't stop as soon as it hit the water."

"And?"

"Arlo left town on the fifth. That watch stopped on the sixth But it could have been in the water for a day, maybe two or three before it stopped. The kid could have been killed before the *Cape Kiska* left town."

He kept his eyes on the road.

"Can I look into it? Can I make inquiries with the manufacturer about its performance in the water?"

He smiled. "Why not? Let's see where it takes us."

Maureen turned to check on CoCo in the back seat. The last couple of sleepless nights had caught up with the shepherd. She lay curled-up on the back seat, a paw hanging over its edge, her eyes closed to the world, seeming happy to ride in the grilled back seat of a police cruiser again. The dog's easy breathing showed that, for her, it didn't get much better than this.

The cruiser followed Airport Beach Road as it turned to hug the coast.

"For whatever reason, Franken felt compelled to send me your police record from Boston."

"Jesus," Maureen said turning to look out the window again. She wasn't surprised since he'd made a point of commenting on it to her yesterday when he picked up Casey's body. She made light of it and laughed. "Am I under arrest?"

"Possession of an unregistered firearm is a serious offense."

"Especially," Maureen quipped, "when you shoot someone with it."

"Clearly, it was self-defense. He's in jail. You're not."

"Still, I got a year's suspended sentence."

"That was your own doing, Maureen, for not explaining how the illegal gun came into your possession."

"I wasn't going to give up the guy who got it for me. The cops wouldn't issue me a permit. I was scared, and for good reason it turns out."

The chief slowed the truck and looked at her. "Why was he after you?"

"My fiancé? Turns out the great guy I met in first base line seats at Fenway Park wasn't the easy going, clever baseball nut I thought he was."

The chief raised a hand from the steering wheel to wave to the mayor who was driving in the opposite direction.

"Did you know that the first ten rows of seats behind the dugout at Fenway Park are the best seats in baseball? I'm talking *any* first base line seats in *any* park. He bought me a beer at an afternoon game when we both should have been at work, but it was the third game in a series with the Yankees. How could we resist playing hooky? Turned out we couldn't resist each other either."

"Did he attack you?"

"When he wasn't the most charming man on the planet, he was a possessive, jealous bastard. He was mean when he was riled. I was naïve…. Heck, I was stupid."

"Did he attack you, Maureen?"

He slowed the cruiser.

"Please don't stop again," she said, wanting him to keep his eyes on the road instead of on her.

"What happened?"

"He grabbed me by the neck and held me up to the wall trying to wipe anything but fear from my face."

She fell silent.

"Then what?"

"What happened? I throttled him with my knee and threatened to call the police. I sent him packing. But when I sent him the engagement ring..." She wasn't going to get teary-eyed about this. All that remained, she hoped, was anger.

The cruiser approached the Aleutian Hotel on the right. The parking lot was full. The fishery meeting attracted a crowd from as far away as Seattle. Instead of pulling into the hotel lot, the chief drove past it.

"He showed up again," Maureen said. "He was enraged that I'd returned the ring." Her finger unconsciously traced a scar along her jaw line.

"Is that where he hit you?"

"With a chair."

Her hand moved from the scar to tuck a strand of hair behind one ear.

"After that, not having a means to defend myself was no longer an option. Unable to get a gun permit, a friend of a friend showed up at my apartment one day with a brown paper bag. He had two guns, a .38 and a .22. We went down to the basement and used some old patio cushions for target practice. I chose the .22. It felt comfortable. Like I'd really use it if I had to."

"And he came back?"

"Yup." Her eyes wandered around the snow-laden landscape, noticing the wind had come up. Its blustering gusts blew the crests of plowed snow banks across the road.

"It was the middle of the night," she said in a monotone. Her words marched forward to tell the tale as if it had happened to someone else. "He broke down the door. I kept the gun fully loaded in the table drawer next to my bed. I grabbed it. He charged. I fired. I shot him in the right shoulder. Low enough, apparently, to cause his lung to collapse."

She'd relived the attack many times. It was chiseled into her memory and, like stone, devoid of feeling.

"He's in a Massachusetts state prison now, and that's good enough for me."

"Except that he's up for parole in six months. What will you do if he comes looking for you? You must worry about that."

She turned the stone face toward him. "If he comes after me, I'm ready to do damage. But in Dutch, I'm as far from him as I could find. Hopefully, he'll be too lazy to track me down if that's even on his mind. And, if he does, I've got Coco."

Maureen looked at the shepherd lying in the back seat. Her stoneface slipped away for a moment, knowing that if she gave the command, the dog would protect her as best she could. Then stoneface was back. "And I've got a gun. This time it's legal."

The chief pulled in front of the vet clinic. "Are you sure you want to go to this fishery meeting, Maureen? I can find this Glass fellow on my own."

Maureen couldn't look at him.

"Are you all right?"

She shook her head. "No, I'm not."

"Is there something I can do?"

"I always thought I was the kind of person that came to Alaska *looking for* something. Now, it seems I'm part of the gang that came here *running from* something."

"Don't be so quick to judge yourself, Maureen. A running person is afraid of life."

He waited, she knew, for her to finish the thought in her own mind. She let it roll around in there, warming to it. She lifted her eyes to meet his.

"Thanks, Chief."

Climbing out of the cruiser with the shepherd in tow, she looked back at him through the open door.

"You know, other than my father, you're the only one that calls me Maureen."

The chief, resting his wrists on the steering wheel again, threw her a smile warm enough to melt snow.

"Seems about right," he said.

Chapter 19

It was mid-afternoon the next day when Maureen pushed open the bar door. She was hoping her day might improve by trashing the Yankees with Andy. The bums had won last night's game, the second in the series.

"Jesus, Andy," Maureen said sliding onto a stool and motioning toward the jukebox. "Love this song, but it seems a little early in the day to be crying in our beer."

Andy laughed and continued washing down the scarred wooden bar. "It seems a little early in the day for you to be in here."

Shrugging, she headed to the glass-domed jukebox, intent on taking control. Neither the music selection nor the technology had been updated since the 1980s, and that's the way people liked it. She dropped in some quarters. When the song ended, the gentle click of another forty-five-rpm record falling into place gave her pulse a kick in the right direction. Her foot began to tap as a drum pounded out a disco beat, soon amped up by horns. Satisfied, Maureen shimmied to the music as she moved across the floor.

Swinging her leg over the stool near the center of the bar, *her* stool, she sang along with the refrain.

Andy already had a beer waiting for her. The bottle, so cold that condensed droplets slid down its long neck, waited to be tipped toward parched lips. Hers.

"Oh yeah." Her shoulders gyrated to the beat.

She took a long pull on the cold beer and set the bottle down. "Did you ever think about how lucky our parents were, growing up during the sixties and seventies with all that great music? A great soundtrack to life."

Andy looked up from cleaning the bar. Not even the twenty-something-year-old customers complained about the jukebox selections. "Not everyone loves disco music as much as you, Mo."

Maureen ignored his comment. She hadn't been doing much smiling in recent days, and the music had lifted her spirits.

"But that doesn't answer the real question," said Andy, letting his washrag stop on the bar right in front of her.

"What the hell are you doing here in the middle of the day?"

Maureen tossed back half a bottle of beer. "Thanks, Andy, but I'm okay."

He tossed the rag over his shoulder and folded his arms in front of his chest.

She ignored him. "The Yankees hammered them with homers last night."

"Yeah, it sucked. But what's ailing you?"

"Last night's game. That's what's ailing me."

"You didn't need to show up in the middle of the afternoon to tell me that." Andy rinsed a beer glass and stacked it on the shelf. "I'm not gonna serve you another beer until you spill the beans."

Reaching into her jacket pocket, she tossed a folded paper across the bar. "I think it might be time to call it quits in Dutch."

Andy opened the paper, read it, and slid it back to Maureen.

"Oh, so you're in the running for a nice gig at an animal hospital in Anchorage. They want you in for a second interview. What's the problem? You've just been given a great compliment and an all-expenses paid trip to civilization. Maybe," he said, "I should have poured you champagne instead?"

Crossing his arms across his chest again, he seemed to be challenging Maureen to look up from her beer.

Her head tilted to face him. "You make it sound so damn rosy."

"Yeah. Well, it's not as if I want to serve you that bubbly because I'd miss you too much. But what's the rest of the story?"

"I like living in Dutch when I don't hate it here. I like warming this stool. *My* stool."

"Jesus, Mo, it's a job interview. Come in and get drunk when they turn you down, or the Yankees win the World Series."

She gathered herself up, making another move at an end run.

"Your parents make it to Woodstock?" she asked.

"Not everyone made it to Woodstock, Mo. But I had an uncle who was at the Newport folk festival when our favorite folksinger went electric and got booed offstage."

She looked down at her beer. "I think I might have gotten booed off the *love train.*"

The crows' feet at his eyes tightened.

"Arlo and I may be on the rocks."

He popped the cap on another beer and set it down in front of her.

"I'm sorry, Mo."

"When it comes to the ratio of women to men here, the odds are good for women, but the goods are, as they say, often odd. Arlo seemed to be one of the exceptions. Or so I thought."

"What does that mean, *or so you thought*?"

The door to the bar opened, shooting a shaft of light across the darkened floor. A lone figure walked to the bar and sat at its far end. Making himself comfortable on the barstool, he looked at Maureen and nodded in recognition. It was Rob Stokes. He was unshaven now and looked unkempt, she noticed.

"He's been in here a lot recently. And I hear, the boat hasn't made a trip to the oil rigs this week," Andy whispered.

"A dead brother can do that to you."

Andy moved to the end of the bar. After a brief consultation with Stokes, Andy poured him a shot of whiskey and a tall draft beer.

He returned to Maureen. "A boilermaker." He looked at the clock. "Poor guy."

Maureen stood up. "Maybe I should keep him company."

"Nice thought but dumb idea." He shot her the stern look of an experienced bartender who knew what he was talking about. "Contrary to pedestrian opinion, misery does not like company."

Maureen was still considering whether it was a dumb idea when Marla appeared at the door. She stood there for a moment, seeming to let her eyes adjust to the dark interior. Stepping forward, she nodded at Maureen and Andy but joined Stokes at the bar. She slid onto the stool next to him. The heel of her cowboy boot hung on the rung of the bar stool.

Maureen sat back on the stool, a perplexed expression on her face.

"So, what's that look about?" Andy asked, drying glasses again.

"I didn't know they were friends." She watched the interaction at the end of the bar. Marla's hand was on Rob's shoulder as if she were trying to calm him.

Maureen thought Marla was probably trying to support one of her charter boat captains that wasn't servicing the rigs as he should. One with a dead brother to mourn.

Washing the last glass in the sink, Andy whisked it dry with the towel and set it on the shelf.

He leaned on the bar. "So I hear you're digging deeper into police work these days."

"Come on, Andy, I just help with forensics when no one else is around."

The door flew opened, and deputy Michele made quick work getting to the bar. If Maureen hadn't recognized the deputy as a friendly face, she would have thought she was about to be arrested.

"The chief wants to see you, Mo."

Both Marla and Rob turned to look.

"Geez, how did you know I was here?"

"Patsy always knows where you are."

Maureen reached into her pocket to pay for the two beers. Andy's palm was up. "Today, it's on the house. *Your* seat will be waiting for you."

She looked at him like she was counting lucky stars. "You know, Andy, you're an exception to the *goods are odd* rule."

"Everyone knows that."

He did it again, made her laugh even as she was getting pulled away from a cold beer and a warm stool. It would be hard to leave this place, she thought, heading toward Michele, who held open the door.

Before stepping outside, Maureen turned back toward Andy one last time.

"The Yankees suck!"

Andy rang the brass bell over the bar. "A round of beer on the house to everyone that thinks the Yankees suck."

The six remaining patrons bellied up to the bar.

Chapter 20

Michele led Maureen into the chief's office. Chet followed them inside. Everyone grabbed a chair. The chief passed a report to each of them.

"It's official now. We have the ballistics report from the state police." The chief's blue uniform shirt was neatly pressed, and the cuffs snapped. He wore a badge. He saw the inquisitive looks.

"I'm picking up Casey Elliot's mother at the airport in an hour." Clearly, that was all he planned to say about that. "This ballistics report confirms two separate weapons were used to kill the sea lions and Ben Stokes: a rifle using a .30-06 cartridge and a .44 handgun."

"Which one took out One-Eye?" Phil asked.

"The .44," Maureen said. She recalled the big fat slug she had pulled from his skull.

"A .44 slug fired from the same weapon was found in one of the sea lions, so I think we have a solid case that they were killed together by the same perpetrators."

The chief stood up and reached for his parka. "I'm heading to the airport now but, Chet and Michele, I'd like you to head to the hardware store and get the names of people who have purchased a .44 handgun or ammo in the past five years. Most everyone in town owns a .30-06 rifle, so searching for owners is not likely to turn up much, but ask for recent ammo purchases."

He finessed his favored gray hat from its home on

top of the file cabinet, looked at it, and dropped it back where he found it. Instead, he grabbed the navy-blue billed cap off a coat hook. It clearly identified him as the *Police Chief* in large white stitched letters across its front. He popped it on and fitted it in place with a practiced motion. Then he looked at Maureen, who was still sitting in her chair, wondering why she was called to the meeting.

"Maureen, I'd like you to phone Franken. Compare notes about the conclusions in the medical examiner's report, that sort of thing." He handed her a business card with an Anchorage phone number.

"Not Franken!" Both hands flew up as if trying to stop a Zamboni from crossing the room.

He looked at Maureen from beneath the bill of his hat, his charmer grin in command. "Be nice," he said. "I'd like to see if we can work with him."

****

Carrying a cup of tea, Maureen curled up in the overstuffed chair near the diesel stove. She eyed the gun on the ottoman. Ever since the break-in, she'd kept the fully chambered .22 on her nightstand. Now it lay in front of her.

Setting the cup down, Maureen disarmed the gun and removed one of the bullets. She'd shot her fiancé with this gun. His attack had traumatized her. But she had no regrets about defending herself and thought she'd done a good job of tossing the whole mess from her life. But that private investigator, a stranger, breaking into the clinic below had brought back unwelcome memories. Feelings of fear and anger had returned. She thought she'd been able to chuck them, but they were just buried. Now they'd returned like zombies coming at her in the dark. And now, just when she needed him, Arlo seemed out of reach.

"Damn it!" She said it loud enough to cause CoCo to jump to her side, ears alert, eyes scanning the room. Maureen rubbed the shepherd's neck.

"Yeah, you're right, CoCo. Call this Franken guy and get it over with!"

She dialed the number , checking her watch to make sure it was not too late.

Franken answered. She told him the chief had asked that she check-in with him about the medical examiner reports on One-Eye and Casey. She passed on what she had learned from two watchmakers she'd called regarding the time and date registering on the face of Casey's water-resistant watch.

"That watch is rated to be water resistant to one hundred meters. Even at one hundred and fifty meters, they said the gaskets might hold for a few days."

She knew that Arlo's boat had left town the day before the date on the watch. The *Cape Kiska* would have had time to get to the location where Casey was found. But if death occurred a day or two earlier, Arlo would be in the clear. She didn't raise this issue with Franken but the chief knew. Instead, she shared what she had learned about of the depth of the pot when it had been dragged up by the trawler. "The captain of the *Viking King* said he was towing at fifty fathoms, about one hundred meters. So, well within the water-resistant range."

Listening to Franken on the other end, she could tell he welcomed this phone call as much as she enjoyed making it. *Blah, blah, blah,* she thought as he smothered her with skepticism from the other end.

"How about Butch Bixby, the private detective who broke into my clinic? Did you find out who he was working for yet? He seems our best link to the killer."

She monitored the pitch of her voice, wanting it to sound as if she were making the inquiry about something that happened to someone else instead of her, her home, her clinic. Her eyes wandered to the gun on the ottoman. She hated that the break-in had made her feel so vulnerable.

"Nothing yet?" She listened to his voice drag on, reminding herself of the chief's admonition to *play nice.*

She was about to hang up when she remembered her conversation with Blackie.

"The harbormaster regularly tests the water temperature in Captains Bay. He said the temperature was forty-one degrees, colder than we thought." She hesitated before completing her thought. "So time of death before discovery of One-Eye may be longer than the two-day estimate your medical examiner calculated."

Blah, blah, blah, she thought again, listening to him rattle on but not share any new information.

Ending the phone call, she was surprised when he signed off saying, "I appreciate the call, Dr. McMurtry."

Maybe she'd misread him? Still, when she hung up, she looked at the phone. "Asshole," she said, rising from the chair.

Rummaging through a box of cassettes until she found the one she sought, she inserted it into the player. Puccini's opera, *Turandot,* filled the room with a swoon of violins. Falling into the armchair, she raised her feet onto the ottoman so that her red wool socks straddled the reassembled gun. She felt the warmth of the stove, flexed her toes, and let her head fall back on the cushion. When

Pavarotti's voice soared to a high C singing the "Nessun Dorma" aria, her toes curled.

Chapter 21

The stark streak of land called the Alaska Peninsula protrudes into the Pacific Ocean like a bold thumb jutting from the fist shape of Alaska. Strewn beyond the thumb are dozens of mostly uninhabited islands called the Aleutian chain. On a map, it appears as if the fist of Alaska grabbed a pearl necklace and flung it westward toward Russia. Set free, the pearls splashed across one thousand miles of sea, creating a porous border of islands between the Pacific Ocean and the Bering Sea. Unalaska Island, home to Dutch Harbor, is the largest island and, situated closest to the mainland, the most accessible.

****

The plane's flight path to Dutch charted an approach from the Gulf of Alaska side where gusting winds had made for a bumpy landing. The gloved hand of Eleanor Stockbridge Elliot rested on the metal railing that led from the plane to the tarmac. She grasped the high fur collar of her parka so that it held tight around her cheeks. An attaché case swung from her other hand.

Ray St. George hung back from the entry, where passengers pushed through the glass door. He recognized Mrs. Elliot immediately, not because of her fashionable outfit in a place where high fashion generally meant clean clothes, but because he had spent time on her social media page in preparation for their meeting. He waited for her to move past the knot of people near the door, then approached her.

"Good afternoon, Mrs. Elliot." He tipped his hat and met her gaze. "Welcome to Dutch Harbor." He extended his hand and held hers warmly.

"Thank you, Chief St. George." Her voice was taut as if held by a leash.

She clutched the handle of the attaché case that hung at her side and took a deep breath.

"Please call me Ellie," she said, struggling to smile.

"Everyone here calls me Chief, Ellie."

He escorted her to baggage claim, where they watched two men toss luggage from a cart. She pointed to her suitcase, and he fetched it. They headed outside to the cruiser parked in the lot out front.

"Would you like to check into the hotel," he asked while loading her suitcase into the back seat, "or go to the station first?"

"The station, I think. I'm anxious to know what you've learned and to be of assistance if I can."

They drove past the hotel and headed to the Unalaska side of town.

Inside the station, deputies glanced up from their desks, offering her looks of sympathy as the chief guided her to his office. He hung her parka on a hook alongside his own. Chet brought her a cup of tea and closed the door as he left.

Ellie sat in the chair opposite the chief, her back straight as a flagpole in a storm. His forearms lay on the desk, his hands folded.

"I am sorry for your loss, Ellie. I know what it is like to lose a son. The pain never really goes away. But eventually, the good memories bring comfort."

"You lost a child too?"

"Yes, in Afghanistan, six years ago. He was a Navy Seal, like me, before I moved to the Navy's criminal command." The chief's eyes moved to a framed photograph of the two of them in uniform together. He turned the frame so she could see it. "We were very close. What about you and Casey? Close?"

"Yes, I think so. We communicated a lot by phone and email, but he never moved back to Chicago after college. He stayed in California until his move to Alaska this year." She took a sip of the tea and looked out the window.

"He lived in California," she said, letting her eyes meet the chief's again. "The last time I saw Casey, we sat around a fire on Carmel beach with his friends, watching the sunset and making s'mores. They got sandy, but nobody cared."

A short splash of laughter washed over her. She leaned back in the chair.

"My son..." The chief looked at his folded hands for a moment, "My son, Tom, was stationed in California too, near San Diego. He'd already made lieutenant when he was deployed to Afghanistan. We rode mountain bikes together. Then we'd play some golf. He generally beat me."

"I guess that's what you mean about the medicinal quality of memories." The choke-hold on her pain failed. Tears streamed down Ellie's cheeks. "But it's not working now."

"It will. One day." He passed her a box of tissues.

Ellie wiped mascara from beneath her eyes.

Then she was all business again, transforming into mother-in-chief. "Have you made progress in finding the person who killed Casey? Or why anyone would want to kill my son?"

"The investigation is ongoing, but I want to be straight with you, Ellie. It's not going to be simple." He shifted back in his seat. "The case is complicated by several factors, starting with the cold ocean water, which makes it difficult to determine time of death."

"What else?"

"The cause of death has been determined to be blunt force trauma to the head." He leaned forward again. "Are you okay discussing these details?"

"Of course." She set her empty cup on the desk.

"He could have been struck with something or hit his head on something. Injuries to the face indicate he may have been in a fight."

"Do you have any leads at all?"

"Yes, we have some but nothing conclusive. Right now, we are trying to piece together Casey's life so we can focus our efforts. On the phone, you said he didn't have an address here and that he lived on a boat, but you didn't know the name. Has the name of the boat come to you since our conversation?"

Her lips tightened. She shook her head. "No, nothing. I told you all I knew."

"You said you two communicated by phone and emails, but we've not located his laptop or phone. So, we have very little to assist us in identifying what he was up to and who he knew here."

"I told you he was working on environmental issues."

"That's a big canvas, Ellie. Perhaps you can help us with some details you recall."

She stood up. "What's going on here? Why isn't the FBI involved?"

The chief remained seated. His voice softened. "We are working with the FBI and the state police. Casey is getting our complete attention."

He took a deep breath. "Would you like me to bring you to the hotel? We can talk tomorrow."

Eleanor Stockbridge Elliott collapsed into the office chair and sobbed into cupped hands.

Her sobs changed as she worked to rein in the tears like easing a horse from a gallop to a trot. The chief pushed the box of tissues closer. She dropped her hands from reddened eyes.

Without a word, she reached for the slim black briefcase leaning against the leg of her chair. She laid it flat on the desk and pushed her thumbs against the two brass clasps that caused it to snap open. She raised the lid, turned it to face the chief, and slid it toward him.

"It's my laptop," she said, blotting her eyes with a tissue. "I'm turning it over to you, Chief. Perhaps you can find a clue in our emails to one another. I've never deleted any, so there are years of Casey's emails stored here. I just ask that you don't read my other emails. Not that they are very exciting, but they are personal."

She pulled another tissue from the box. "My husband could not leave his law office for the trip. But I want to help," she said, blotting mascara from beneath her eyes.

The chief lowered the lid of the briefcase. "Thank you, Ellie. This will be very helpful. May I ask my staff to transfer your email exchanges with Casey to our computer here at the station? Then we can return your laptop."

Ellie nodded. "Yes. Please do."

Chet was summoned and asked him to make the

transfer.

"I suspect you'd like to check into your hotel soon. But before I bring you there, perhaps you can tell me your best understanding of the reason Casey came to Dutch Harbor."

"He wanted to save the world," she said wistfully, still dabbing beneath her eyes. "He thought the best way to do that was to protect the oceans. It's in the emails."

"Anything else? Did he talk about people he met here or specific projects he was working on?"

"I can't recall specific names, but there might have been some references made in the emails. And, of course, specific reference is made to his birth mother, who he met with in Anchorage."

The chief blinked, a look of surprise on his face.

"Yes, we adopted Casey as an infant. We've always supported his efforts to track down his genetic parents. He located his birth mother earlier this year and met with her in Anchorage on his way to Dutch Harbor."

"And the father?"

Ellie raised an eyebrow. "She didn't seem to know who it was except that he was a fisherman. It's all in the emails."

Chapter 22

At sixteen hundred feet, Mt. Ballyhoo hardly qualifies as a mountain, but it looms over Dutch as if it were a mighty one. In summer, it rises from the sea in a gown of tall green grasses bejeweled in swirling blue lupine. But in winter, its treeless shape, armored in snow and ice, is angular and masculine.

****

The snow had stopped around midnight when it left town on a strong blow. Quiet now, the morning sunrise shone as a pink glow. Maureen's snowshoes pressed into the fresh snow, crushing fragile crystals under her weight.

An October sunrise in Dutch arrives around nine thirty a.m., so, technically, she was off to a pre-dawn start at nine. By ten thirty, she was halfway up Ballyhoo, leaving large oval snowshoe prints in her wake. They were quickly destroyed by CoCo as she leaped to snatch snowballs. She heaved another snowball, this one sailing long and high. CoCo demolished it.

Maureen was anxious to reach the peak of Ballyhoo. From that perch, she'd be able to see Mt. Makushin in all its regal glory. It was one of many volcanoes in the Aleutian Islands where earthquakes regularly rolled beneath the surface. Sometimes it coughed up an eruption of soot through conical vents. But today, it slept peacefully beneath a snowy blanket, unlike Maureen, who, of late, felt like a volcano on the verge of a sooty outburst. *Arlo, not Arlo. Anchorage, not Dutch. Tending to murder, not puppies.* It wasn't just a crossroads she had to navigate. It was a six-car pile-up. Glad to be on Ballyhoo, she climbed toward its peak. She wanted to get outside her head.

When her cell phone rang, she considered ignoring it. She wanted to get to the top of the mountain and breathe deeply. She wanted to pretend she was listening to Enrico Caruso on a wind-up Victrola. She wanted her troubles swept out to sea. But she planted her ski poles and fumbled inside her parka for the phone.

It was Kate, calling from Seattle. Maureen perked up. Kate might have news about the dead sea lions she'd packed off to the marine mammal lab two weeks ago.

She answered the phone.

"Four days, one hour, and thirty-six minutes." Smugness radiated from Kate's voice.

"What?"

"I know you, Mo. You're always digging for more data. And I've got more. It's in my hands, on this piece of paper." Kate rattled the paper in the air, generating a boosted audio effect.

"What are you talking about, Kate?"

"Time of death," she said, her voice resonating a deadpan cadence. "Time of death before we discovered the dead sea lions and Mr. Ben what's-his-name...on the beach."

"Ben Stokes. AKA, One-Eye."

"Yeah...One-Eye."

Maureen could hear the smile in Kate's voice. It spread all the way across the Gulf of Alaska and halfway up Mt. Ballyhoo.

"Incredible, isn't it?" Kate said, "to have such precision?"

Maureen used her free hand to wad together a snowball. "I'm confused," she said. "How'd you determine the time elapsed since the animal was shot?"

"Telemetry. It's all about tracking by satellite." Kate sounded cocksure.

"Telemetry tracking?" Maureen threw the snowball long and high.

"Steller sea lions are endangered, so there's a lot of research invested in determining their life history and how they die. Some devices track where they travel and how deep they dive in search of food. The device we found embedded inside the animal tracks the sea lion's body temperature until it dies."

"Go on."

CoCo was digging in the snow, looking for a white ball.

"This is the cool part," Kate said, still sounding confident she had a good thing up her sleeve. "Once we removed the device from the body, exposing it to the atmosphere, it was able to signal the satellite causing all the temperature data to be downloaded. Now we've got a mountain of data."

"Why didn't I find it?"

"It wasn't in the adult female you worked on. We found it in the juvenile male."

"I don't get the link to the cause of death."

"If the body were ripped apart by a killer whale, instantly releasing the capsule, the temperature would immediately nose dive, and we would know that it was a victim of predation. We've found a lot of these. With natural deaths, the temperature decline may take days as the body decays."

Maureen wondered where this was going. She looked toward Ballyhoo's peak.

"But there's more…" Kate said seductively.

"I'm waiting." She launched a line drive toward CoCo.

"No matter how the animal died, the device can tell when it died. The sensors will show when the body temperature begins to decline, especially in a smaller, juvenile animal with less blubber."

"Holy shit!" Maureen stamped on the snow with her snowshoes to pack an area for CoCo to lie down. Kate had her full attention now. "I get it. Four days, one hour and thirty minutes before we discovered it on the beach, its body temperature went on a downhill sleigh ride."

"You got it, Mo! On *September 27 at 5:30 p.m.,* the data tells us the animal died. That's the time the heat-detecting capsule began tracking a constant decline in body temperature."

Maureen gazed down at CoCo, who rested her head on a hiking boot still lashed to her snowshoe.

"Based on what you've told me, Kate, death seems to have occurred earlier than the medical examiner's estimate. The whole investigation has been wrongly focused on a date two days later than it actually occurred."

"Science is a wonderful thing," Kate said wistfully.

"Heck, yeah! You know it. I know it. And now Franken's gonna know it."

"What do we do now?"

Maureen's gaze moved from Ballyhoo's peak toward the harbor below, filled with boats, fish plants, and noise.

"I'll contact the chief," she said. "If you could get me a copy of the report, I'll get it where it needs to go."

"I'll email it to you."

"This is a big deal, Kate. Other than knowing the same gun that killed One-Eye was also fired at one of the sea lions, we've made little progress on his death... until now."

"Consider it done."

Maureen tucked the phone in her parka, grabbed her ski poles, and redirected her snowshoes so that they faced downward toward the harbor noise. She surprised herself by feeling relief even as she turned her back on Ballyhoo. It was as if One-Eye had cut into her painful dance with Casey Elliot that always seemed to head back to Arlo. Too close for comfort. Like she'd been dancing cheek to cheek with Casey's corpse. The corpse of One-Eye seemed more distant, less able to wrap its hand around her waist.

****

Maureen hadn't done much grinning in the past week, but when she came through the door of the police station, she got about as close to it as a person robbed of reasons to smile might manage. She felt the folded email message from Kate in her pocket, knowing the information would vindicate her call about One-Eye's time of death. She'd already checked the harbormaster's roster of boats in town two and four days before Ben was found. Two days before, the weather was great, and the harbor was nearly empty. Four days before, the weather was ripping. Many boats were at their berths.

Chet looked up from his desk. "Hey, Mo, who you picking for the World Series game tonight?"

"The Yankees will face rock solid pitching from the

mound tonight." She leaned over his desk. "Life is good."

She'd called ahead, so Chet knew the chief was expecting her. He chuckled and pointed his head in the direction of the chief's office. "He's all yours."

Maureen gave the door a cursory rat-tat-tat and stuck her head inside. He was on the phone but flagged her in.

"It's Marla," he mouthed to Maureen. Within a minute, he said goodbye, hung up, and turned his attention to her.

"The shipping company has no record of Casey working on their supply ships," he said, "but Marla says Lightning Strike Oil might have sent him as an oil rig crew member aboard one of the chartered boats carrying supplies to the rigs. So, there's more footwork ahead. She's making inquiries."

"I've got news." She removed Kate's email from her pocket and waved it in the air.

Folding his hands on the desk, the chief studied Maureen. "You look like Christmas arrived early."

She laid the email in front of him. "That's for you, but I'll tell you what it means. It means that I was right about One-Eye's time of death, and the medical examiner's office in Anchorage was wrong."

The chief looked puzzled.

She shrugged her shoulders. "Yeah, I'm sounding juvenile, but that Franken fellow is a jerk. I'll try to be more mature when I finish gloating."

He laid a hand on the folded paper giving it a pat. "Tell me about it."

Maureen recounted the marine mammal lab's report on the telemetry device they found on one of the sea lions that unequivocally pinpointed the time of death to four days, one hour and thirty-six minutes before they found the beached carcasses, including One-Eye Ben.

"I'll make sure Franken is updated," the chief said, trying not to smile. "We can singe the bridge but not burn it down."

"I'll take what I can get." She leaned back and relaxed. "Okay, I'm done gloating."

"I'm impressed, Maureen. It's nice to have someone in the orbit of this office able to track down details that move the investigation forward. Unfortunately, it means I'll have to send the deputies out to re-interview everyone about what they'd seen or heard *four* rather than *two* days before the body was found."

He wrote a note to himself and looked up. "Good work," he said.

"Mrs. Pynchon told me she saw a skiff near Swallow Reef about that time. It had a yellow line painted around the hull, just above the water line. But I don't know how much that will help us find the killer. I noticed the harbormaster's skiff has a yellow line. I've seen Marcus poking around in it at all hours. He was all the way out at the ISI dock the other night."

"I'll ask Michele to talk to Blackie about skiffs with yellow paint at the waterline, including his own."

The chief stood up and headed to the file cabinet, removed a folder, and brought it to his desk. Flipping through it, he found the memo Blackie had sent him and laid it on the desk. He ran his finger down the dates on the right-hand side of the paper and stopped when he came to the date *September 27*. He pointed it out to Maureen.

"Two days before we found him, there were no

boats tied to the two tramper buoys at the far end of Captains Bay," he said, indicating the list of tramper vessels in town that the harbormaster had sent over. "But on September 27 there was a Russian cargo vessel tied there."

"Russian?" Maureen immediately thought of Viktor and his brother.

"Michele can follow up on these leads with Blackie. But before we start investigating, there's something else I want to discuss." He turned toward his computer and worked the keyboard, sending a document to the printer in the corner of his office.

"Could you grab that for me, Maureen?"

She pulled it off the printer and tried to hand it over.

He waved her off. "Read it."

She skimmed the document and looked up at him. "This is an application for a state coroners license."

"I understand you're heading to Anchorage in a couple of days." His folded arms lay across his chest. "I'd like you to be part of our team, Maureen. It's different than a medical examiner. A coroner does not have to be a medical doctor. But you will need some training."

Her jaw dropped.

"Why don't you stop at the state office building while you're in Anchorage for that vet hospital job interview and talk to the health department about the coroner position."

Still standing, one hand holding the application, the other on her hip, she remained speechless.

"It's nice to have options," he said. "Fill out the application if you think it might work for you. It shouldn't interfere with your job in Dutch as a veterinarian."

Maureen wasn't sure what to think. She still did not know whether she wanted to make the move to Anchorage.

The chief leaned back in his chair, knitting his fingers together behind his head and giving his elbows an expansive stretch. "I need a coroner in Dutch."

Now *he* was smiling.

"And I've set up a meeting for you with Casey's birth mom while you're in Anchorage. Since you'll be there, I thought this meeting better done in person than over the phone." He slid her a paper with the address and phone number scribbled on it. "She's expecting you." He shared with her what he had learned, including information that Casey's father may have been a fisherman. That nugget set Maureen's head spinning.

Chet poked his head in the door.

"Got something here, Chief."

It was his turn to wave around a piece of paper. "Take a gander at this. I don't know what to make of it."

He explained it was one of the email communications between Casey and his mother.

"Right there," he said pointing to the email exchange. "He asks his mom to find out the ownership of the *Cape Chirikof LLC.* "

He looked at the chief and then at Maureen before he laid down a second piece of paper. "Here's her response."

Chief St. George picked up the paper and read the email exchange. "It says Rob Stokes is not the sole owner of the *Cape Chirikof.* His brother, One-Eye, owned half of it."

Chet rubbed his hands together. "A motive, perhaps?"

Chapter 23

Maureen walked with Dr. Kittredge down the brightly lit hall of the Anchorage veterinary hospital. Blue jeans poked from beneath the stiff hem of his starched white smock. A shock of blond hair was combed back behind his ears and grazed his shoulders. He looked like a surfer gone serious. They stopped in front of a glass door. A sign overhead identified it as the entrance to the imaging lab.

Opening the door, he led Maureen through a small office area and waved at the young woman behind the desk.

"Hi, Chad," she said, smiling as they made their way past the entrance into a narrow corridor with glass doors on either side.

Stopping at the first door, Kittredge reached for the handle. "This is the MRI imaging area."

It was not in use, so Kittredge introduced her to the sleek cylindrical machine. He rested his arm on it as if admiring a surf board. "Have you ever used one of these sweethearts?"

"Only in med school."

He gave her a look of surprise. She got that a lot; people always wondered why she'd attended med school before switching to veterinary medicine. She never said why. Tic-tac-toe pet love, was why. Love and loyalty, courage, and strength. So simple. So in the moment.

Unlike humans, all wound up.

"There's a CAT scan and two x-ray machines farther down the hall," he said.

Gesturing toward two chairs along the wall, he continued. "But let's sit down. Perhaps I can answer questions you might have about the equipment and the job."

Kittredge leaned forward in his chair, resting his elbows on his lap with hands clasped in front. Maureen could see this was the let-your-hair-down part of the interview process.

"First of all, please call me Chad." He smiled, then did his best to be charming. "This is a great place to work. We're fully loaded with a great staff and awesome equipment."

The doctor let his eyes rest briefly on the MRI scanner. Then back to her. "What would you like to know about working here?"

She knew this was the best-equipped veterinary hospital in the state and that it provided services to many rural communities. Most villages were in remote locations, some still on a honey bucket system of sewage retrieval, a feature that did not attract resident members of the medical community. In fact, that was why she was here. The job she'd applied for was as coordinator of rural services. As coordinator, she would manage the rotation of village visits.

"Why is the position vacant?"

"The current coordinator is heading back Outside. It wasn't the job. Living in Alaska takes a toll on those separated so far from family and friends. But ask him yourself." He pulled a business card from his pocket, scribbled a name and number on it, and passed it to

Maureen.

"The schedule?" she asked, intrigued by working in the Bush. "How much time here? How much time working in the villages?"

"Well, as coordinator, you'd have a staff of two other veterinarians. The three of you would be covering most of western and central Alaska that's off the road system, excluding Bethel, Kodiak, and Dutch Harbor, where they have resident veterinarians."

Maureen wondered whether they'd find someone to replace her in Dutch. They'd been without one for several years before she arrived.

Kittredge continued. "You'd probably be traveling to the villages about half the time."

She leaned back in the chair. Spending time in the villages is what had drawn her to the job opening. She was still trying to assess the other half of the job, the working in Anchorage half, including what it would be like to work with the surfer dude doctor.

"You'd often travel by small plane and sometimes stay in a villager's home. It's a great way to see the real Alaska, the one few ever see."

Maureen asked about the villages and whether they had medical facilities. As an example, Chad described a village located at the mouth of the Kanektok River, where it flows into Kuskokwim Bay and the Bering Sea. The area surrounding it was flat, grassy tundra pocked with swampy ponds in the summer and inaccessible except by plane or boat. In the winter, only planes and snowmobiles got you there.

"It's a fly-in destination for legendary salmon sport fishing. So, bring your fishing rod and waders."

He told her it was a small Yupik community that

swells in size for several weeks in the summer when the salmon are running, and villagers from the delta region arrive to let loose their gillnets from small, outboard motor-driven, aluminum skiffs. In summer, families set up fishing camps along the river bank where they catch and slow-smoke salmon fillets on open-air racks. Veterinarian visits are scheduled once a month, he said, using a room at the town hall.

"All the medical equipment is mobile and travels with you as the visiting veterinarian," he said.

"But you've been to the Bush, working in Dutch and servicing the surrounding villages on the islands and the peninsula. That's why you rose to the top of the candidate list pretty quickly. The difference here is that after your travels, you get to come back to Anchorage." He raised an eyebrow as if to say that was a no-brainer step-up from Dutch.

Maureen was still trying to size him up. "What do *you* do when you come back here?"

"*Me?*" His face lit up as if pizza had been delivered. "Snow board in the winter. Hike in the summer. And I'm in the Anchorage opera chorus." He laughed at her expression of surprise. "A tenor. We're doing *Carmen* next month."

Maureen watched him stand up, hands in his white smock. "Let's swing by one of the operating rooms," he said, nodding toward the west wing of the building.

She was intrigued and asked him about the opera schedule as they walked down the wide, window-lined corridor.

"Wait," she said. "I sent a bluetick coonhound here. He needed amputation of his right hind leg. Can we visit him? His name is *Blue.*"

They found the dog resting in a recovery area on the second floor. Maureen checked his chart. "Looks like he's recovering well." The dog was sleeping, so they didn't disturb him.

Farther down the hall, they entered a room with a viewing window. They looked down into an operating room. Three doctors hunched over a sedated moose. It lay on its side but with its upper hind leg tethered in a sling that hung from the ceiling, giving the surgeons unobstructed access to the abdomen area. The abdomen was covered except where an incision had been made.

Maureen had no experience with moose but had field dressed injured horses. If she had a specialty outside domestic house pets, it was tending to the semi-wild horses in Summer Bay. The trick was to tend to the horses in the herd without the big roan stallion shaking his mane and pawing at the dirt. Bringing a bushel of apples helped divert his attention. Often they'd been apples left at the clinic by One-Eye. She'd miss those horses if she took this job. She'd miss those apples no matter what she did.

The operating room below them was stocked with sophisticated equipment, none of which was in her Dutch Harbor office. An array of bright surgical lights hung above the table, and a fully loaded anesthesia cart was parked alongside the moose's head.

Maureen thought about her antique X-ray machine and the surgery table parked in the far corner of her basement office. If she'd had just some equipment like this in Dutch, she'd have been able to operate on Blue herself.

But watching the action below, she couldn't help wonder why the moose wasn't hanging in a meat house.

****

Maureen walked across the parking lot looking for a puny white sedan, the only rental available for this last-minute trip. There it was, the pint-sized runt of a car, parked between two giant SUVs armed with studded snow tires meant to show the road who was boss. The two-story animal hospital loomed behind her. She reached for the car's door handle. They'd offered her the job. She had a week to inform them of her decision.

She drove down Lake Otis Parkway, passing the University of Alaska on her way downtown. Maybe dinner at the Eagle's Nest? Perched atop The Captain's Hotel where she was staying, views from the Eagle's Nest would be spectacular. A steak and a rich cabernet to celebrate? To celebrate what, another tough decision to make? She turned onto G Street and pulled alongside the Evolution bar instead. It was already busy as the after-work crowd filtered into its dim confines. She found an available stool at the small horseshoe bar and counted herself lucky.

Unwinding a blue cashmere scarf from around her neck, Maureen looked around the crowded drinking hole. The tall tables in the windowed alcoves by the street were plugged with people, some standing, some sitting, all drinking. Most still wore jackets, now unzipped or unbuttoned. The packed room extended around the back of the bar and past a jukebox that blasted rock music loud enough to compromise most conversations.

Maureen nodded to the bartender so that she came her way. The short woman with a puffy hairdo leaned in to take her order. She ordered her usual Boston bottled beer. "And a hotshot."

"Make that two but hold the hotshot on mine," said a man's voice behind her.

Maureen looked over her shoulder to see Franken flash his badge at the guy sitting next to her, signaling it was time for him to move.

"What are you doing here?" Maureen's expression did nothing to disguise her disappointment.

"The chief told me you were coming to Anchorage," he said. "I expected you to stop by the office in follow-up to our phone call. Hearing nothing from you, I had you tailed from the pet hospital. Here you are, and I'm off duty." He motioned to the worn leather stool next to her. "May I sit down?"

"You tailed me?" Maureen laughed. The beer and cinnamon hotshot arrived just in time. She drank the shot and chased it with a swig from the cold bottle.

"Our medical examiner re-examined the data," said Franken, removing his black leather gloves. He laid them on the bar. "He concurred with your preliminary report on the cause of death for both victims and has revised the estimated time of death on Benjamin Stokes."

Maureen noted that he said this without contrition. He should be apologizing to her, damn it.

Franken continued, "It turns out the telemetry data you passed on helped us get a break in the Stokes case." He took a swig of beer. "Good job."

That's more like it, she thought. "Have you made an arrest?"

"Not yet. But the telemetry data you sent tells us that we were wrong about the time of death. You were right to be skeptical. Now that we know the killing occurred two days earlier than we thought, new evidence has come to light."

"Like what?"

"Well, for one thing, there was a longline vessel anchored in the far end of Captains Bay at that time. The crew heard what could have been shots fired near the reef and saw a skiff in the area. It was reported to the harbormaster but ignored by us because the timing was off. And, according to the chief, a woman who lives near the reef also saw a skiff about that time. She gave a good description of it."

Maureen felt smug. And why not? She'd been the one who got the description of the skiff from Mrs. Pynchon. Clearly, the chief had shared her report with Franken, which was the right thing to do even if she hadn't yet warmed to the idea of working together with him.

"Have you found the owner of the skiff?" she asked.

"Not yet. But we will."

"What about the Russian cargo vessel?"

"The FBI's checking it out."

He took a sip of his beer. "Thanks to the telemetry information you dug up, the new time of death makes these facts pretty darn important."

"Glad I could help, Franken." Maureen allowed her bottle to clink with his but didn't crack a smile. She noticed he looked more relaxed without his trooper hat standing at attention on top of his closely cropped hair. He'd probably left it in the patrol car parked in front of a nearby fireplug. She figured he must have been tailing her himself. How else could he get to the bar so quickly?

Franken took another sip of beer. "I like Alaskan beer better than this Boston beer."

"Yeah, well, I like the Boston Red Sox better than… Oh yeah, we don't have professional sports teams in

Alaska." She faced away from him toward the TV tuned to the fourth game of the World Series. She wondered when he would leave so she could watch it.

He followed her eyes to the television screen. "The Yankees suck, right?"

Maureen's head turned in his direction, an eyebrow cocked. She looked him over again. He must be in his forties. Big hands, she thought, like a pitcher.

"Yeah, they do." She set her beer down on the bar. "What can I do for you, Franken? You've invested some effort in finding me."

He set his beer on the bar next to hers. "Call me Joe."

"Okay, Joe."

"Everyone knew Ben Stokes was a drug addict," he said, looking directly at Maureen. "What no one knew, or no one should have known..." He paused, lowering his voice. "...that he was also a confidential informant. He was helping us with a drug probe in Dutch. An important investigation. FBI in the mix."

Maureen was shocked and angered. "Don't you think the chief should have been informed?"

"He was informed but not included in the investigation. And he was prohibited from sharing the information about Stokes, even with his deputies. It's our investigation, and we don't want it screwed up, simple as that."

Maureen thought Franken looked like a jerk again. "Sounds like a clear motive for his murder."

"Yes, it does."

"Why did One-Eye become an informant?"

"We made him a promise, a deal to protect someone. A promise we intended to keep, but it appears word may have gotten out despite our best efforts to keep it confidential."

"You mean because he's dead, you think someone leaked that he was an informant?"

"Yes, it seems likely that it got out. As you said, it seems a probable motive for murder. I suspect the killer never thought the body would wash up on a beach."

"So why are you here? Was it a trick to see the expression on my face so you could blame the chief for blabbing it around?" Maureen took another sip of beer. She was angry. "Since I didn't know about it, I guess you can't pin that tail on his donkey."

Joe Franken reached into the inside pocket of his jacket, pulled out an envelope, and set it on the bar.

Maureen looked at the envelope. "Another rap sheet on me? Keep it."

Franken stood up and dropped some cash on the counter. He tucked his hands into his jacket pockets. "I thought I'd save you a trip."

She ignored the envelope.

"Who hired the private detective that broke into my clinic? That's a big lead that no one seems to be tracking."

She expected him to say they still didn't know or that it was a police matter and none of her business. She was crafting an indignant response when he answered.

"Lightning Strike Oil Company. We're looking into it."

She noticed he didn't seem sore at her. Her smart-ass attitude seemed to slide off his back. He grabbed his gloves and slipped them on. "See you around," he said.

She watched him slip through the crowd and disappear out the door without looking back.

The bartender set a fresh beer in front of Maureen.

What the hell was in the envelope? It was long and white. Her name was scribbled on the front. She held the envelope up to the light hoping for a clue to its contents. A string of unhelpful red chili pepper-shaped decorative illuminations hung from the ceiling above her head. She tapped the envelope on the bar and fanned her face with it. Then, without ceremony, lifted the unsealed flap, removed its contents, and unfolded the document.

It was an application for a state coroners license. Someone had already filled in items on the application. Name: Dr. Maureen McMurtry. Location: Dutch Harbor, Alaska. References: Detective, Joe Franken.

Chapter 24

While the American Revolutionary War raged in the colonies, the British officer, Captain James Cook steered the three-masted sloop-of-war, *Resolution*, up the coast of Alaska in search of the Northwest Passage. The great explorer pushed north, navigating the waters surrounding Anchorage, now called Cook Inlet. He mapped the Alaskan coast all the way to the Bering Strait and into the Chukchi Sea. After several failed attempts to continue farther, the *Resolution* turned south, anchoring in Dutch Harbor to re-caulk the ship's leaking timbers. A hotel in Anchorage stands near a handsome statue of the explorer that overlooks the waterway named for him. The lobby and corridors of the hotel are lined with floor-to-ceiling murals of the great explorer's exploits, including encounters with aboriginals from New Zealand.

****

Maureen finished her latte admiring a Māori warrior, his detailed tattoos on full display. She chucked the empty coffee cup in a garbage can and headed outside into the icy-cold weather.

She watched her breath vanish into a smog that hung over Anchorage. Something called *atmospheric inversion* traps the arctic air when a cold front arrives, causing frigid temperatures and carbon dioxide to be capped by warmer temperatures above. It was another item in the negative column when it comes to urban living at higher latitudes where carbon emissions occur. But the drama of the Chugach Mountains that guard the city's eastern perimeter is impressive. Admiring them, Maureen took a deep breath. That craggy range, she thought, upstaged the worst things about Anchorage.

She tossed her suitcase in the trunk, planning to head to the airport as soon as she finished interviewing Casey's birth mom at a strip joint. She slammed the trunk closed, irritated by the whole business. A strip joint, really? But maybe she would learn something that brought her closer to identification of Casey's real killer and farther away from the circumstantial evidence implicating Arlo. That's what she hoped for but she'd heard the father might be a fisherman, and that nagged at her.

She headed up L Street into the kind of neighborhood where you wouldn't want to raise kids. Clutching the steering wheel with gloved hands, she appreciated that the defroster seemed to work overtime to keep the windshield clear.

Pulling into an empty parking lot covered in ice and sand, she didn't need to check the address. An enormous wooden sign hung over the western saloon-styled architecture and announced it in foot-high lettering. She looked at her watch: *11:00 a.m.* She was right on time and should have no trouble making the afternoon flight to Dutch.

It was dim inside the windowless joint, but it was lit well enough that Maureen could see red leather upholstering on the couches and chairs arranged around tables. At the center of the open room, an elevated stage was lit from above. At its center was a dance pole. The stage was surrounded by red leather fencing to keep the patrons at bay.

There were no patrons now, just a fellow mopping the floor and a woman on a stepladder at the bar. She wore pressed jeans, boots, and a crisp white blouse that tucked in at the waist where a narrow leather belt held everything in place. Her long blonde hair was drawn back in a French braid that trailed down her back. She appeared to be taking inventory of the liquor.

"You must be Dr. McMurtry?" she said, still facing the wall of liquor bottles that were lit from behind. She turned around, revealing a smiling face framed by silver hoop earrings.

"It's not rocket science," she said before Maureen could answer. "We're closed to customers at this time of day, and Police Chief St. George said you'd be here around eleven."

She stepped down the ladder, left her notepad on the bar, and extended her hand. "I'm Shelley Ferris, floor manager of this establishment and, apparently, the biological mother of a murder victim. Sorry, don't mean to be glib, but it's a lot to take in."

"Mo McMurtry." Exchanging the handshake, Maureen noticed her own unmanicured look. Not just her no-nonsense nails, but the sturdy cut of her wardrobe: a turquoise turtle neck, jeans, and hiking boots. "I'm sorry for your loss."

Indicating a stool, Shelley Ferris invited Maureen to sit at the bar. "It's not really a loss to me. I only met him once, about three months ago, and there were no embraces involved. But how can I help you, Doc?"

"We're hoping to find out more about Casey and, perhaps, a motive for his murder. We don't want to leave a stone unturned."

"Well, I can tell you right now, I didn't do it!"

They both laughed while Maureen unwound her cashmere scarf and laid it on the bar.

"But you may have been the last person he talked to on his way to Dutch. Perhaps he said something about his plans that might lead us in the right direction."

"You want a cola?"

"Please." Maureen unzipped her leather jacket but left it on. She didn't plan to stay long.

Moving behind the bar like it was her living room, Shelley grabbed two highball glasses and filled them with ice. "Well, he'd contacted me by email saying he thought I might be his biological mother and could we meet when he was passing through town."

She filled one of the glasses with soda from the tap. "Of course, I was shocked. But I agreed. I was looking forward to it until I met him."

She pushed the glass of soda with a practiced touch so that it slid to a gentle stop just in front of Maureen. Satisfied that she'd served up her customer, Shelley shifted her stance. "I could see the minute he came in here that he was disappointed."

She nodded, confirming her recollection. "Yeah, I was not the mother he hoped for. But he's already got a mom to brag about, so why does he need another? Right?"

She stopped and smiled. "I've got two great sons here in Anchorage. Even though they're teenagers, they seem to like me."

Maureen took a sip of her cola. "What about the father?"

"I'm married to him."

"I meant Casey's father."

Shelley walked around the bar and sat next to Maureen. "You know, I was a *newby* back then."

She saw the confused look on Maureen's face. "A novice stripper." She gave Maureen a frank, these-are-the-facts-of-life look and made sure it registered.

"Okay." Maureen nodded, maintaining a poker face. She wasn't some naive idiot just because she didn't know stripper slang. And she had her own views about the shaking booties of strippers and professional football cheerleaders. As far as she was concerned, they helped keep the lights on in a misogynist world. But she kept it to herself. Her face remained still as Shelley continued.

"This kid came in and paid a lot of money for me to do table dances for him. Every night."

Maureen took another sip of her soda and worked on her poker face some more.

"It was back in the oil pipeline boom days. The place was packed every night." Shelley turned and stretched an arm magnanimously to indicate the full expanse of the room. "There were dozens of girls working here. He could have asked for any of them. But, no. It was always me." Her voice edged upward at the end as if lifted by pride.

She sipped from the glass of cola and set it down on the bar. Her back was straight. Her posture, perfect. "It gave me a lot of confidence."

She reached for the pack of cigarettes on the bar and pulled one out so that it came to rest on her lips. The pink lacquer on her nails glowed when she flicked on her lighter.

"That's important in this business." She inhaled deeply and pursed her lips to direct the exit of smoke away from Maureen's face. Then she relaxed.

"He wanted to date me, to take me away from it all. It went on for a few weeks. Then one night, I found him waiting for me in the clinic parking lot when I left work to go home. He climbed out of a pickup truck. I remember that. He looked pretty good for four in the morning."

"What was his name?" This was the question she'd shown up to ask.

"Yeah, we spent the night together. He was sweet, a real gentleman." Then her voice caught an edge. "But wouldn't you know it? One night together and I got pregnant. I knew he'd offer to marry me, but I didn't want that. I was just a kid. We were both kids. So, I never told him. I went back to my parents in Illinois to have the baby." She took another drag from her cigarette. "I gave him up for adoption as soon as he was born. And now you and I are sitting here wondering who killed him."

She looked at Maureen. "Maybe you're wondering if that sweet kid who swept me off my feet for a night twenty-five years ago might have had something to do with murdering this Casey kid. Am I right?"

"It's a lot to take in, isn't it? After twenty-five years, the son you had to give up comes back into your life, snubs you, and then turns up dead."

"Yeah, the whole episode stinks. I've spent twenty-five years trying to forget it. I only allow myself to remember the father was a kind man. Something I can call on when I start slapping myself around for getting pregnant."

"Nice thoughts are good to have," Maureen said with an encouraging smile. But she was still annoyed Shelley hadn't answered the question. *Who's the damn father?* A fisherman, she'd been told. She squirmed her seat, again hoping to gain information that would cross Arlo off the suspect list rather than raise him to the top.

"Well, Doc, it used to be nice. But now it's feeling like you think Mr. Awesome might be the killer. That he killed my son…his son." She stubbed out her cigarette.

Maureen laid her hand on Shelley's. "We're trying to follow the crumbs, Shelley. Maybe Casey reached out to his father. Maybe Casey said something to him that might provide a clue about what was going on in his life that would cause it to end so violently."

"I did this," she said, tears welling up. "I set this ball in motion by getting pregnant."

"Look at me, Shelley." Maureen's poker face was gone. "Nothing could be further from the truth." She waited, her heart aching for the poor woman who'd been a victim herself. "You okay?"

Maureen handed her a cocktail napkin.

"Holy crap! I don't know what got me going there." Shelley wiped mascara from under her eye. "Of course, it's not my fault!" She sat up straight on her stool. "I guess I feel guilty because I didn't much care for the kid. Truthfully, he was arrogant and looked at me like I was a loser for working here."

Her gaze surveyed the expanse of the leather-clad room. "But I'm in charge here. I do a terrific job, and it's behind a desk, not up there anymore." She nodded toward the stripper's pole on stage.

"You don't have to convince me," Maureen said. Then she tried again to get the information she'd come for. "Casey's dad, did he have a name?"

"The truth is," Shelley reached for Maureen's arm. "I didn't tell Casey his father's name because I don't recall it. After pushing it away all these years, it vanished." She looked toward the ceiling as if trying to pluck memories from somewhere up there.

"He was a fisherman."

"Yes, the chief shared that with me." Something new, please, Maureen thought.

Shelley became excited as if discovering a trail of cookie crumbs. "That's where his wad of cash came from. King crab, he said. Dutch Harbor, he said."

Maureen began to feel queasy. Arlo had fished king crab twenty-five years ago.

"He was tall," said Shelley trying to remember more details. "And handsome. He had a tattoo."

"A tattoo?" Maureen said. She recalled the ship bursting through a cresting wave that wrapped the bicep of Arlo's right arm. *Please something else. Please lead me in another direction.*

"Yeah, unusual at that time, but you see them everywhere now." She opened the top button of her white blouse and pulling it aside, exposed a tiger seeming to leap from the far corner of her clavicle. "I think his might have been a ship, but, you know, it could have been an eagle. I really don't remember."

"I see." Maureen leaned back and began to describe Arlo aloud who, at forty-four, was age-eligible to be Casey's father. "Tall. Dark hair. Tattoo on his upper right arm."

"Yeah! It was high on his arm…here." She patted her upper arm. "Like I said, I really don't remember what it was. But I do remember the wavy dark hair." Shelley seemed to take pleasure in visualizing him.

Maureen didn't feel good. Her thoughts traced the contours of Arlo's tattooed ship on his muscled arm, his wavy dark hair now salted with silver. The crab pot. The permit numbers. The skate survey. The broken finger. She was ready to vomit.

She'd come, hoping to help vindicate him. Now she wondered, had she been screwing the once-lover of this stripper and the father of a dead man whose murder she'd been investigating? *Could Arlo be the killer, now with some bizarre family motive? Get a grip,* she told herself. *Get more facts.*

"Do you recall the color of his eyes or other defining features?" She felt relieved she could talk like a normal person.

"He was dreamboat handsome like that actor what's-his-name who once played a doctor on a Chicago hospital show...except for the glass eye. But that's wha..."

Maureen was stunned. "Glass eye?"

"Yeah. He wore it like a badge of honor."

Is it you One-Eye?

"What?"

Maureen didn't even notice she'd said it aloud. Her mind raced.

"Could his name have been Ben? Think carefully now."

Shelley's eyes scouted the ceiling for memories again. "It...it could have been." Her face, an anguished question mark, met Maureen's. "I'm sorry, I really don't know. It's...buried. I can't believe it."

"Did you describe him to Casey? Mentioning the glass eye?"

"I think so...yes, I did."

Maureen sat back on her stool, ashamed of herself. "So, he had a glass eye and George Clooney-like good looks?"

"Yes."

It's time to apologize to Arlo, thought Maureen. He had neither.

Chapter 25

It was dark when the plane touched down in Dutch, and arctic temperatures had swung south to grab the island in its frozen grip. Maureen navigated her suitcase across the icy parking lot like a race car driver, eager to get to the *Cape Kiska* and apologize to Arlo. The windshield of her truck looked like the face of a glacier. She leaned the suitcase against the pickup and fumbled in her pocket for the keys.

Maybe the *Cape Chirikof* was still tied-up near Arlo's boat, thought Maureen as she struggled to get the key in the iced lock. She could swing by the boat and ask One-Eye's brother, Rob, if he knew about Casey and Ben. *No harm asking, right?*

The key lock was frozen. She frisked herself in search of a lighter all the time chasing ideas around in her head.

If Casey confronted One-Eye, perhaps it led to an altercation between a father and his abandoned son.

She found a lighter in her parka chest pocket.

The chief was right about Arlo, she thought, flicking the lighter unsuccessfully. He had no motive to kill Casey.

The fact that Casey was found in one of his crab pots, that his fist was beat-up and finger sprained, that some permit numbers on his boat were the same as noted in Casey's diary, that the timing and location of the skate survey were similar to the time and location of Casey's murder; these were all circumstantial evidence. *None of it mattered without a motive.*

A flicker of spark and the flame sprang from the lighter. She held it near the lock until the ice began to melt. Then she banged the lock with her gloved hand. The ice fell away, allowing her to maneuver the key into the hole and unlock the door.

She was convinced of Arlo's innocence and wanted to prove it to others.

"Arlo deserves an apology." She said it aloud. Opening the truck door she tossed her suitcase onto the cab's bench seat like it was a bale of hay. Pumping the gas first, she tried the ignition. She got the high whiney sound everyone hates to hear on a cold day. She pumped again. Casey was killed *after* Ben. *Jesus, he could have killed One-Eye.* But had they even met? She didn't know. It was like chasing her tail.

Frustrated, she waved the thoughts aside and tried the ignition again. This time the engine turned over. Looking around the inside of the cab, she realized the windows were covered in ice. Turning the defroster on high, she sat in her ice cave, thinking about forgiveness.

Forgiveness from Arlo. To forgive her, Arlo would have to pardon her inclination to take shortcuts in her thinking. He'd have to forgive her wavering trust in him. She knew it was a lot to ask. She pulled down the visor and looked in the mirror. The anguished face of a human being looked back at her.

"Geeze."

She flipped it up and called Patsy, planning to tell her she'd be late to pick up CoCo. No answer. She left a voice message explaining she'd been wrong about Arlo and was heading to the boat to tell him so.

"I don't know how it will end," she said.

She reached under the bench seat for the ice scraper, but when she looked up, she realized the defroster had done its job. She engaged the gears and made it to the road without the tires spinning out.

The moon shone over the pearl-colored mountains across the bay when Maureen walked down the deserted ISI dock. Work was done for the day, so the drone of laboring engines had fallen away. Crews were either eating dinner aboard their boats or in town at a restaurant or bar. It was quiet as she made her way down the dock, except for the sound of a skiff slowly motoring along the outside perimeter of the boats. She approached a tall stack of pallets parked on the dock near the stern of the *Cape Kiska*. A dim light was on in the galley, but the wheelhouse and back deck were dark. It looked deserted. Her heart sank.

Rowdy music from another boat tied three boats down the dock put a dent in the silence. She stepped back far enough to read the boat's name on the bow. Lit by a dock light against the inky night, she could see it was the *Cape Chirikof.*

"Why not?" she said, hoping Arlo might return by the time she finished her visit to Stokes' boat. She headed there, stopping near the bow where she could see Rob in the wheelhouse.

She walked to the boat's midsection. The tide was low, forcing Maureen to climb down the dock ladder to access the darkened back deck. She stepped on the railing, jumped to the deck, and headed inside the house, where she encountered Viktor and his brother. They were eating a pair of steaks to the beat of a heavy metal tune.

"Hey, doctor lady," said Viktor, a nasty grimace on his face. "What you want now?"

Still holding a steak knife, he stood up from the galley bench seat.

Maureen stepped back. "I'm here to see Rob," she said, wishing CoCo were at her side.

She was halfway up the stairs that led to the wheelhouse when he responded. She could almost feel the heat of his breath when he moved to the stairwell and growled behind her, "Maybe you leave us alone."

She found Rob shutting a safe and spinning the tumblers. He closed the cabinet door and turned to face her, a look of agitation on his face.

"What can I do for you, Dr. Mo?"

"I'm sorry, Rob. I saw the light on…" Instead of unzipping her jacket, she shoved her hands in the pockets, already feeling that coming aboard was a mistake.

He raised a corner of his mouth in an awkward grin. For a second, she could see a flash of the Clooney-like good looks that his brother may have had a long time ago.

"You want a drink?" He didn't wait for an answer. Opening a drawer, he pulled out a pint of whiskey and two paper cups. "Is bourbon okay?"

Watching him, she saw his hand quiver while pouring the brown liquor into the cups. She figured he was still devastated about One-Eye's death.

"Normally, there's no booze on the boat, but normal isn't normal since Ben…" He passed Maureen a cup but didn't bother to finish the sentence. He led her to the small table framed by an upholstered bench.

"I'm sorry, Rob. I didn't know Ben very well, but despite his...troubles, he seemed a good man. He used to leave apples at my clinic for the horses out at Summer Bay."

Maureen let the whiskey swish around in the bottom of the cup. She wondered if Viktor would explode into the wheelhouse. And Rob, why did he allow Viktor and his brother on the boat? *Was she paranoid?*

Rob stared into his cup. "Yeah, Ben was a good guy when he had enough drugs to keep him high. That was the trick, how to keep him high without killing him. Ben," he said, looking up at Maureen, "was hooked on the adrenaline of fishing and the flash of money long before heroin got him. But the pain meds for his lost eye took him down the road to drug addiction. He kept trying to kick it long after the rest of us had given up. Gutsy."

The last word choked in his throat, making Maureen's heart ache like someone had pinched an aortic valve. She wondered if he knew that Ben might have had a son.

She sat at the table, still letting the whiskey swirl in her cup. Her eyes wandered around the wheelhouse, noting a framed picture of Rob and his brother Ben on the wall. Together they held up a barn door-sized halibut. Whoa, she thought, Ben *had* been good-looking in the old days.

She cleared her throat.

"Had Ben changed at all recently? Did he seem excited or agitated? Afraid?"

Rob leaned back on the bench, startled. "Why?"

"He was murdered. Something must have changed to make him a target. Did you notice anything different about him?"

Reaching for a pack of cigarettes, he lit one.

"He *did* seem different." He took a deep drag and seemed to relax. "Like he was nervous and excited all at once. He even talked about getting clean again."

"When did the change in behavior begin?"

Rob exhaled, seeming to give himself time to think about it.

"A couple of months ago," he said. "The last time I saw him, he seemed unusually happy. I didn't know what to make of it." His voice trailed off. "Now, I'll never know."

Maureen thought about One-Eye's work with the FBI. She hoped Rob would one day learn about the bravery of his brother and that, perhaps, Ben had a son. She wanted to ask him if he recognized the name Casey Elliot. Her mouth even opened. Then she told herself it was time to keep it shut. Leave it to the chief. It was his job to ask about Casey and why he might be interested in the ownership of Rob's boat.

Instead, she offered hope.

"I just learned news in Anchorage that I plan to share with the chief in the morning. It may help the police find your brother's killer."

Rob's brow crumpled like a dented fender. "What did you find out?"

She regretted her words immediately. "I'm sorry, Rob. I'm sure the chief will keep you abreast if anything comes of it."

"Ben is my brother. I have a right to know."

"I'm sorry. I shouldn't have said anything." She stood and turned to leave.

Rob shot from his seat and grabbed her shoulder. "Tell me. I have a right to know."

Maureen pushed away his hand. "Stop," she said, her heart racing.

He surrendered. "I'm sorry. Really. I don't know what came over me."

She backed away toward the stairs, not knowing what to make of Rob's outburst.

"I'm sorry I bothered you, Rob. It was my fault." She turned and headed down the stairs, where she bumped into Viktor lurking at its bottom. He'd been listening, she figured. *The sneaky bastard.*

"Leave us alone," he said, glowering at her.

Maureen couldn't get off the boat quickly enough. She scrambled up the ladder to the dock. Walking briskly, all she could think was, *I screwed up again*. She seemed to be leaving a trail of apologies in her wake these days. And now she hoped to make the most important one—an apology to Arlo. The *Cape Kiska* was still dark, but perhaps Arlo was sleeping. She hoped so.

Climbing down the ladder, she heard the skiff again. Its wake caused water to lap against the barnacle-covered pilings. She eased herself onto the deck and walked through the dim galley, lit only by a light over the stove. She moved up the stairs to the captain's quarters. Empty. But the room was filled with his scent. She sat on the edge of his bed and inhaled it, wondering if a good cry might make her feel better.

She slapped her knees and stood up. "No, no it wouldn't." She'd said it aloud. "But who cares!" She felt like o*ne big screw-up.* Purposely, she shouted it. "One big screw-up!"

Making her way out to the darkened back deck, she thought she heard someone above her on the dock and hoped Arlo was returning to the boat. But he never appeared. And when she climbed up to the dock, no one was in sight, just the distant lights of the ISI warehouses. She was headed in that direction when steps charged from behind the pallets. An arm wrapped itself around her neck. It squeezed her throat. She began to choke.

Unable to breathe, she grabbed for a face she knew was there. It escaped her. Gasping for air, she chomped down hard, digging her teeth into an exposed wrist. The arm held firm around her neck and began to drag her toward the dock's edge. She dug in her heels, desperately trying to save herself. Her boots kicked without traction on the ice. Her arms flailed. Her strained voice struggled to scream for help. "Helb…"

Thrust over the edge, she struck her head on the bow of a neighboring boat before making a loud splash. The frigid water stole her breath and stabbed her with lightning strikes of icy pain. Disoriented, she tumbled deeper into the cold, dark sea.

Chapter 26

Eric Petersen stood on the back deck of the *Viking King* smoking a cigarette. Tied at the dock, they would unload gear in the morning and head home to Seattle. Stroking his brown bush of beard, he imagined the cleansing sensation of a shave. He drew another drag on the cigarette and was wondering if this would be the year he would quit smoking when he heard a muffled scream for help off the bow. Then a heavy splash. He reacted immediately. Running to the galley door, he pushed it open long enough to yell, "Man overboard!"

He flew up the ladder, each pull of his arms, each push of his calves propelling him toward the bow. Throwing off his jacket and deck slippers, he scanned the surface of the water looking for signs. But there was nothing to see in the dark.

Having practiced many emergency drills, the crew flew into action. Captain Jack defied the pull of gravity in his movement up the stairs to the wheelhouse, where he flipped the switch turning on high-voltage sodium lights mounted high on the stack. They lit up the boat forward and aft like searchlights from above.

The flood of light allowed Eric to see now. The small, circular formation of waves seemed to originate from a spot four feet off the bow. They lapped against the hull. And then, there it was…a cluster of bubbles popped to the surface. He dove into the inky expanse knowing he had just minutes to locate the person and get out of the water before both of them succumbed to hypothermia.

The captain switched on the hydraulics and moved outside to the upper deck controls. His head looked toward the gear high above his head. He began lowering the cabled hook from the boom. One of the crew reached for the cell phone in his pocket and called 911. The other grabbed a life sling off the side of the house and was hanging over the bow when Eric broke the surface. He used one arm to swim and, with the other, he held Maureen.

Her head hung like a dead fish over Eric's elbow. He signaled to the crew that he was good to swim toward the back deck where the winch could haul her out of the water with the life sling. The sling was tossed over the side and lay waiting on the surface.

Freezing water had already begun to drain the strength from Eric's limbs, but he kicked and stroked with one arm until he arrived at the sling. Maureen's body was limp as he placed it over her head and under her arms. Satisfied that all was secure, he spun his index finger in a screw motion, signaling the captain to bring her up. Slowly, the winch began to haul Maureen out of the water. Her body hung, twisting in the air. Water poured from her clothes. When she was alongside the railing, the crew pulled her over and laid her on the wooden deck.

Kneeling at Maureen's side, the captain removed the sling while surveying her body for injuries. Blood ran down her face from a three-inch gash on her forehead. She didn't seem to be breathing. Hoping to feel a pulse, his fingers found the soft hollow area next to her windpipe.

"Nothing," he said.

Emerging from the water, Eric climbed up the stern ramp and crept to her side. A crew member threw a blanket over his shivering shoulders and another over the woman lying on the deck.

The captain tilted Maureen sideways so that her chest was braced against his shin. He used the side of his clenched fist to pound her upper back and water from her lungs.

Nothing.

He tried again.

Nothing.

This time he pounded harder like her life depended on it.

Nothing.

The captain looked up at his crew. "I think she's dead."

Eric reached for her shoulder and rolled her on her back. Perhaps water had come from her lungs while she hung in the sling, he thought. He held his hands together, so the heel of his palms faced downward on her solar plexus. And pushed hard as he began to administer CPR.

Nothing.

He drew her chin down to open her windpipe and pinched her nose shut. Pressing his purple lips to hers, he blew air into her mouth. And again…and again.

She gasped.

Smiles lit the four downturned faces that huddled over Maureen.

"Bring some more blankets," said the captain, his hands rubbing hers.

Her eyes opened. She searched the cluster of strange

faces that hovered above her.

Eric recognized the look of panic and confusion. He'd rescued someone once before. Leaning in close so she could hear him, he whispered, "You're safe now."

One of the crew approached with a pile of blankets he'd grabbed from their bunks. Eric covered Maureen, carefully pulling the blankets to her chin. He folded another and tucked it under her head.

Water dripped from Eric's beard as he looked down at her. "Damn, if it isn't Dr. McMurtry, the vet lady who examined the dead body we pulled up in the crab pot."

****

The ambulance siren wailed its tragic tune reminding everyone within a mile radius that they could be next. Dutch is a town of heavy equipment and people undeterred by hard work and hellish conditions. Mother Nature straddles the harbor's geological exit to the ocean, one leg planted on sturdy Cape Cheerful and the other poised on the pronounced peak of Priest Rock. It's as if she could kick over the rock if she wanted to, but she prefers to position her foot there and dare mariners to pass under. At least, that's what it feels like when the sky is steel gray, and the wind is whipping up a tantrum. So, when something bad happens to someone else, folks in Dutch generally feel lucky it's not them.

"You're going to be okay, Doc."

Maureen opened her eyes. The place was a blur of bouncing lights. She couldn't move beneath the straps that crossed her chest and thighs. A distorted face approached. Maureen's shoulders backed up to her ears in a defensive cringe.

The face leaned in closer. Still wary, she felt she knew him.

He held her hand. "It's me, Doc. Jeff, your favorite medic. You fell in the drink, but you're okay."

She could see him now, a sandy-haired fellow, more familiar but still blurred.

She looked around and realized she was in an ambulance. The straps held her to a gurney as the vehicle sped down the road. Two clear tubes curved over her cheeks enroute to her nostrils and jiggled there with each bump.

Jeff squeezed her hand. "Really, you're going to be all right."

She could not manage words. They were not able to crawl from deep in her throat.

He looked at the regulator on the portable tank. "Do you need more oxygen?"

She shook her head. *Oh, how her head hurt!*

He bent closer to the wound, carefully removing wet hair from her forehead to get a better look at the bandage he'd wrapped there to stop the bleeding.

"You managed quite a blow to your head during the fall,"

Pressing against the restraints, she raised her head, trying to talk.

"It's okay," he said. "Try to relax."

Instead, she struggled to pull her arms free of the restraints.

Her voice was husky and barely audible. Jeff leaned in closer to hear her.

"Someone tried to kill me." Her head fell back on the pillow.

The young medic stiffened.

"Call the chief." Her head was pounding. "Please."

Maureen's eyes rolled back in her head. Her grip on

the straps went limp, and her eyelids fluttered shut.

****

Maureen woke in a hospital room. Tubes ran from her body to machines that monitored her vitals. She could hear the slow, steady beep behind her head. An IV bag hung above her shoulder. Its liquid entered the vein on the back of her hand. Tubes of oxygen still invaded her nostrils. Chief St. George sat in the corner reading *The Dutch Harbor News.* She watched him turn the newspaper's page.

"Chief?"

He looked up, put the paper down, and was at her side.

"How are you feeling?" His hands on the bed's safety rail, his brows pressed together, he looked down on her bandaged face.

She managed a smile. "Groggy, but without a care in the world. I must be sedated."

"Yes," he said. "But you nearly drowned, and you've got a gnarly gash on your head. They stitched it up."

His faced changed from paternal concern to police chief business. "I want to hear how it happened. Do you feel up to it?"

"What are my vitals?"

The chief read her the pulse and blood pressure numbers.

"Sounds like I'll survive. Did they give me a CAT scan?"

"No, they'd prefer further evaluation be done in Anchorage and want to medevac you there tomorrow." He let that sit for a couple of seconds. "I think it's a good plan, Maureen."

She reached for her forehead to feel the bandage. "How long have I been here?"

"About three hours." He waited to see if she had more questions before launching into his own. "Jeff said you told him someone tried to kill you."

"Yes." She told him about being grabbed from behind. Of someone clamping her neck. The bite on the wrist. Of being pushed off the dock. The freezing water. Of sinking. The darkness. The fear.

"I thought I was going to die. I couldn't breathe." She turned her head sideways on the pillow and took a slow, deep breath.

Looking up at the chief, she spoke softly. "Someone must have saved me."

"Yes, you were rescued by the crew in a neighboring boat. The same crew that hauled Casey Elliot out of the ocean."

She managed a smile. "No kidding."

Reaching for her hand, he squeezed it to get her full attention. "Now tell me what you can recall about your attacker."

He carefully laid her hand on the sheet and pulled a pen and notebook from his pocket.

"I never saw him," she said. "He didn't say anything, so I can't tell you what he sounded like. He wasn't trying to rob me or wrestle me to the ground. He pushed me off the dock."

Her eyes squeezed shut as if trying to erase the memory.

"Did he seem large or small, tall or short?"

"I didn't see him."

"Are you sure it was a man?"

"It felt that way."

Maureen watched him scribble notes on his pad. "I seem to have pissed off a few people during these murder investigations."

Engaging the bed-positioning controls, she raised her torso to a less prone position. She reached for a glass of water and sipped through a straw. Then she turned toward him, embarrassed.

"I went to *Cape Kiska* to see Arlo. He wasn't there. On the way, I stopped by the *Cape Chirikof* to see Rob."

The chief frowned.

"I know, I shouldn't have gone." Her voice began to falter. "But I had just learned that One-Eye might be Casey's father."

She stopped, seeing his face go from bad to worse. But he seemed to be waiting for more information.

"That's what I learned from Shelley Ferris at the strip club," Maureen said. "She couldn't remember the guy's name, but she recalled he fished out of Dutch and that he had a glass eye."

Her voice became strained. "I was curious because it might be connected. I wanted to know if Rob knew his brother might have a son."

The chief froze.

"I know. I know. You told me not to go asking questions on my own. But I didn't ask him about Casey. I kept my mouth shut." She looked at him with pleading eyes. "Please do not be angry with me. I already know I fucked up. I…"

The chief wasn't looking at Maureen anymore. She watched his attention move to the monitor when the escalating heart beats and blood pressure caused the beeping to quicken.

"That's enough, Maureen," he said gently. "It's

okay. We'll talk in the morning."

"But…" Her face was a picture of disappointment with a big fat bandage taped to it.

He flipped his notebook shut and looked down at her. "Really, it's okay. I already know about your interview with Ms. Ferris. She called me."

The beeping began to subside. The chief continued. "I've asked the medical examiner's office to see if there's a DNA match. They've still got both the bodies. Everything else can wait until you get some sleep."

Her face relaxed, a faint smile resting there.

"Get some sleep. I'll be back in the morning."

"Franken." She struggled with the memory. The beeping quickened again. "He tracked me down in Anchorage."

"Yes, I know. We can talk about it in the morning."

"He told me about One-Eye being a drug informant."

He reached for her hand again. "I'd like to put you on an airplane tomorrow. Get a CAT scan in Anchorage. Visit your folks. Sit on a beach somewhere. Once we've solved this, come back. I'll meet you at the airport myself."

She began to protest but reminded herself she'd nearly died.

He reached for his jacket hanging on the back of the door.

"Wait," she said, turning her cheek on the pillow to face him. "I didn't see who tried to kill me. But I smelled something…"

He pulled on his jacket and returned to her bedside. Both hands rested on the bed rail. "What smell?"

"I don't know," she said, visibly fading again. "Not

the sea, not the boat…"

"Once you've gotten some sleep, give it more thought."

He gave her a reassuring smile and picked up his hat. "I've got Chet posted outside. He'll be here all night."

Chapter 27

He walked with his head bent, the wide brim of his hat protecting him from the wind. A flapping jacket did its best to shield the clutch of daisies in his hand. He pushed open the glass door of the health clinic and sailed across the lobby. His clean shirt and eager gait set him apart from the tired huddle of people that sat slumped in chairs around the lobby's edge.

Arriving at the front desk, an Aleut woman raised her eyes above the computer station.

"I'm here to see Dr. McMurtry." His broad smile lit up a freshly shaven face.

She looked him over. "You here on business or pleasure?"

He held up the daisies.

"Okay then," she said, nodding her head toward the hallway. "Last door on the right. Room 255."

Following her directions, he made his way down a long hall that ended near a small formation of chairs underneath a window. When he placed his hand on the door knob, a police officer jumped up from behind an open newspaper.

"That's far enough," he said.

Eric instinctively backed up, raising the daisies over his head in surrender. "I'm here to see the Doc," he said.

Chet approached the deckhand with the authority of a deputy on duty. "Who are you?"

"I pulled her out of the water," Eric started to reach inside his jacket, but, seeing Chet stiffen, he opened the flap, fully exposing a breast pocket. "My wallet."

He pulled out his ID and passed it to Chet. "I wanted to see how she's doing."

Chet looked at his various licenses and handed them back.

"Wait here," he said and opened the door a crack to see if Maureen was awake. "You've got a visitor. Are you up to it?"

Chet opened the door wider so she could see Eric. "Know this guy?"

Maureen looked him over, wanting to place him but unable to make the connection.

"It's me, Doc, your guardian angel."

"I'm sorry, but I'm still a bit foggy in the head." She tapped her skull with an index finger. She waved him in closer, wanting to get a better look. He removed his hat.

"Concussion, huh? I'm not surprised," he said, looking at the bandage on her head.

He looked familiar. She held up her hand, signaling she did not want any hints. "I know you," she said. She wanted to sort out the swirl of memories herself as if by connecting the dots, she might understand what had caused her life to skid off the tracks.

"Somebody saved me…"

Eric nodded and whipped the daisies out from behind his back. "Thought your room might need some cheering up." The sun shone through the windows and lit the blossoms, still springing in the grip of his calloused hand.

"You brought me flowers. Daisies. The happy ones!"

Maureen reached for the green stems and dropped them into the glass of water on her tray. The bouquet fell into a relaxed formation.

"I love them. Thank you..."

"Eric Petersen, ma'am." He saw her eyes widen in protest. "I mean, Doctor McMurtry."

"Ma'am, no. Doctor Mo's better. But I think you saved my life, so you better call me Mo, like the rest of my friends." She leaned forward, closer to him. "You brought me Casey's notebook."

"And his teeth," he said, pulling a chair up to the bed. "You're right, Dr. Mc, I mean, Mo. I work on the *Viking King*, the boat that brought up that kid in a crab pot. I came by your office with his notebook and teeth."

"And you pulled me out of the water."

He nodded.

"Thank you!" She reached over to squeeze his hand, her face overwhelmed with emotion. "You saved my life."

"They say that when you save someone's life, their life becomes your responsibility."

"Don't you believe it! But I'd like it if we were friends."

"All righty then. I'd like that."

She relaxed, almost feeling normal.

"So, what's going on around the docks? Am I the subject of much gossip?"

"More like speculation. Everyone is wondering why someone would want to kill the local vet lady."

"Oh, no."

"The police are all over the *Cape Kiska* and the *Cape Chirikof*. Search warrants, yellow police tape. The whole thing. It's CSI, Alaska style."

"Oh, no!"

He looked at her, perplexed by her reaction. "They're going to get whoever tried to kill you."

Maureen pressed her fingers to the bandage while Eric filled in the details.

"I don't know why they boarded the *Cape Kiska*. But I'm not surprised they boarded the *Cape Chirikof*. People steer clear of that boat, especially those Russians."

She looked up. "Why?"

"They can barely tie that boat to the dock, yet they landed top crew jobs. They don't belong here. They speak Russian most of the time. Keep to themselves."

"That's not exactly scary."

"I'm just saying, they're not real fishermen. I'd never crew with them. And they disappear on a skiff most times that they're in town."

"A skiff?"

The door flew open, allowing Patsy and CoCo to romp in with a flourish.

"Hey, girlfriend, you look like shit, but you're alive and I'm loving it." She pulled up a chair on the other side of the bed.

CoCo placed a paw on the blanket. Maureen scratched the shepherd's ears.

"Hello, girl."

Then the chief entered. He looked around at the unexpected crowd. Acknowledging them, he moved to stand at the foot of Maureen's bed.

The room became silent.

He pulled an airline ticket from his pocket and passed it to her. "They are waiting for you at the hospital in Anchorage. They'll do a CAT scan and give you a thorough exam. I just spoke to your mom. She wants to meet you there. She talked about a trip to Hawaii afterward." He stopped, seeming to let his look of concern do the rest of the talking.

Maureen read the ticket twice. The second time giving her an excuse to avoid the chief's gaze until she was ready.

He spoke softly now. "I'll bring you back when we've solved it...when it's safe for you."

Maureen held the ticket in her hand as if calculating its weight. He was trying to protect her, she knew. And someone had tried to kill her. That was real. And they might try again. But her efforts *had* made a difference. She felt invested in both victims whose bodies she'd examined, whose cause and time of death she'd determined. She didn't want to let them down. Or herself.

She lifted her eyes to meet his.

"Thank you, Chief," she said, "but I'm not running this time."

****

After two days in the clinic, Maureen was ready to leave. She sat in the corner chair of the room, tying her boots when the door opened. It was the Aleut receptionist delivering a bouquet of flowers. She eyed the opulent floral arrangement as it moved across the room to the windowsill.

"Thank you, Amilee."

"Someone must like you," she said and closed the door behind her.

The roses and zinnias clamored for attention, but Maureen was reluctant to approach the bouquet. She had not heard from Arlo. She reached for a rose and bent to smell it. She read the card.

"Get well soon, damn it! The City of Unalaska is praying for you." It was signed by the mayor. She imagined his mischievous grin. She knew she would have to meet with him soon about renewing her contract with the city or giving notice that she was taking the job in Anchorage. She didn't expect to get a bouquet of flowers if it was the latter.

She was appreciative that the mayor had thought of her but disappointed she'd heard nothing from Arlo.

She reached for the clothes she'd been wearing when she arrived. Patsy had brought fresh things to wear while these hung in the closet to dry. She was stuffing them in a gym bag when someone knocked at the door.

"Come on in." She kept packing the clothes, pushing them hard into the gym bag as if trying to bury the dark memory of their circumstance.

A vapor of diesel fuel fumes filled the room. She spun around hoping to find Arlo at the door. But it was Sully, the engineer, standing there dressed like a deckhand taking a break from the engine room: grease-smeared sweatshirt and jeans pocked with the handiwork of battery acid. His hand extended stiffly in her direction. It held a dense arrangement of Stargazer lilies.

"Arlo wanted you to have these." His voice was frosty as if he'd meant to say, *leave him alone.* "He's in Anchorage, but he's glad you're okay. He asked me to bring you flowers."

"Thank you, Sully. Please tell him the flowers are much appreciated." Her smile fell flat when met with Sully's sour face. "Why is he in Anchorage?"

"Boat business," he said.

When he turned to leave, Maureen called to him.

"Sully, please..."

"I'm sorry," she said. "I don't know why they issued a search warrant for the boat. It's not something I wanted."

"I'll let him know," he said on his way out the door.

Maureen could tell he thought the boat's troubles were all because of her. She thought he was probably right.

Sticking her head in the cluster of lilies, Maureen inhaled deeply. She hoped their intense fragrance would release the knot in her stomach. Instead, her lungs, still not recovered from the near drowning, coughed at the effort to fully inflate them.

Amilee stuck her head in the door announcing that Maureen's ride had arrived. Maureen flung the gym bag over her shoulder and grabbed the three bouquets. She was eager to leave this episode behind.

The door to Patsy's truck flew open, and Eric leaped from the shotgun seat. He grabbed Maureen's bag and flowers and held open the front door for her. She climbed in. Eric hopped in the back seat next to CoCo. The dog stepped all over his lap, her tongue trying to lick Maureen's cheek.

"Welcome back to the world, Mo." Patsy stepped on the gas, causing the truck to lurch onto the road.

Maureen braced herself against the dashboard and laughed. It felt good.

She turned to face Eric in the back seat. "Well, well, Eric. What are you doing here? Thought you were heading to Seattle."

Patsy and Eric exchanged conspiratorial glances.

"Like I said before, Doc, now that I've saved your life, I'm responsible for it." He looked at Patsy for support. She nodded encouragingly, her arms manhandling the steering wheel.

He finished his announcement with panache. "You're looking at your bodyguard!"

"Hey, wait just a minute." Maureen looked from one to the other.

"No, you wait a minute." It was Patsy. Maureen could see she was about to get as manhandled as the steering wheel. "You heard the chief. He knows what he's talking about, and he's okay with this. Your life is in danger. And Eric here is a big strong fella who knows how to handle a gun."

"I've got a gun and dog," protested Maureen. "I can take care of myself!"

"You think you can take care of yourself. And that's admirable and true most of the time. But the fact is, Mo, you'd be dead now if Eric hadn't saved your ass."

Maureen turned to look at him.

He smiled. "If you don't mind, Doc, I'd be honored to get you through this tough time. Then I'll be on my way."

She watched the way he stroked CoCo's ears, easily winning the shepherd to his side of the argument.

"So, it's settled," Patsy said. "Eric, here, is with you until this murder shit is sorted out or you take a vacation to some stupid, sandy beach. Your choice."

"Okay, he can sleep on the couch."

The green pickup slowed at the turn into the parking lot.

Patsy parked at the front door of the clinic. "Now, both of you get going. I've got work to do."

Maureen and Eric headed upstairs to her apartment. Stepping into the kitchen, she looked around. It had been a long time since she'd been home. She'd been to Anchorage, she'd nearly drowned, and she'd been laid-up in the hospital for a few days. They moved to the living room and tossed their bags on the couch.

"How about some coffee?" She headed to the kitchen, not waiting for a reply.

Her nose sniffed the old milk in the fridge and, satisfied, poured some in the container for steaming.

She ground the beans, scooped them into the espresso maker, placed a china cup beneath the spout, and flipped the switch. She set it atop a saucer and passed it to Eric.

"Sugar?" One for him, one for her. She directed him to a small square table.

Looking over the rim of her grandmother's china cup, she eyed his good looks and confidence. He was ready to take on the world but too naive to know what he was getting into, she thought.

She rested the cup in its saucer and thought it might be up to her to save him.

"Good?" she asked.

"Yep." He smiled politely.

"I want to thank you again, Eric, for saving my life. But you don't have to do it twice."

He seemed too sure-footed. She could see it written all over his face, his posture, the patient tapping of his boot on the kitchen floor.

"No, I mean it," she said. "I appreciate that you and Patsy have cooked up a plan for my safety, but I'm okay. Now that I know someone's trying to kill me, I'm prepared."

She stood up and left the room. Returning with a gun, she laid the .22 on the table between them.

"I know how to use this. And I will not hesitate to use it if necessary."

Eric picked it up, popped the cartridge, and removed a bullet. He held the narrow, one-inch brass casing up for her examination.

"This won't stop an angry man like the one who tossed you in the drink." He dropped it on the table as if it were a poker chip.

Maureen looked over at the shepherd lapping up water from her bowl.

"And don't forget my dog. CoCo's an alarm system armed with a platoon of teeth to take down any intruder." Hearing her name, the dog looked up. "She took down a burglar in my clinic."

"What if she gets shot trying to protect you? Don't be stubborn, Doc. Please, just accept my help."

"What if you get shot trying to protect me?"

"Just having a big thug like me around will keep trouble away."

"I couldn't live with myself if you got shot because of me. It's not going to happen, Eric. But, thank you."

She knew his arguments might make sense under different circumstances, but these murders could go unsolved for a long time. He needed to get home, and she needed to take charge of her life. But something he'd said made sense. She stood up and reached for her jacket.

He grabbed his. "Where we going?"

"It's time to buy a bigger gun."

She pointed at the couch. "And bring your duffel bag."

"Why?"

"Because I'll be dropping you at the airport when we're done."

Chapter 28

Pushing open the door of Sycliff's Hardware Store, the pair passed a circular rack of wool-lined jackets and flannel shirts, a row of steel-toed rubber boots, and a wall lined with a display of power tools, until they reached the back corner where Harold Iverson worked at a desk beneath a *Guns and Ammo* sign.

"Hello, Harold," said Maureen as she guided Eric toward the counter. "How's Greta?" She'd treated his rabbit for an overgrown tooth during the summer.

Harold looked up from a crossword puzzle, a pencil in one hand and a cup of tea in the other. "Oh, she's fine now. Her cheek's all mended."

An animated smile lifted the silver handlebar mustache, so it brushed the bottom of his bulbous nose. Gnarled hands pushed him out of the grease-stained office chair. "But, hey, how you doing, Number Six? The pet food department is upstairs." He snapped his suspenders to punctuate his own joke.

"Well, Harold, I'm looking for a gun, and I brought my friend Eric here to help me."

"Nice to meet you, sir." Harold extended his hand, giving Eric the hairy eyeball. "Glad to hear Number Six has a friend but no cutting in line."

Maureen responded to Eric's quizzical look.

"Harold, here, has been married five times. He says if he ever marries again, I'll be his next wife...Number

237

Six."

She leaned over and kissed the cheek the old man had tilted toward her.

After getting his kiss, Harold turned to look back at Maureen. "So. Guns. That's serious business. What are you looking for?"

"Something to stop an angry man at close range." There was an edge to her voice.

Harold reached for her hand and held it. He eyed the bandage on her head. "I heard about your trouble, Mo."

"I'm just taking precautions, Harold." She gave his hand a squeeze and slowly drew it away. "But thank you." She meant it. People wanting to take care of her. It seemed a curious thing at her age.

Eric looked down into the display case beneath the counter. "I thought it might be a good idea to start with a 9mm and a .22 automatic."

"Sure," Harold said, "but a .22 won't stop an angry man at any range."

"She's got a .22 automatic," Eric said patiently. "So, I thought it might be useful to get it out for comparison purposes."

Harold nodded, unlocking the glass case and reaching for the guns. He laid both on the counter in front of Maureen. "Your friend is right, Number Six. This 9mm is one of the best pistols in the world. Fast, reliable. Police forces everywhere love this hunk of high-tech polymer."

Maureen picked up both automatics, measuring their weight in her grip. She put down the .22 and popped the clip from the larger gun. "How many rounds?"

"Fifteen," Harold said.

With his thumbs hung in the front pockets of his

jeans, Eric seemed to assess how she handled the gun. "That ought to stop an angry man if he's not smart enough to high-tail it as soon as he sees it." He turned toward the older man. "Could we see some ammo, Harold?"

Harold laid two boxes of cartridges on the counter.

Maureen appreciated that the two men, one old and one young, managed to be helpful without mucking it up with condescending quips.

Harold reached into the cabinet again. "Unless you're gonna spend time at the range getting used to the 9mm, Number Six, that may not be the gun for you. A revolver might be a better ticket."

He reached for a short revolver and handed it to Maureen. "The snub-nose is easy to conceal."

She turned it so it fit handily in her grip. "It's lighter. But it doesn't look like it would scare an angry man. Maybe I need something bigger?"

The three of them stood around, looking at the glass case.

"How about that one?" She pointed to the biggest bad boy lying there.

The brows of both men rose in unison.

Harold reached into the case and took out the 44-magnum automatic. He pressed the cannon into her palm.

Maureen's hand sank under the weight of it. She laid it on the counter.

"How about that one," she said, pointing to a steel revolver with a curved wooden handle.

"That's a .38 special," said Harold, picking it up. He blew on the barrel and polished it with his shirt. Passing it to her, he said. "A sweet gun in the right hands."

Holding it in her grasp, Maureen rolled open the cylinder, spun it to check the chamber, and clicked it shut. She pulled back the hammer.

"If I was an angry man," Eric said, "I'd leave now."

He folded his arms, watching her handle the firearm. "Looking good," he said.

Maureen laid it on the counter. "I'll take it. And please throw in a shoulder holster and two boxes of cartridges."

She passed him a credit card. "If it's okay, Harold, we'd like to use your firing range in the basement?"

"What's mine is yours, Number Six."

Passing her boxed purchases to Maureen, Harold tilted his head in the direction of the hallway. "The door is down the hall beyond the storage rack of taxidermy equipment." He handed her a key. "You be careful, Number Six. We only got one vet in this town."

After an hour's practice, they left the store and stood in the parking lot under a darkening sky.

They walked across the windswept lot toward her pickup, its gray paint job blending in with the dim horizon. The small boat harbor stretched out beyond the bank. Most of the skiffs and small recreational boats had been pulled out of the water for the winter.

Eric stopped at the snowbank where the truck was parked and waved Maureen over. He rested one hand on her shoulder as he pointed toward the floating dock with the other. "That's the skiff I told you about."

He pointed to a sturdy workhorse of a skiff with a center steering console and a distinctive stripe of yellow that circled the boat near the water line.

"That's the skiff the Ruskies power around in when the *Cape Chirikof* is in town." He turned toward her.

"Let's go check it out."

Maureen looked at the metal walkway heading down to the float docks. Then at her watch. Shaking her head, she turned around toward the truck.

"If we don't leave now, you're going to miss your plane."

Eric stood with his arms folded at the chest, not moving an inch. "This is what I'm talking about. This is why I should stay. You cannot be sneaking around on your own."

She looked at him, his earnest eyes pleading his case. She could trust him, she knew. And she appreciated that he wanted to protect her. But she knew she'd be putting him in harm's way. This one was on her.

Maureen opened the door to the driver's side of the cab and threw the box onto the bench seat next to Eric's duffel bag. She climbed in and started the engine. And waited. Eric relented and climbed into the cab.

"Look," he said. "I can sleep in the clinic lobby, so you've got your space. No one can get to you without going through me first."

Maureen gazed out the windshield at the small boat harbor. What did she do to deserve his generosity?

"I've got to do this myself, Eric. I've got my reasons, but you only need to know two. Number one." She held up a single finger. "You risked your life once to save mine, and I am not going to have you risk it again. And, number two." A second finger emerged. "You had to rescue me from drowning because I acted stupidly. I'll not be stupid again."

She could see him looking her over, trying to assess how determined she was to reject his protection.

"Going to the skiff alone is stupid," he said.

"Yes, I know."

"I'll be back next month to work on the boat's engine. You better be alive enough to pick me up at the airport."

She engaged the truck's gears, her eyes on the rearview mirror as she backed out of the parking spot.

"I will," she said, turning onto the road that headed to the airport.

****

It was dark and freezing rain had begun to fall when Maureen returned to the boat harbor. Through the windshield, she looked out over the array of docks, their wet planks glistening beneath overhead lights. She could make out the silhouette of the lone skiff parked on B dock.

Loading the .38 with six rounds, she slipped it into her shoulder holster and climbed out of the truck. CoCo leaped out behind her. Keeping her promise to Eric, Maureen had fetched the dog on her drive back from the airport. So she was not alone.

"Okay, partner, let's see what we got here." CoCo stopped to look at her as if questioning the wisdom of the mission. "I gotta try, right?" Maureen said in her defense. "I've mucked it up and gotta see if I can fix it." She was eager to find evidence that would nail down One-Eye's killer and, perhaps, lead to Casey's killer and clear Arlo. She felt the two murders could be linked after learning Casey might be One-Eye's son. If she couldn't apologize to Arlo, perhaps she could help clear him.

A half dozen cars were parked in front of Jean's Tiki Hut Diner. Maureen could hear patrons inside laughing as she and CoCo headed down the gangway to the docks.

It was low tide, and it smelled that way. She could

hear sea lions barking out on the breakwater and water lapping against the floating docks as she made her way toward the skiff. Her hands in her pockets, she felt the .38 in the holster under her arm. CoCo's tail waved stiffly in front of her. The dog was on sentry duty.

She approached the skiff with caution. Walking along its twenty-foot length, she checked out the gear packed along its gunnels. Oars, life vests, a cooler, bucket, fuel tank. All the things you expected to see.

Maureen turned back toward the gangway. No one there. She scoped out the other docks stretching into the gloomy harbor. Nothing. She pulled on the pair of latex gloves she'd stuffed in the back pocket of her jeans and slipped over the rail into the skiff.

"Stay," she told Coco. The dog stood at attention as did the hair along her spine.

Even at night, Maureen could see the skiff was well maintained. She turned toward the steering console and was startled by the decal stuck on its front. *Lightning Strike Oil. Innovators in Offshore Drilling.* So that's who owns the skiff, she thought. She snapped a photo with her phone, using the flash, so the decal was legible. Why are the Russians using it?

She continued surveying the floor of the boat. She picked through rags stashed beneath the console and found nothing. She headed toward the bow where other items were stored. She saw a cigarette butt. She reached for it. Then reconsidered. Best to leave it for the chief to retrieve with a search warrant. She took a photo of it with her phone. A non-filter.

The flash of the camera reflected on something tucked back under the triangular platform in the bow. It barely stuck out beneath the coil of line stored there. She got down on her knees for a closer look. It was a shell casing.

Suddenly, the skiff shifted. Maureen reached for her gun, the curve of its wooden handle resting in her hand. She scanned the docks for a human figure. Nothing. She could see the glow of lights from the distant parking lot and hear the subdued chatter of voices leaving the diner. Feeling reassured, she knelt in the bow again, positioning her phone to take a shot of the shell casing. When the camera flashed, the stern of the skiff plunged downward, slamming Maureen against the steering console. Water exploded in all directions. CoCo barked wildly. Maureen struggled to face the stern.

Separated only by the console and a bolster seat, she found herself face to face with a sea lion so large it filled the back half of the boat. Its cavernous mouth was lined with teeth that chomped at the air as if spring-loaded. CoCo's barks became ferocious as she waited for an attack command. But none came. Maureen knew the big bull would make quick work of the three-legged shepherd.

"Stay!" she commanded.

The sea lion's hot breath smelled of dead fish. He shook his great mane causing water to spray down on her. Then, leaping in the air, the bull braced both flippers atop the steering console. He towered over Maureen.

Backing herself into the bow, she found the grip of her gun. Pulling it from the holster this time, her arms shook as she stretched them in front of her. She pulled back the hammer. CoCo barked insanely.

Aiming the gun at the bull's neck, she had a clear shot. The sea lion roared, his mouth open like a bat cave. His eyes found Maureen's. She blinked. The bull closed its mouth. Maureen raised the gun toward the sky and fired shots into the air. Turning on his hind flippers, the bull dove into the sea. But not before another barrage of bullets fired at the beast as it slid beneath the surface.

Maureen looked up on the dock to find the dark silhouette of two men, their guns drawn, their feet surrounded by a scatter of brass casings.

CoCo growled through bared teeth.

"Hello, doctor lady, we meet again."

Over her galloping heartbeat, Maureen recognized Viktor's voice.

He waved his big gun. "Maybe you like boat so much, you want to go for ride."

Maureen's finger still on the trigger, she rotated the gun in his direction until it was aimed at his crotch. She knew an attack command to CoCo would be the last command the dog would hear. Instead, she hoped the gunfire and barking dog would attract the attention of others.

Viktor's brother, Arseny, swung his gun in her direction. "What de fuck you doing in boat?"

Maureen's finger tightened around the trigger. She thought she'd fired three rounds in the air, so she had one remaining for each of them and one to spare. Even if they took her out, Viktor's sex life would be over, and CoCo would sink her fangs into the other.

Ignoring the dog and Maureen's weapon, Viktor stepped closer. Waving his gun in her direction, he smirked. "You trespass on private property. Maybe you steal something?" He looked at his brother, and the gun he held pointed at Maureen's head. "Shooting a thief. Not a crime, I think."

"Neither is shooting two armed men pointing guns

at you."

"But which one?"

"You," she said. "I choose you."

Viktor stepped back.

Behind the silhouette of the two men, a small crowd had gathered in the parking lot. Four figures scrambled down the gangway.

One yelled, "Everyone all right out there?"

Maureen's galloping heartbeat slowed to a trot. She holstered her gun with one hand and reached upward with the other, indicating to Viktor she wanted an assist in getting out of the skiff.

"*Is* everyone all right?" she asked.

He yanked her up by the hand.

She knelt to rub the barking dog's neck. Quieting the dog, she also managed to surreptitiously grab a shell casing from the dock.

Arseny shook his head in disgust and tucked his gun away. "Lady, mind your business."

Viktor stepped closer. So close she could smell his cologne. It smelled familiar. She couldn't place it but didn't care. All she wanted was to get far away from this pair.

Gunsmoke hung in the air as she and CoCo walked quickly toward the gangway. Out near the breakwater, the corpse of a sea lion popped to the surface.

Chapter 29

The chief lived three blocks south of the onion-domed Russian Orthodox church in a white clapboard house. The lights were on when Maureen parked out front. Her hair was wet and tangled when she knocked on his door.

The chief answered the door. He wore reading glasses and held a newspaper opened to the crossword puzzle. Her sudden appearance made his brow jump. She'd never been to his home before.

"Are you okay?" he said, opening the door wider and motioning her inside.

"There's a shell casing and a cigarette butt in a skiff owned by Lightning Strike Oil," she said.

She saw the question in his eyes and told him what happened.

He shook his head. "You should have left the island, Maureen."

"I'm sorry," she said. "But I'm sure the Russians are involved in the death of One-Eye, and with Lightning Strike owning the skiff, the two murders may be linked. I feel it in my bones, Chief. We just can't prove it."

"And there's the rub."

"What about the Russian cargo ship?"

"The FBI found no shady history. It's clean as a whistle."

"And what about Lightning Strike Oil? They own

247

the skiff. What's their stake in all this?"

"I've had Chet rattling their cage ever since we learned they hired Butch Bixby, the P.I. that broke into your clinic. And with Casey nosing around offshore rigs, there may be a link. But, Maureen, your investigation of the skiff on your own was inappropriate." He looked at her over his reading glass.

"I wasn't alone. I brought CoCo and..." she opened her jacket and showed him the holstered .38.

"You're lucky to be alive."

"It wasn't luck, Chief," she said knowing it was CoCo's barking that had saved her. "What about a search warrant? Can you get one for the skiff? I have a photos. And this..." She passed him the casing she'd retrieved from the dock.

"Are you sure you didn't touch anything?"

She held up her hands, still encased in latex gloves.

****

Maureen's bedroom was quiet except when interrupted by the kind of rhythmic snoring that signals deep, enviable sleep. CoCo's snores rose like the soulful sound of a cello on the down stroke of a bow. Maureen's head rested sideways on her pillow. Her mouth let loose the purr of a pennywhistle when her body turned. Her arm fell across Arlo's shoulder, where the sonorous tremble of a trombone erupted from deep inside his chest.

Arlo had come by earlier. He was parked outside Maureen's clinic when she returned from visiting the chief. She'd climbed out of her truck and walked to the driver's side of his. He'd rolled the window down.

"We can't just go on having sex and barbequing fish together," he said.

"I know," she said, "we're not kids anymore."

"Trust," he said. "It's something we gotta have."

"I'm sorry," she said. "I know you didn't kill Casey. It's not what I meant when I asked if he'd worked your survey charter."

"What did you mean then?"

"I was told he'd gotten a job on the skate survey. I wanted to cross it off the list, is all."

"If you had to cross it off the list, it means you thought it a possibility."

She looked down at her wet boots, knowing she didn't trust her judgment when it came to men.

"You're right," she said.

"I didn't know Casey," he said, his hands still clutching the steering wheel like he might drive away in the next moment. "He didn't work for me on the charter or any other time. Even with some evidence to the contrary, can't you trust that I'm not a killer?"

"I do," she said. She pulled her jacket tighter and studied his expression. Trust. If it had a face, she wondered, what would it look like?

Arlo dropped his hands from the steering wheel. One hand reached out the window and lifted strands of damp hair that hung over her head wound. "You don't look so good."

He tucked the strings of hair behind her ear.

"The trust thing," she asked, "Can you see it in my eyes now?"

Using both hands, he drew her face toward him. "So, is it true? Someone tried to kill you?"

She nodded.

He ran a finger along her tightened jaw. "You're scared but not willing to admit it, I bet."

"I'm angry that someone tried to kill me. Like they felt they had a *right* to end my life. *My* life. *My* right."

"I'm sorry, Mo. I shouldn't have thrown you off the boat. I was mad…and stupid. I should have been here for you."

She took a step backward. "Where were you?"

He laid his hands on the steering wheel again. "First, I was in Anchorage. Then I had to fly to Seattle to get boat parts I needed."

"You could have called. It would have helped to know you were in my corner."

"I sent flowers," he said, not looking at her now. When he turned to face her again, his face looked pained.

She nodded, knowing the answer. "You were still mad."

"I was stupid."

She opened the truck door. He stepped out and pulled her close.

"Lots of stupid going around," she said, resting her cheek against his chest.

Upstairs, he kissed her neck. His hands slipped off her shirt and cupped her breasts. He pressed them together, moving his lips from one nipple to the other. She unbuttoned his shirt, pressed it back over his shoulders, and pushed him onto the bed.

Chapter 30

Toby held the coonhound in his arms. Blue was back.

Maureen knelt down beside the six-year-old. "They did a good job fixing him up in Anchorage."

The dog licked the boy's face until Toby laughed.

Maureen looked at his dad. "The recovery time will frustrate Toby and Blue, but do your best to keep the dog at rest. Just let him out to do his business. No running yet. Bring him back in two weeks, and we'll go from there. He'll hate the plastic cone around his neck, but keep it on."

He rested his hands on the boy's shoulders. "Thanks, Doctor Mo."

She walked them up the stairs to the clinic door wishing she had decent equipment, the kind that would have allowed her to do the surgery herself. Not every animal would be as lucky as Blue in surviving a traumatic trip to Anchorage. *Blah, blah, blah,* she thought, making fun of herself. For now, she was glad to see the profile of the coonhound in the back seat, still licking Toby's face as they drove away.

Maureen circled her desk and sank into the chair. She felt good after last night's sweaty sex and sound sleep with Arlo. Maybe, she thought, they had a chance.

She pulled a file from the bottom drawer of her desk, the one with brochures of veterinary equipment. Her wish list. She thumbed through it, finding the surgical equipment that would have allowed her to do the amputation. At a minimum, she would need anesthesia and monitoring equipment. Noting the price information, she dropped the file back in the drawer.

She stared at the empty exam tables that had attracted so much use in the past few weeks. Dead bodies aside, the place had been broken into, and she'd nearly drowned. And last night's confrontation at the skiff would have cost her another sleepless night propped up in bed with a bad book and a loaded gun if Arlo hadn't come by.

"Nothing's simple!" She slammed the drawer shut.

Checking her messages, she listened to a voicemail from the chief. "Call me," it said.

Her fingers dialed-up the station's number.

"Good morning," she said when her call had been put through to his office.

"You sound chipper. How are you feeling?"

She felt better, she told him. And it wasn't a lie. The chest pain from the water in her lungs had subsided along with the overwhelming lethargy. But it was the night with Arlo that had worked the real magic. She left that part out of the conversation.

"Good," he said. Silence hung in the air as if he were thinking before he spoke. "I've got a fellow here that flew in from Anchorage to see you." She could hear him tapping a pencil on his desk. "It's Butch Bixby, if you'd like to meet with him."

"But Bixby…"

"Yes, I know he broke into your place. Just tell me *no*, and you won't see him until your day in court."

"Jesus, Chief." Her knee began to shake under the

desk like a squirrelly animal. She pushed down on it with her hand.

"He's here and wants to apologize to you, Maureen. *No* is a good answer."

Trying to think it through, she was slow to respond.

"I'll tell him you refused to see him."

"Actually, Chief, I'd like to hear what the creep has to say." She stroked the shepherd. "Send him by. And tell him CoCo is here ready to take him down again if necessary."

"I want you to come here for the meeting."

Maureen opened her desk drawer and looked down at the loaded .38. She figured that if she could survive an encounter with the Russians, she could handle a meeting with a guy who wanted to say he was sorry.

"I'll be okay, Chief, really. I have CoCo, and I'm ready for him this time."

"Either you come to the station, or I'm sending him back to Anchorage."

"I can't leave the clinic. I've got two appointments scheduled here after lunch. Send him over now... Please, Chief, I want this apology."

****

The laptop was open on her desk when Bixby arrived. Maureen grabbed CoCo's collar when the shepherd leaped to her feet. A growl rumbled from deep in the dog's throat. She recognized him.

"I've been expecting you, Mr. Bixby," she said, still holding the dog's collar. She noted he was shorter than she was and had a lot less hair.

"Please call me Butch."

Maureen released the collar knowing the dog's head was back in her police training. CoCo sat at attention, and so did the hair on the shepherd's back.

Typing in Bixby's name on her laptop, Maureen had already checked his record online. It hadn't taken long to read.

"It says here that twenty-three years ago when you were nineteen, you had a DUI, pled guilty, spent three days in jail, and paid a fine. It appears you learned your lesson because there's nothing else here. So, what happened?" She put down the lid of the laptop and looked at him, "What happened to cause you to break into my clinic?"

"I'm sorry, Dr. McMurtry." He clasped his hands together on his lap. "I have no excuse. Just stupidity."

She sat and waited, thinking a lot of that was going around.

"I hadn't had a big client like Lightning Strike for years. The kid was sneaking around on their oil rig. They hired me to find out what he was up to."

"The kid?" asked Maureen, knowing who he meant but wanting to hear it aloud.

"Casey Elliot. He was hired as a cook's assistant on one of Lightning Strike's oil rigs in the Chukchi Sea. Lightning Strike had camera footage of him rummaging through office desks. Like I said, I was hired to find out what he was up to."

"So, what did you find?"

"I checked him out online. No record. But his social media page opened up a whole new world."

"Environmentalist." It wasn't a question.

"Yeah, how'd you know?"

"I've been asking my own questions about Casey. But I'm surprised to hear he was rifling through people's private offices." She looked at Bixby. "That's a criminal offense."

Bixby nodded. "Guilty," he said. "I was wrong, and I'm sitting here saying it."

Maureen looked him up and down. "How'd you know Casey was in my clinic?"

"I'd heard through an old friend in the state police office that he'd been brought here and that a notebook had been found on him."

"Franken?"

"No, he's as tightlipped as they come. But someone in his office mentioned it in passing. He said they were looking forward to retrieving the body and his possessions from your office."

"Why didn't you just wait until it got to Anchorage and ask your friend what it said?"

"Simple. I was told the information would not be available while the murder was still under investigation. That's not what I was being paid for. Lightning Strike hired me to avoid surprises."

She waited.

"It was a huge error in judgment. I'd planned just to snap pictures of its pages but panicked when I heard something upstairs. I ran out with it. It's not something I'm used to doing."

Still waiting, she joined Bixby in looking at CoCo. The dog showed her teeth.

"I'm sorry," said Bixby turning his attention back to Maureen. "Very sorry." He reached inside his jacket pocket, removed an envelope, and passed it to Maureen. He seemed embarrassed. "Please accept my apology and the apology of Lightning Strike Oil."

Opening the envelope, Maureen pulled out a check. "What is this?" She looked up at him, her fleeting respect for his apology boiling into anger. "I hope it isn't a bribe of some sort."

"I thought you might react this way. I am not asking that you drop charges. I'm not asking for anything. It's to make up for the scare I caused you. I screwed up."

"This is a lot of money, Mr. Bixby." She passed the envelope back to him. "I wasn't planning to sue anybody if that's what you or Lightning Strike are worried about."

"Please reconsider."

She stood up. "I think it's time for you to go."

CoCo bared her teeth again.

"Stay," Maureen commanded. She escorted Bixby up the stairs and out of the clinic. She watched him drive away in a banged-up white rental car beneath afternoon skies so dark he'd turned on the headlights.

CoCo was still at attention when Maureen returned. She bent down and scratched the dog's ears, letting CoCo lick her face. Falling back into her chair, she eyed the plastic jack-o-lantern on her desk and reached inside for a candy corn. She'd neglected getting fresh candy for this year's Halloween. Popping the orange and yellow wad of sugar into her mouth, she let her molars have their way with it. She spat the year-old candy in the garbage.

"What am I doing!" She opened the bottom drawer and reached for the file she'd been thumbing through. Grabbing her truck keys, she raced out the door in pursuit of Butch Bixby. Thunder bellyached from the sky, and windshield wipers swiped at pinging hailstones. She spun out of the parking lot.

By the time she reached the turn onto Ballyhoo Road, she was going fifty. Barely tapping the brakes, she made the right-angle turn by sliding across the intersection, causing the rear of the truck to crash into a snow bank. Down shifting, she pulled forward and brought the truck back on the road. Gunning it, she barely made the curve where Ballyhoo bellies out toward the bay. She was pretty much out of control when she saw Bixby's rental car ahead.

She pulled alongside him, honking her horn. He navigated his wreck of a car to the side of the road. She jumped out of her truck.

"I'll tell you what," she said, hanging over the open window at a horrified Bixby. She handed him the brochures of the equipment she wanted. "Buy this surgical equipment, donate it to the clinic here, and we'll call it square."

"What?"

"Just do it before I change my mind."

He took the brochures.

She swatted at the hailstones stinging her cheeks. "So, tell me, what's the connection between Lightning Strike Oil and the *Cape Chirikof*?"

Sweat collected around Bixby's receding hairline.

"Lightning Strike," he stammered. "Lightning Strike charters the *Cape Chirikof* and two other vessels to bring supplies and crew to the rigs."

Maureen already knew that. She waited for more.

"Casey got back and forth to the rig aboard the boat."

Maureen clutched the window's edge while gusts of wind blew her hair in wild formations. "Are you saying Casey rode aboard the *Cape Chirikof* to get to the rig?"

"Yes, he was scheduled to return to the rig. That's when Lightning Strike planned to confront him. But the captain said he never showed up."

"Never...showed...up." She said it slowly,

struggling to place it in the sequence of events. "Why does Lightning Strike let them use its skiff?"

"Why? What are you thinking?"

Her hair flew across her face like wildfire. She looked skyward and hollered into the storm. "I don't know!"

Her phone rang.

****

By the time she arrived at the small boat harbor, the wind seemed to have amped up its game, blasting spitballs of hail on its path through town. Sleek gray clouds galloped across the sky not wanting to be left behind.

She parked between a police cruiser and Patsy's truck. Donning a hooded sweatshirt, overalls and boots, she snatched her medical kit and headed toward the breakwater where the Harbormaster's office had directed her in the phone call. A gathering of people lined the shore. Some worked with ropes to haul the massive sea lion's body from the water.

Maureen stood above the animal. Her shoulders slumped. She was unable to answer Chet when he asked if she needed anything. She just shook her head. The bull's bulbous head and shoulders lay on the crushed rocks. Strands of his wiry mane fell away from its head. His sharp teeth looked less menacing than they had while slicing the air above her last night, thought Maureen. She knelt to measure the animal's length and estimated his weight at near a ton. Sending a text to Kate at the marine mammal lab, Maureen asked what she would like done with the animal. It would be another tragic but treasured find for them.

Michele, Jeff, and Patsy aimed the full wattage of

their flashlights on the animal.

"Tell Arlo thanks for the ivory," Michele said.

Maureen looked up from the carcass. "Thanks for what?"

"For delivering the ivory from my cousins on St. Paul island."

Maureen's gloved hands moved over the glistening fur, searching for the gunshot wounds she knew she would find. "Yeah, sure. I'll tell him."

The first two bullets had pierced its neck. Blood oozed from the wound as she worked through the layer of insulating fat and a rope of muscles that had stopped the bullets. Removing them with expert cuts, she hoped they would match the one that killed Ben. Or the casing found in the skiff.

She could hear Michele calling the chief to report the find. When the call ended, Michele said she'd been called to the station.

"The chief wants to see you when you're done here. Bring the bullets with you."

It took Maureen a half hour to locate two more entry wounds and remove the bullets causing the forearms of her sweatshirt to be covered with blood. It had taken a lot to kill this beachmaster. Despite his attack on her the night before, she felt sick seeing him there, his life at sea ended.

She was packing up her medical bag when Kate responded to her text using an outburst of exclamation marks.

Pack in ice!!!! Ship by air!!!! Immediately!!!!

She moved to stand next to Patsy and shared the message.

Batting hail stones away from her face, she yelled

into the wind. "I've already got a boom truck from the High Seas plant headed this way. They'll get the beast in a sling and onto the flatbed. Have Kate call the plant manager. He'll make sure it gets packed and shipped to her specifications."

"Thanks." Maureen held up a bag of retrieved bullets. "I'm headed to the station."

Chapter 31

When she opened the door to the station, Maureen knew something was wrong. Chet's eyes averted hers and his lips were pressed together like he'd made a pledge not to talk. Michele, pulling handcuffs from her desk, shot Maureen a look of sympathy.

She found the chief in his office. He stood behind his desk, a .357 magnum in one hand, a fistful of bullets in the other.

"What's going on, Chief?"

He laid the gun down. "This is police work, Maureen. I can't involve you in this."

"Sure you can." She stuck her blood-soaked forearms into the pouch of her sweatshirt. "I've assisted in this investigation and"—she raised an eyebrow— "am being recruited by the local police chief to be the town's coroner."

"You're good," he said, acknowledging her point. "But, right now, you're the local vet and...you're in too deep."

Maureen's eyes wandered around his desk, looking for clues.

A document faced the chief but was upside down for her. She tilted her head, trying to read it. And there it was, waiting like a deep pothole you knew would bust your axle. Her voice was slow. She asked again. "What's going on, Chief?"

"It just arrived from the state police office."

It was an arrest warrant with Arlo's name on it. The chief told her he had no choice but to carry it out. He explained Franken had sought the arrest warrant for Arlo when the search of the *Cape Kiska* turned up Casey Elliot's fingerprints in the galley.

"I know it's personal, Maureen." His statement hung in the air. "Hard as it is, the best thing is to cut yourself loose from this investigation."

"Seems like you've already done that for me."

"True-enough. But your buy-in helps."

She slid her hands from the sweatshirt pocket, pulled out a clear plastic bag of bullets, and dropped it on his desk.

"That's real evidence," she said, pointing to the five lead slugs. "I just pulled these from the sea lion the Russians killed last night. Compare those with the ones I removed from the sea lions found in Captain's Bay and One Eye."

She tapped the bag with her finger. "And there's a brass casing laying in the bow of the skiff. It's the same skiff with the yellow paint job along the water line that was seen by Mrs. Pynchon in the far end of Captains Bay the night One-Eye is thought to have been shot." She stopped. "Remember the yellow paint chips I removed from One-Eyes' hair?"

He nodded.

"It's the same skiff Eric has seen the Russians using when in town. The same skiff that…"

The chief held up his hand. "After your visit last night, I was able to secure a warrant to search the skiff. We've already gathered the evidence and sent it to Anchorage, including paint samples, the casing, the cigarette butt, and a blood stain found on its tie-up lines. They're checking to see if there's a match with Ben's blood and the paint found in his hair."

Over Maureen's shoulder, he motioned for the new deputy, Tyler, to come to the office. Passing him the bag of bullets, he asked him to take high-resolution photos of the bullets and send them to Anchorage for immediate analysis.

He turned back to Maureen. "Are we squared away now?"

"Casey could have been on Arlo's boat for any reason. Applying for a job, anything. Fingerprints don't prove a thing."

"They prove he was on Arlo's boat when Arlo says he wasn't."

The chief waited, not ignoring the pain in her eyes.

"The fingerprints are circumstantial, Chief. Please don't do something…" Her eyes fell to the half-loaded gun that lay on his desk, and whispered, "fucked-up. Really fucked-up."

He reached for her hunched over shoulders. "This warrant is not about the murder of Ben Stokes, Maureen. It's about Casey Elliot. And it's not just his fingerprints that link Arlo to Casey's death. There are just too many arrows pointing in his direction."

Michele and Chet continued gathering gear, their eyes drifting in the direction of the chief's open door but careful not to intrude on the dust-up they knew was shaking in there.

"Casey was found in Arlo's crab pot, Maureen." He knew she knew that fact well enough, but he wanted the cumulative weight to sink in. "The vessel monitoring system shows his boat was working grounds near where the body was found. He returned with a banged-up hand. And his assault record. Stuff you already know."

Then quietly, he put the last weight on the scale. "And now Casey's fingerprints in Arlo's boat. It's just one circumstance too many."

"He's right-handed."

"I'm sorry, that's not good enough," he said.

She watched him finish loading his gun.

"Casey was scheduled to hitch a ride to the oil rig aboard the *Cape Chirikof*." She wouldn't give up.

"*Scheduled*, is the key word, Maureen. We've checked it out. Rob Stokes says Casey never showed up. I'm sorry, Franken wants us to take Arlo into custody before the fleet leaves tomorrow. We've been told he's at the bar."

Maureen closed her eyes.

He looked over her shoulder at his deputies. Chet and Michele stood at their desks, slipping on their jackets and adjusting their holsters. Tyler, the new hire, looked at the chief hopefully.

"Sorry, Tyler, you wait here to see if there's a response from Anchorage on the ballistic evidence we just sent them." Then, turning to Chet and Michelle, he gave further direction. "Okay," he said. "The state police have sent the arrest warrant. It's our job to carry it out, no matter what we think."

"I'd like to be there, Chief," Maureen said.

"If you're asking me if you can accompany us while we make the arrest, the answer is no. This is police business. But it's a public bar, and I can't stop you from going." He stopped to look at her. "If you're asking me whether I trust you not to warn Arlo...the answer is, yes. Just keep your distance. I don't want you to get hurt,

Maureen."

He waited before looking away. He knew the word *hurt* had two meanings, and he wanted her to know that he knew one of them could not be avoided.

When he motioned the two deputies into the office, she knew it was time to leave.

****

Music throbbed from the jukebox and the place was thick with smoke when Maureen arrived. The barroom was so packed with people it was hard to tell where the dancing began and the hanging around ended. Maureen slid sideways between gyrating hips and flailing arms.

She found Andy at the far end of the bar, passing two pitchers of beer to a patron. He made his way toward her, ignoring requests for drinks along the way. He didn't arrive empty handed.

He placed a bottle of beer in front of her. "The Yankees winning the series in six games. This beer's on the house."

She hadn't even watched the game.

Andy looked closer. "Are you all right?"

Maureen wished the bar were empty so she could tell him the truth.

"Thanks, Andy. I'm okay." She looked around the room. "Looks like a rowdy crowd tonight."

"Yeah, folks have been holed-up in town too long. That and the World Series finale; it's a perfect recipe for mayhem." He nodded toward Marcus, bussing empty glasses and pitchers on a tray to the bar. "I'm glad to have Marcus here to help out tonight."

Maureen reached for the beer.

She saw him checking out the bloodstains on her sweatshirt.

"This?" she said, holding her forearms up like a surgeon. "I just came from digging bullets out of another sea lion."

She took a long pull from her beer. "I'm tired, and I'm thirsty, is all."

"Another dead sea lion? Jesus." His eyes stayed on her as she scanned the crowd.

She was only half in the conversation. "Is he here tonight?"

"Arlo?"

"Yeah, Arlo." She was embarrassed to ask, knowing she had spilled her guts to Andy about what seemed to be a breakup at the time.

"He's upfront, near the window." He nodded in that direction. "I think he's hanging with his crew."

Maureen took another pull on her beer, her eyes studying the far perimeter of the bar until she spotted him. Then she turned to Andy. Leaning over the bar, she whispered. "There may be trouble tonight. Just a heads up."

"What's going on, Mo?"

"I can't say. Probably not a problem, but thought you might want to be prepared." She picked up her beer and disappeared into the crowd.

Andy moved to the cash register and opened the drawer beneath it. The .22 sat there just as it should, uncluttered and within easy reach. He closed the drawer and reached under the bar for a knob that allowed him to ease down the volume of the jukebox.

"You, hey you! Barkeep guy. Bring us two Scotch whiskeys. Straight up." It was Viktor and his brother Arseny. Andy ignored them. But Lillian poured them two shots of the worst Scotch on the shelf and collected their money.

Edging her way through the crowd toward the window facing the bay, Maureen dodged a barrel-sized guy shoved by another patron. She ducked a moment later when the big guy threw his beer bottle across the room in the general direction from which he'd first been shoved. "Asshole," he yelled as he charged back across the room. Lillian moved from behind the bar and was throwing the drunk out the door when Maureen locked eyes with Arlo.

He sat in the booth closest to the window with his three crew members. His hair was combed back like he'd just taken a shower. He wore his denim jacket, the one lined with sheepskin. She recalled its rich smell, clean but savory. A pitcher of beer and some shot glasses sat on the table before him. Arlo raised a glass of beer and waved her over.

She wished she could move through the crowd toward that booth, packing a pitcher of beer in her hand and anticipation in her heart. Instead, she raised her bottle, giving Arlo a nod and a smile before turning away. It wasn't easy.

She moved toward the jukebox. *To hide? To betray Arlo's trust? But he's innocent. He doesn't need to run.* She'd argued with herself all the way over in the truck. She believed him innocent and would help prove it after the arrest. The chief trusted her not to warn him. *But stay away? That's impossible.*

At the jukebox, she was surprised to see Rob Stokes there with Marla. Rob leaned against the jukebox, a sullen look on his face as he perused the music options. On his far side, Marla cradled a glass of red wine in her hand. Smoke rose from the cigarette in her other hand.

"I didn't know you smoked, Marla?" Maureen said, parking herself next to the jukebox.

Marla shrugged. "Sometimes it helps." But when she noticed the gash on Maureen's head, she looked concerned. "Are you okay?

"Yeah. They'll be taking the stitches out soon."

Rob looked up from the jukebox and gave her forehead a once over. He seemed to have forgotten their awkward meeting on the *Cape Chirikof*, the night she'd been jumped.

"Glad to hear you're on the mend," he said.

His skin seemed sallow and his eyes weighed down by dark bags beneath them. She thought that mourning his brother's death had damaged his health more than her near brush with death had damaged hers.

He pointed to the menu of songs inside the glass hood of the jukebox. "I can't find my song."

She hadn't seen him this melancholy before. And he seemed half drunk.

"Are you okay, Rob?" she asked.

He nodded, passing her some coins. He named the song he wanted played. "Can you find it for me?"

"Yeah, sure. Let me play it for you."

She flipped through the menu. Finding the song, she deposited the coins slowly. *Ding...Ding...Ding...* She was in no hurry.

Soon the song began. It was a ballad. The kind that drowned you in a sea of sorrow.

****

Chief St. George, Chet, and Michele entered the bar quietly. No guns drawn. No announcements. Wearing clearly marked police jackets, they wove their way to the bar and flagged down Andy. His expression didn't hide the fact that he was surprised to see them.

Maureen watched the chief speak to him.

Andy nodded toward the window where Arlo sat with his crew.

Most people hadn't noticed the police. But as they moved through the sea of bobbing heads, the noise began to subside, and gradually, the crowd parted, making way for them. By the time the chief and his deputies stood in front of the booth inhabited by Arlo and his crew, the place was pretty quiet, except for the weeping melody that floated from the jukebox. Andy turned down the volume.

Arlo sat with his back to the wall on the inside corner. "What can I do for you, Chief?"

"I'd like you to come with us, Arlo. I'm arresting you on suspicion of the murder of Casey Elliot. Please step out of the booth."

Arlo set down his glass of beer. "You got the wrong guy, Chief."

Chet began to shift nervously. Maureen could tell he was wondering what might happen if Arlo refused to come quietly or if his crew members raised a ruckus. Michele stood next to Arlo's nephew, the crew member with the blond dreadlocks. Maureen thought she seemed positioned to grab his shoulder and push him down if he made trouble.

"Please step out of the booth," the chief said again.

Sitting next to Arlo, Sully nervously adjusted his cap. He seemed to be waiting for a signal from his captain, Maureen guessed. Maybe he was wondering if this might require him to stand and fight? She knew he would do anything for Arlo.

No one moved.

"You're innocent until proven guilty in a court of law, Arlo, you know that. But we have enough evidence for a judge to issue this arrest warrant. We'll see where it goes from there."

"Seems like I need a lawyer, Chief."

"You do. And you can call one from the station, or one will be provided to you."

Arlo's eyes searched the bar until they landed on Maureen. His darkened gaze asked her questions she could not answer. But she did not turn away this time.

"Okay," he said to the chief. He nudged Sully to let him out. Sully seemed to resist. But Arlo persisted, giving him a no-nonsense nod to move aside. Sliding across the bench seat, he stood up.

The chief motioned to Chet to step forward. Then he looked again at Arlo. "Would you put your hands behind your back so we can get these cuffs on and move out of here?"

"No problem," he said. Arlo knew the routine. He'd been arrested before, but he'd thought never again. He put both hands behind his back and locked eyes with Maureen again. She returned his gaze, her dark eyebrows sloped steeply like gashes across her brow.

Chet cuffed Arlo and gently nudged him forward toward the door. All eyes were on the procession as they passed by the jukebox.

That's when Tyler, the deputy left behind at the station, swung open the front door of the bar. Waving a paper over his head, he yelled. "Chief, I've got another warrant here!"

Commotion broke out among the crowd causing it to press against itself. Patrons began to shout in panic. Some fell to the floor. Chet spun around. He raised his pistol toward the ceiling and fired.

"Hands up! Where we can see them! Everyone! Now! Hands up!"

Chapter 32

The crowd cowered beneath the hoisted gun, their hands raised to the ceiling. When the chief instructed Chet to holster his weapon, folks took a deep breath and lowered their arms.

Tyler handed the chief the second warrant. He read it. Looking up, his eyes searched the crowd until he found Viktor and Arseny toying with their drinks at the bar.

He walked toward them and stopped a few feet away. "You are both under arrest for the murder of Benjamin Stokes." He looked from one Russian to the other. "It seems ballistics tests did you in. One of the guns you fired on the sea lion last night was the same one used to kill Ben."

Rob pushed past Maureen, shoving Marcus and his bussing tray aside. Empty glasses flew from it and shattered on the floor as he lunged toward Viktor and Arseny. "You killed my brother!"

The last step was too close. Viktor grabbed Rob and twisted him around so that he faced the crowd. They gasped when Viktor pulled a switchblade and held it to Rob's bare white throat.

Arseny whipped out his own switchblade and swept it back and forth in a menacing motion. His eyes bulging with panic, he pleaded with the chief. "We not kill brother."

Every boot and sneaker in the bar stepped carefully back as the two Russians edged closer to the door, Rob still in Viktor's clutches.

Viktor and Arseny, their eyes focused on the police officers, didn't see Andy slip the .22 from the drawer. He held it behind his back, where he chambered the first round. In a single motion, he swung the automatic forward and shot Viktor in the leg. The crack of gunfire stunned the crowd.

Dropping Rob, Viktor spun to meet his new adversary. With a flick of his wrist, Viktor let loose the knife so that it flew directly at the bartender. It pierced Andy's shoulder and stuck there.

Ignoring the knife, the former linebacker launched himself over the bar. He rushed Viktor and slammed him to the ground. The Russian fought back. But Viktor was no match for the thrust of Andy's forearm that once pushed loose pigskin from the hands of charging running backs. Straddling Viktor, Andy forced the Russian's arms to the floor over his head.

Arseny dropped his knife. His hands shot into the air, signaling surrender. "We not guilty. Please, we kill no one."

Chet slapped cuffs on Arseny while Maureen helped Rob off the floor. Victor lay at their feet until Michele hoisted him up by the collar and cuffed him. Maureen could smell his spicy aftershave, just as she had at the skiff. It reminded her of something. What was it? She looked at his exposed wrist. Tooth marks.

Mine! she thought, recalling now the same smell when she'd been thrown from the dock.

"We not shoot him!" Arseny screamed.

"Shut your mouth," commanded his brother.

"Not us," Arseny said. "We drive boat. Not shoot."
His eyes searched the room. "Her."

Everyone turned to look toward the jukebox where Marla was standing, smoke curling up from a cigarette in her hand.

"She said we take One Eye out to scare him because he rat to cops. She come too." Arseny's eyes met the chief's. "So we shot sea lions and talked rough with him."

Viktor strained against Michele's hold. "Shut your mouth."

"One-Eye stupid. Play brave." Arseny looked at Rob now as if trying to convince him it was his brother's fault. Then he looked toward the jukebox again. "But boss lady take gun and shoot him in head."

Rob's eyes ballooned as he stared at Marla in disbelief.

The chief motioned to Tyler. "Arrest her."

Taking a last drag on the cigarette, she dropped it on the floor. A non-filtered cigarette like the one in the skiff, Maureen noted.

"I can't believe it, Marla," Rob said, his voice strained by anger and disbelief.

Holding her narrow wrists forward to be cuffed, she said nothing.

Viktor laughed. "Why you so mad, big brother? You ran Marla's drugs to oil rig." He stopped to smirk. "And you killed Casey kid."

All eyes were on the Russian, his face pinched into a cruel smile. "Yes, I watch from the wheelhouse window when you stuff kid in crab pot and use crane to drop him in sea. Bye, bye, Casey kid."

"You lie," Rob screamed. "You killed him when

you found out he knew about drug deliveries to the oil rig."

Rob backed up slowly toward the bar. All eyes followed him there and watched him reach for the neck of a beer bottle. He'd grabbed it with his left hand, Maureen noted. She stepped toward him.

He slammed the bottle on the bar. Sharp shards of glass now pointed in her direction.

She nodded toward Viktor and Arseny. "They don't know how to use the crane on your boat, do they Rob?" She'd been in the wheelhouse when he'd been asked by Viktor to operate it.

Rob looked around the bar, his eyes inviting everyone into a jury box. "They're too stupid," he said. The corralled jury seemed to nod sympathetically.

"So they couldn't move the crab pot, could they?"

"Stay away," he said.

"They didn't kill Casey, did they?"

Running a hand through his tangle of hair, Rob's gaze turned to Marla. He looked at her and began to sob.

"First, the kid wanted to know if the oil company was in on the drug runs. Then he wanted to know about Ben. Was he in on it? I told him, no, it was just me and the Russians. I left Marla out of it." His pained eyes turned to Marla again, wiping tears from his cheek. "I had to do it or lose everything. My boat. My house…My family."

Maureen watched Rob still waving the broken bottle in her direction. "Then what happened?" she asked.

"The kid told me he was Ben's son and that he knew Ben owned half the boat. And that now that Ben was dead, he should inherit his father's share. That would keep him quiet, he said. He went on and on about how he planned to use the profits to stop overfishing."

A murmur rose from the crowd.

"Yeah," he said, looking at the crowd. "I told him there was no overfishing in Alaska. But he didn't care." His eyes became fierce again. "He didn't care what I said. He said if I didn't share half the profits, he would expose me and the whole drug operation."

The crowd waited.

"That snot-nosed kid…He got all disappointed to learn his mother and father were a stripper and drug addict. It was like he wanted half my boat, so he got something out of a bad deal. But the jerk's not half the man my brother was."

"What happened then?"

"He left the wheelhouse and went out on the deck for a smoke. I followed him." He raised his chin defiantly. "I…"

A hush fell over the crowd.

"It was an accident. Don't you see?" He looked around for acknowledgment from the crowd. Most just looked star-struck, hanging on his every word. "I slugged him. He fought back. His head hit one of the steel gussets bracing the crane." He stopped to search the faces of the crowd again. "It was the gusset that killed him, not me."

"Then you used the crab pot to dispose of your nephew's body?"

Rob's eyes pleaded with Maureen for understanding. "Yes. We had a couple of pots on board to catch a few crabs for ourselves."

"Arlo's pots?"

"I don't know. We just grabbed them from the pot graveyard outside of town."

He stopped to give Arlo a look of apology. "I'm

sorry, man." He dropped the bottle at his feet.

The chief stepped forward and slipped his hand around Rob's upper arm. "It's time to come with me." He looked around the room. "Okay, folks, go home."

Maureen watched the chief cuff Rob. The world seemed to shrink around them as if it were just the two of them at the quiet center of a noisy room. It seemed intimate and fragile, she thought. She watched Rob lean into the chief's shoulder and whisper in his ear as if sharing a secret. But she could hear it. "You'll find a rifle in my gear shed. Should be prints on it," he said, nodding toward Viktor. "He likes to shoot sea lions with it."

The chief clicked the cuffs shut and squeezed Rob's shoulder as if acknowledging a pact. Then he threw Maureen a set of cuff keys.

"Cut him loose," he said motioning toward Arlo.

Arlo turned his back to Maureen, allowing her to unlock the handcuffs. He spoke to her over his shoulder.

"Trust? You could have warned me, Mo. You could have made a phone call, walked across the damn room. But nothing. Thanks for nothing."

She unlocked the cuffs and whispered in his ear. "I didn't think an innocent man needed time to run."

He turned toward her, a look of disappointment on his face. She saw it. She knew what it was. It wasn't trust. She watched him walk away. He never looked back. *Sex and BBQs. Turns out they'd not shared much more than lust and a hot charcoal grill.*

Chapter 33

Andy's large frame leaned against the bar next to Maureen. Blood oozed from around the switchblade still planted in his shoulder. A darkening stain spread like the petals of a red corsage pinned to his gray flannel shirt.

Tyler, Chet, and Michele pushed the prisoners past them and out the front door. With Rob in tow, the chief paused next to Maureen.

"Secure the crime scene," he said with an atta-girl grin and left with the others.

Only Maureen and Andy remained in the emptied bar. An ambulance siren wailed in the distance.

Maureen made him sit down on a bar stool. She could feel his heart still racing when she unbuttoned his shirt to look at the wound.

"Don't move," Maureen commanded as she separated the blood-soaked flannel from the wounded flesh. Blood seeped slowly from beneath the knife's ivory handle.

"You know who the real hero is?" Maureen said while patting the wound with a clean, moist cloth.

"Me, right? I jumped over the bar and nailed that crazy Russian."

"Yeah, you were awesome, Andy. But the real hero in all of this was One-Eye, the drug addict. He put his life on the line to save his brother. Even now, it might get Rob a reduced sentence. People are not always what they seem."

She gave the wound a closer look now that it was cleaned up. "You're lucky," she said. "This appears to be just a muscle wound. No arteries cut. No bones shattered. It's best if we keep the knife in place for now, so we don't cause further damage by unplugging things." She looked him in the eye. "Make sense?"

Maureen could see his pupils were fully dilated.

She moved behind the bar, filled a glass with water, and placed it in front of him. "Drink this."

He chugged the full glass in seconds. "Now bring me some whiskey, Mo."

The ambulance siren grew closer.

Maureen reached for a green bottle on the shelf over her head and passed it to him.

He splashed whiskey over the wound and winced. Then he took a long pull from it.

Wiping his lips, he offered her a reason to smile. "The Yankees suck, right?"

She knew he was trying to cheer her up, going for the standard feel good remark by a Red Sox fan. Like everyone else, he'd seen Arlo walk out on her. But still... "Not today, Andy," she said. "Today they won the World Series. Today the Yankees are the best damn team in baseball."

"Hmmm," he said, taking another pull. "You're not gonna start sporting pin stripe pajamas are you?"

"Nah." She reached for the whiskey. "I'll be a Red Sox fan till the day I die, but I may give up on dating for a while." She let the whiskey warm her throat. "Right now the thought of a man in my arms gives me a headache."

She handed the bottle back to Andy.

"Yeah, well," he said, looking at the knife lodged in his shoulder, "the thought of *anyone* in my arms gives me a headache."

He'd done it again, made her laugh when it seemed impossible.

Maureen took the whiskey from him and set it on the bar.

She handed him another glass of water. The glass was tipped to his mouth when the bar door flew opened. Two EMTs hauled a wheeled gurney into the room.

"Glad to see you, Jeff," Maureen said.

He opened Andy's shirt to take a closer look at the knife implant. "We'll take care of it at the clinic."

They directed Andy toward the gurney. The big guy sat down on it, then swung his legs up and lay down. While the EMTs strapped him in, he called over to Maureen, still behind the bar.

"Look up on the shelf over your head. There's a surveillance camera there. It's always on, taping everything that happens between the bar and the front door. Give the tape to the chief for me, will you?"

"Consider it done." She reached up, pushed the eject button, and out it popped. She held it up for Andy to see.

"Thanks, Mo." The EMTs rolled him toward the door.

"Wait. Stop," Andy ordered. "So, are you gonna take that job in Anchorage?" He looked at her with anxious eyes.

Maureen walked to the gurney and reached for Andy's hand. "The deadline to accept the job passed today," she said. "So you're stuck with me."

He let his eyelids fall shut and sighed.

She tucked the hand of her friend onto his chest,

careful not to touch the knife. They both smiled, already looking forward to the next time they would see each other over a cold beer.

The EMTs carried the gurney down the steps and into the hailstorm, leaving Maureen alone in the bar. She was surprised to feel happy. When the jukebox played its next song, her toes began to tap.

"This song about Folsom Prison," she said, leaning across the bar to turn up the volume, "never makes me blue." With a grin broad enough to block thoughts of another misread man, she snapped on latex gloves. Her step was lively as she secured the crime scene.

She found a pen next to the cash register and used it to pick up Andy's .22. Next to the jukebox, she retrieved Marla's non-filtered cigarette ringed with a deep shade of red lipstick. The bottle broken by Rob, she handled with care. She was slipping the shell casing from Chet's fired weapon into a bag when the front door burst open.

Maureen slowly turned toward the door.

Relief. It washed over her like sunshine when CoCo pushed her way past Patsy and leaped toward her. The shepherd's tail waved, her haunches quivered, and her eyes shot Maureen a laser look of love.

"I heard the good news," said Patsy, sliding onto a bar stool.

"That we got the bad guys, and Arlo is innocent?"

"Well, yeah. But Andy called me from the ambulance. He told me you turned down the job in Anchorage." She threw her arms straight in the air, signaling a touchdown. "Wahoo!"

Maureen laughed, glad she could finally look at it in the rearview mirror.

"What do we have here?" Patsy asked picking up the

bagged gun.

"Evidence," said Maureen, dropping it, the cassette tape, the casing, the broken bottle and cigarette butt in a box. Leaning over the bar, she grabbed the key she knew hung there.

"Sounds like police business," Patsy said as the two women, the dog, and the box of evidence headed for the door. Maureen took one last glance around the emptied barroom, turned off the lights, and opened the door.

With the jukebox crooning about not seeing sunshine since who knows when, they stepped into the wailing wind.

A word about the author...

The author and her family are long time participants in the Alaska fishing industry. In addition to fishing for halibut, salmon, crab, and cod, she's been a journalist, a fisheries specialist for the State of Alaska, and a fishing company manager. Halibut bought their first home in Kodiak. She's traveled to most ports in Alaska including small villages on the Yukon and Kuskokwim rivers and above the Arctic Circle. She survived a boat that went down off the coast of Kodiak, and many fishery management meetings. And she's been to Dutch Harbor many times experiencing a *white knuckler* airplane landing there as well as her fair share of beer at the Elbow Room, famed as Alaska's most dangerous bar. While the characters in this book are completely fictional, they thrive in an authentic setting. The author loves Alaska, the sea, a well-crafted sentence, and her family.

Printed in the USA
CPSIA information can be obtained
at www.ICGtesting.com
CBHW051038031223
2315CB00005B/77

9 781509 252237